HOUSE OF ROYALE

SECRET KEEPERS SERIES #4

JAYMIN EVE

Jaymin Eve

House of Royale: Secret Keepers Series

Cover: Tamara Kokic
Editing: Hot Tree Editing and Lee from Ocean's Edits

STAY IN TOUCH

Stay in touch with Jaymin:
www.facebook.com/JayminEve.Author
Website: www.jaymineve.com
Mailing list: http://eepurl.com/bQw8Kf

For Family.
Those you're born with, and especially those who come into your life
when you need them most.

1

"*A*valon! Are you okay?"

I could have cried at the sound of Dr. Spinner's concerned voice. It was such a welcome relief after walking almost ten miles to get across the island. Doc was seventy-eight years old, retired, and living alone on the edge of Lanai. He was also one of the only friends I had, and I really needed a friend right now. And a medical practitioner, apparently.

Pulling himself up from the rocker he sat in for most of the day, he waited for me to hobble up the three front steps to the small porch. "I had a bit of a run-in with some ... rocks," I told him. The bleeding had mostly stopped at this point, but red lines still trailed along my skin.

He squinted at where I was holding my arm, his expression giving away nothing. I couldn't tell if he believed my story or not, but I was really hoping it wouldn't be obvious that it was actually a stream of bullets that had cut me up. "Could you have a look and stitch me if needed?"

Doc didn't ask any more questions. He was very good at minding his own business, and somehow still getting all the information from me. Psychology—or more accurately, reverse psychology—would have been a good career option for him if he hadn't gone into medicine.

I followed him into his home, which looked exactly the same as the last time I was there. It was an old plantation house that had seen better days, simply furnished, but had an amazing view—ocean as far as the eye could see from every room. Doc never spoke much about his past, but I knew he'd lost his wife and daughter in a boating accident and now he just sought peace and quiet, waiting out his days until he'd be reunited with them.

I wasn't sure why he'd taken a liking to me, but he'd patched up my hand years ago when a shark had mistaken me for the fish dinner it had been aiming for, and ever since then it'd felt like he was looking out for me.

"Come into the back room, that's where my kit is," he told me, shuffling forward.

The worn wood floors creaked as we crossed them. Doc waited until I was seated before he started to prod at my left bicep. I was almost certain the bullets had just grazed me, but I was already trying to think of what I was going to say if he discovered one buried in there. "This doesn't look like rocks," he murmured.

"I was in the water," I explained. "Figured it was rocks, but it could have been anything."

Like a stream of bullets.

"Right," he murmured again, still prodding me.

It hurt like a bitch, but I didn't complain. I was used to pain, always getting scraped up and knocked around by the ocean. That's the price I paid for getting to ride the tides and waves of the beautiful sea. I would literally rather be dead than not glide with the ocean creatures. Of course, this injury could not be attributed to anything except wrong place, wrong time. They'd been shooting at that girl I'd found hiding under the rock ledge, and I'd gotten hit in the process.

No regrets in saving her though. I had special abilities in the water, far beyond anyone else I'd ever seen; it was my duty to help when I could. I'd saved more people from the ocean than I could count.

"You will need some stitches," he finally said after prodding, cleaning, and muttering over my injury some more. "Hold still, I'll give you a shot to numb it."

I shook my head. "No. No drugs. You know I react badly to man-made pharmaceuticals. I'm just going to have to tough it out."

His brow furrowed, just slightly, which was the only indication that he was unhappy. The thing I loved the most about this old guy was the way he took everything in his stride. All the weird, fucked-up happenings in the world ... he just kept on trucking.

I closed my eyes as he inserted the small curved needle, mentally going to the ocean. It helped keep the pain at bay, and by the time he'd made the four or five precise stitches, rubbed some cream over the top, and bandaged me up, I was feeling much better.

"So..." Doc leaned back in his chair, crossing his arms over his slightly rounded belly. "How have you been, Ava? Do you need a place to stay?"

The answers to those questions were always the same: *I've been existing*, and *Yes, I need a place to stay*. But I was afraid to be a burden, so I would never force my company on him.

"I've been fine," I said. "Working at the sanctuary, and lifeguard duties. You know how it is."

Deflection and avoidance often worked, but not this time.

Apparently my "rock" graze had worried him. "I'd really like you to stay here for a few nights ... just so I can keep an eye on you. There is always a possibility of infection."

Swallowing hard, I tried not to let my relief reach my face. If he knew how badly I wanted to stay, he'd feel obligated to make it happen—as a permanent arrangement. But I knew Doc liked his privacy, his alone time. I would never want to take that small peace away from him. A few nights was okay, though, especially if he insisted.

"I guess that's a good idea," I conceded. "Just until we know there won't be any complications." We were acting like I'd just had open heart surgery rather than a small cut, but I was too worn-out right now to put my big girl pants on and walk out the door.

He bustled off to make up the sofa, which was under the huge bay windows that lined the front of his house. He wouldn't let me help, so I just hovered close by, staring out at the blue sea. I'd get to sleep with the view of my favorite place in the world.

"Can I shower?" I asked him after a few minutes. "I'll just leave this arm out."

He nodded, his almost bald head shiny in the afternoon light through the window. "Yes. A bit of water won't hurt it."

I'd showered here before; I knew the bathroom well. "There are new razors and toothbrushes in the same place," he called when I was about to close the door. "Feel free to use them while I grab you some clothes."

"Thanks, Doc," I returned, shutting the door.

I actually didn't have much body hair ... probably because I had so much hair on my head that it had to balance out somewhere. But a toothbrush would definitely help. Mine was in my bag, which was, again, at the lifeguard tower. I hadn't

4

had a chance to go back for it yet, which meant I was going to be in these clothes for a while.

Worse things have happened, Avalon. My motto for the past six months, ever since my parents had basically packed up their lives here, leaving on a yearlong cruise around the world. They'd sold our house, left me with enough money for a rental, and waved goodbye. Apparently I'd been holding them back all this time, and it was bon voyage, *see you never.*

The money for the rental had lasted long enough for me to get a job, but not a permanent house. I'd stayed with a few friends until they'd had enough of me. It hadn't been my intention to mooch, but there was very limited work around this tiny island for an eighteen-year-old who'd barely finished her senior year and had no skills to speak of. If I could tell people about my abilities in the water, that would have made a difference, but the one thing my mom had warned me about was never exposing those unique traits to the world.

They will hunt you down and experiment on you, Ava, she'd always said.

Lifeguarding ended up being a last resort, and as long as I kept my speed modified, I was never singled out. But they also only had part-time hours for me, and the money was really low. So I bummed around, sleeping where I could, often in the tower after shift.

One day I'd get my life together. Not today, of course, but one day.

When the shower stream got nice and hot, I stepped under, then immediately had to adjust it to colder, because I loved the idea of a hot shower more than the reality. I took in a deep breath of the doc's shampoo, which I knew he only kept for me on those rare occasions I showered here. Firstly, it was my favorite kind: ocean blend, in the aqua bottle. And secondly, he was almost bald.

As soon as my waist-length hair was wet, its silvery gray changed to an almost rainbow-like color. I had no idea why my hair did this under the water, but it had happened for as long as I could remember. I usually wore my hair tied back tightly or under a swim cap when I was on lifeguard duty, because a rainbow sheen was kind of hard to explain.

Within five minutes, because I didn't waste water, I had shaved, washed my hair, and brushed my teeth. Doc knocked on the door as soon as the water cut off. "Some clothes out here for you," he said, then I heard him walk off.

I wrapped one towel around the heavy length of my hair and used a second for my body. Padding over to the door, I eased it open and dropped down to grab the small pile. They were his daughter's clothes; he'd never thrown away anything of his family's. This wasn't the first time he'd offered them to me. I couldn't bring myself to say no when he was trying to look after me. While I was somewhat disturbed wearing dead people's clothes, they really didn't need them anymore.

The shorts and shirt were a little small. Judging by the photos, his daughter had been quite a few inches shorter than my six foot height—as were most women. So right now I was wearing a midriff top and short shorts that hugged my butt cheeks. Almost fashionable. And since I was used to wearing swimmers—or nothing in the ocean—the shortness of my outfit really didn't bother me.

I quickly washed my clothes in the sink so I could put them back on tomorrow.

"Thanks so much," I said when I found the doc on the deck. I hung my clothes across the railing and together we watched the sun setting.

"You got your bandage wet, girl," he muttered. Guy was always muttering, and I loved it.

Glancing down, I wrinkled my nose at the wet patches across the white bandage. "Whoops, kind of forgot about it."

He didn't seem too bothered, probably because it was warm enough here, even at night in December, that it would dry soon. Along with my hair, which would become a long mess of thick waves. Luckily it never knotted up, and I'd be back in the ocean soon enough so there was no point worrying about it.

"I'm going to make some lomi-lomi salmon for dinner," Doc told me, and then without another word went back inside.

I followed, trying to ignore the ache in my arm and the confused thoughts in my head. For some reason, the face of the girl who had been in the water wouldn't leave me. She had stirred an unusual level of protective instinct in me. Maybe it was because she was so tiny. She'd been strong though, fighting the current.

I hoped she was okay. I'd left her on the main patrolled beach, just out of sight, keeping an eye on her from far out. When she'd gotten to her feet and stumbled to help, I'd left. I didn't understand why they'd shot at her in the first place. It was unusual to have gun violence here. Lanai was a very laid-back island.

Doc distracted me when he handed me a cutting board, small knife, and some very red tomatoes. "Dice them up," he said. We finished the salad in silence. He added the salmon last, and we ate out on the deck. No point having a stunning view if you weren't going to enjoy it. I grew restless after dinner, wanting to head into the water, but the injury was tiring me enough that I thought some sleep was the better option.

I'd just have to be satisfied with the view of the ocean through the windows.

THE NEXT MORNING I was up with the sun. Just before it actually, which was my preference. I liked to see the dawn of each new day; it reminded me I was still alive. Despite my family completely giving up on me, I was not giving up on myself.

Doc was awake. I heard him shuffling around, but I couldn't wait any longer. I needed my morning swim. Running barefoot, I ditched my denim cutoffs, leaving just the shirt and my underwear on. When the cool water washed around my ankles, everything inside me felt better. Stronger. My head cleared, and the worries that had plagued me faded away.

This was what I lived for. Something my very straitlaced parents did not understand. They were both astronomers; they cared for the sky. Neither of them even knew how to swim. I often wondered where the hell I'd come from. Were they really my parents? But no doubt if I'd been adopted they would have dumped me long before I was eighteen.

I just didn't fit in their lives. Luckily, I had my own version of a family.

Under the water.

Once I was far enough out, I took a breath and dived. Despite the low light—the sun was still rising—I could see as clearly down here as I could above. There was none of the disorientation other swimmers spoke of, no need for goggles or masks. My eyes never hurt either. For years now I'd wondered if I was one of those genetically advanced humans, like from the movies. A fish person or something. Humans had originally come from the water, so maybe we were evolving to go back there. What other explanation could there be?

Fish swam around me, and I ran my hands gently over them. The scars on my left hand were amplified under the water; I was lucky to still have full use of it. Doc told me I should have lost the hand, that there had been too much damage for a recovery, but even at the age of seven I'd insisted on trying to save it. And somehow the dead tissue had almost regenerated. It wasn't immediately clear when you looked at it; most of the damage was on my palm, but my hand was in a permanent half-claw position from the scar tissue and internal damage. It was functional, though, cutting through the water with ease. And that's all that mattered.

I'd had one or two guys kind of freak out when they saw it, like it meant I was damaged goods. I'd be lying if I said that sort of judgement didn't hurt, but I just went back to the ocean. No one judged me there.

As I swam faster, I sent out the call I'd mastered, almost like echolocation, along with a series of clicks that told my friends I was out and ready to swim. The pod of six dolphins met me about a hundred yards offshore and kept pace with me as I dived through the rolling blue waves. My mind shut off and I just existed. We went for miles. I lost track of how far we swam, but I could no longer see land.

It was only when Jojo, the smallest of the females, started clicking at me that the sound of the boat registered. I usually paid close attention to those things because humans would freak out if they saw me swimming like this with a pod of dolphins. Ducking down deep, I left the surface for the world below.

Some days I imagined never having to return, just living forever under the water. I had no problem eating raw fish and seaweed, and I could swim for hours, but I still needed to breathe and sleep, and I hadn't figured out a way to do both safely.

Forgetting about the boat, I made my way toward the cathedrals. I didn't come here as often as I'd like because it was very touristy, but right then I needed to see the lights. Just for the clarity their natural beauty brought me. Halfway there the dolphins said goodbye, in their way, and I waved before lowering my head and swimming as fast as I could. I always swam with my eyes open so I wouldn't miss anything. Millions of colored fish, the lazy glide of the turtles, sharks doing their predator thing—the only creatures in the blue to scare me. Just a little. Mostly because they were king and I respected them.

When the familiar rocks came into sight, some of the tension in my chest eased. Whatever the events of yesterday, this was grounding. It was weird that I couldn't get that chick's face out of my head, but since I'd never see her again, it was better I just moved on.

She was just a girl I helped; nobody special.

2

I got an hour's exploration in before the thrum of another engine disturbed my trip through the lights of the underwater cathedrals. It was probably time for the tourist boats to start, which was my signal to get out of there. I rose to the surface for one more gulp of air, then dove down again and was about to start swimming when an unusual noise caught my attention. Turning in the water, I tried to determine what it was.

Definitely not an engine—it almost sounded like something was zooming through the water the same way I did, only much faster. Since I'd never seen another human move at those speeds, or animal for that matter, I wondered if it was a projectile of some description? A missile ... maybe?

A missile? Not many missiles usually shot around the Hawaiian Islands. Had I missed an announcement about Navy drills in this area? Was war about to start? Were we under attack?

Or was it possible that this was linked to yesterday? Did those maniacs with the guns decide to up their arsenal?

My first thought was for the dark-haired girl. *She's nothing to you, Avalon.* Seriously, one would think she was my sister, that's how worried I immediately was. *Not family.* Not. Family. If I repeated it enough, hopefully it would sink in. Apparently I was so hard up for a family now, I was simply going to create a fantasy world where I had one out there, waiting for me.

Diving lower to hide under some of the rocks, I waited to see what was coming through the water. A more intelligent person would have gotten out of there, but I was pretty confident in my underwater abilities. If this was a threat, I'd be able to get away in time.

Spiraling water was the first thing I saw, and whatever was moving at those speeds was hidden within that spiral. I was already holding my breath, being under the water and all, but it felt like everything inside of me was on edge waiting to see what could move that fast.

Excitement, fear, and anticipation warred inside of me, but despite the small part of me that dreaded what I was about to see, I didn't leave. Just before it neared the first rocks, the turbulent water started to ease, then slowed and stopped completely.

Holyseashellshit!

A long pair of well-muscled arms came into view, followed by the rest of a male body—thankfully, because it would have been some sort of horror story otherwise. I thought I'd been pretty well hidden in my crevice, but as soon as he stopped moving, his gaze shot straight to where I was, our eyes meeting through the water.

Fuck! I should have taken off when I had the chance, because apparently there was a massive, blond, tanned, muscled man who could swim even faster than me. And he was heading right in my direction. *Go!* a part of me screamed over and over, like it could propel me into action. But I couldn't seem to move. I'd have to eventually; I was going to run out of air sooner or later. But right then I found myself edging out of the rocks and into open water, dancing—that's what I always called it when I was upright under water—closer to him. He danced the same way I did, drifting forward as if gliding.

At first I was fascinated by the hypnotic blue of his eyes. They were almost electric. As we moved even closer together, I noticed small slashes of deep green that bisected right near his iris, like the ocean had crashed into his eyes and he bore all the colors of it. His hair was blond, but not like the gray tones of mine, more yellow, and it almost looked like he had tattoos on one side of his head and neck, partially hidden by his thick hair.

Wait ... was that a rainbow sheen? He had a freaking sheen, just like me. I froze, my brain unable to comprehend that I might finally be meeting someone like me. Of course, I wasn't stunned enough not to notice all of his golden skin stretched over heavily roped muscles. He was not as lithe as most swimmers I'd seen, but he moved gracefully. His lower half was still covered in swirling water, so I couldn't see anything but his broad chest.

My lungs started to protest then—the first sign that I needed to start thinking about getting some air. The first discomfort usually meant I had a minute left, maybe two. I was only about fifteen feet down, so it wasn't a big deal.

The boat noises from before roared over our heads, and then the engine cut off, almost directly over the top of us. Unease flickered inside of me. A boat and a speed-swimming stranger made me nervous. I had the sudden thought that I was in a very vulnerable position right now.

I'd just decided to take off when he lifted his right hand

and pursed his lips like he was going to blow me a kiss. I blinked as a bubble formed on his palm. It drifted away from him toward me, growing larger as it moved. I wasn't sure what to do; I couldn't look away. Not even when it grew bigger than my head. I expected it to pop when it hit me, and I closed my eyes waiting for the impact.

But there was no pop. Instead it enclosed my head, trapping me inside.

The water drained out of it in an instant and I sucked in a deep breath, able to breathe again. *Holy freaking hell.* What was happening right now? How could he control water like this?

And why hadn't I swum away yet?

A small waterspout shot off my bubble, spiraling toward the guy, and then he too wore a bubble around his head.

"What's your name?"

A deep voice echoed around my new little air pocket, and if jumping under water was possible, I'd have been six feet higher than usual. *How in the....* Did he just talk to me?

"I don't understand." I felt stupid speaking like this.

His reply was almost immediate. "My name is Xander," he started, his voice accented and rumbly. "I don't want to scare you, but we are running out of time. You need to come with me for your own safety."

Creepy. Seriously, this was too creepy. Even for me, the girl who wanted to live in the ocean. I decided to see if I could break free from the bubble. I had enough air now to swim a decent distance. I might even make it to shore.

"Wait," he called as I started to back up. "I know you're scared, I get it, but you should know that the girl you saved yesterday ... she is just like you. An advanced human."

I knew it! I knew there had to be a reason I felt a connection to her. I wasn't just a crazy needy person. But how was it possible that the two of us ended up in the same bad place together? I slowed my retreat, giving him one last chance to speak.

"The people shooting at her, they are looking for you as well. We're the only ones who can protect you. I'll explain it all if you come with me now."

I wanted to believe him. I was almost desperate to place my trust in this gorgeous stranger. But I wasn't that naïve. Just because someone told you they were the good guys didn't mean they were. I'd learned that the hard way with my parents. They'd abandoned me, which had hurt more than I expected, considering they'd always acted like I was a burden they'd been saddled with. Then, on top of that, a lot of friends had given up on me as well, mostly because I couldn't live the surfy life anymore. I had to work. I had to be responsible.

I was a little scarred and jaded from the entire thing.

"Why should I believe you?" I asked, the back of my head pressing against the bubble. "You could be lying just to get me to go with you."

I heard and sensed his frustration as he bit out, "Wouldn't I have just grabbed you? I'm faster than you could ever be in the water, so if I wanted to take you by force, I would have already."

That was a fair point.

"Who's in the boat?" I changed the subject. Somehow I knew the boat was his. He'd just been way too unconcerned about it sitting above.

"Maya, the one you rescued, and her mate, Chase."

My burst of excitement at knowing she was close by, an advanced human like me, was overshadowed by my confusion over the word *mate*. Were they like ... Australian or something? We had tons of Aussie surfers over here, and they called their

friends *mate*. Like buddy, pal, dude. But not only did this guy
—Xander—not have an Australian accent, he also hadn't said
it like they did. His inference was boyfriend, but I'd never
heard any person call someone's boyfriend a *mate*.

"Just get in the boat. We'll tell you the entire story and then
you will understand." He sounded a little less pissed now,
more resigned. "I promise no one will touch you. You can dive
over the side anytime you want."

As tempting as it was to see Maya again and explore the
connection between us, my self-preservation won out, and I
regretfully said, "I can't. Sorry. I just don't trust you.
Later, dude."

Water started to churn around us then, and I knew I'd
lingered too long.

"Don't run..." was the last thing I heard before my head
was out of his bubble and I was swimming as fast as I could. I
hadn't forgotten his statement that he was much faster than
me, but I knew these waters better than anybody. Ducking and
diving, I used the tunnels to my advantage. I wanted to call for
the dolphins, but putting them into possible danger was a
really shitty thing to do, so I refrained.

Somehow, though, they knew. Dark shadows closed in
around me, and I could have cried at the familiar company of
my favorite pod. I clicked in greeting, and they returned the
gesture as we dashed across the sea. I had no idea if he was
behind me. I wanted to look back and check, but it felt more
important to keep powering forward.

We were still out very deep, and it was dark below me, so I
didn't notice the churning water until he was close. Damn. It.

He wasn't going to leave it alone, that was very clear. The
only question was: would I make it to land before he caught
me? When the swirling water shot straight up, I tried to get out

of the way. With a normal human I would have had no trouble, but he was too fast. It felt like steel bands wrapped around my body, holding my arms down against my sides. I kicked hard, but he was too strong.

The dolphins turned to come after us, but I sent out a last call, warning them away. I would not have them hurt because of me, and this Xander seemed desperate as he flew through the water, holding me tight against his chest. He wasn't even using his arms and somehow still moved at rapid speed.

The boat came into view again; he aimed straight for it, shooting up out of the water just before we would have smashed into the side. I sucked air in as I flailed through the sky, before another pair of arms caught me, arms as strong but slightly-less muscled than Xander's. My new captor had skin that was a deep, rich, stunning brown, a few shades darker than the kidnapping bastard under the water.

"Sorry about that," a smooth, accented voice said. "Xander can be a bit of—"

"An asshole," I spat.

I struggled in his hold, expecting to be dropped. Instead I found myself gently seated in one of the padded captain's chairs. A familiar face pushed past the guy and stopped right in front of me. "I can't believe we finally found you! The stone kept changing locations all morning. I thought it was faulty."

Maya. She looked Asian, maybe half, with creamy brown skin and straight dark hair. Her eyes were blue, though, and she had a straight-up American preppy accent. I was just staring at her, not speaking. "Thank you for saving me," she tried again. "Honestly, if you hadn't been there, I would be dead now."

The dude behind her made a deep rumbling sound—he must be Chase, her *mate.* He was clearly very upset by those words. His hand brushed across her arm and she tilted her head back to see him. I lifted my gaze to look at his face for the first time and I almost gasped. *Holy sweet hotness*, he was beautiful, all cheekbones and hard lines and perfect features. Together, as a couple ... they were almost too pretty.

"Who the hell are you guys?"

I did briefly wonder if I'd asked the right question. Maybe it should have been "what" instead.

"I'm Maya, and this is my boyfriend, Chase," she said, focusing on me.

"Boyfriend? Or mate?" I asked, because I couldn't help myself.

Her eyes got really wide then. "You already know about us? How? Did your parents tell you? Where are they?"

She shot each question off rapidly, and before I got a chance to answer, the boat rocked. At first I thought it was wake from another vessel, but it was the Poseidon-looking asshole. As he pulled himself gracefully onto the fancy boat, I found myself lurching to my feet.

The water fell away from his lower half to reveal normal, well-muscled legs to match the rest of him. A very naked rest of him. Maya must have known, because she'd turned away as soon as he stood up. I, on the other hand, did not.

Well ... he was definitely a normal male. Actually, normal didn't quite fit. I'd seen my share of naked guys—you couldn't surf or swim in Hawaii without seeing more than a few male goodies—but there had been none like Xander.

It was a real shame he was a fucking douche.

"You threw me into the boat," I snarled, taking a step forward while he pulled on a pair of board shorts. *Do not be distracted. Do not be distracted.*

"You didn't listen to me," he shot back. "I told you we

weren't going to hurt you. I told you that you were in danger, and you still took off like an idiot ready to die."

Excuse me? Was he actually for real right now?

"Well, I guess since you *told me*, I should be apologizing right now for doubting you, a complete stranger who can create air bubbles to talk under the water." I shook my head while pasting on a broad, fake smile. Then I flipped him off.

Maya made a small squealing noise. "Air bubbles? I want to see that."

Xander shot her a smile and his face softened slightly. "They're called exprendo channels. They form a link, almost like an underwater cell phone."

While they were distracted, I eyed the side of the boat. I was pretty sure I could dive over the edge from here.

"Don't even think about it, human." Xander's warning slammed into me with force. "There is no way you can outswim me, even with a head start. I'll just keep bringing you back, so you might as well hear us out."

I spluttered. "Human? What in ... did you just call me *human*? Like you're not...." I trailed off as the implication of what I was about to say registered. Why would he call me human like that unless he was something other than a human?

"I'm human," Maya jumped in, her voice higher than it had been before. I pulled my attention from the guys and turned it to her. "I'm exactly like you."

I swallowed hard. "And these two?" I tilted my head toward the unnaturally beautiful and unnaturally tall and unnaturally perfect guys. *They aren't human.* Somehow I knew they weren't, but I needed to hear her say the words.

"They're Daelighters." She didn't hesitate, but her voice was very soft, like she was trying not to spook me.

"Daelighters ... what does that mean? Are they fish people?"

It was the only thing that made sense to me. Like mermaids. But I didn't want to call them that in case it was offensive. No doubt movies had badly represented them.

"No." Maya shook her head. "Only Xander is of the water. Chase is a forest guy. Trees are his thing."

My head felt a little fuzzy, which might just be adrenaline, or it might be because I was trying to figure out how trees were his "thing." What did that mean?

"You're confusing her." Xander's deep voice sent a shiver down my spine. I wanted to say it was disgust, and part of it was, but another part went deeper than that. Something I was determined to ignore. "You need to explain from the beginning, so that she—" He cut off, eyes drilling into mine. "What is your name? I don't want to keep calling you *she* and *her*."

"Avalon," I replied, without thought. "Ava." I should have said *Mind your own business, fish face*, but I really didn't want to insult the fish. They were amazing. "Ava Shortlin. Although, since my parents all but abandoned me, I guess I don't really have much of a family to go with the family name."

Maya gasped before reaching out to touch my arm. She was the only one I'd let get close enough to do that, but I still flinched back before she could make contact. "Sorry," she said, retracting her arm. "I just hate that I'm the only one of the four who managed to make it to this point with parents intact."

"The four?"

Did I really want to know what that was? Maybe I should have kept my mouth shut.

"We'll tell you everything," Maya assured me. "But we need to move back toward land. Is that okay?"

"Because I'm in danger?" I asked, dubious.

Chase nodded. "You and Maya both. The Daelighter and humans who attacked you yesterday are actively searching, and we don't want to just sit around and wait for them to find us."

Half of me was screaming no, but the part wanting to learn more about these people was slightly stronger. "I will stick around," I decided. "As long as you don't try anything weird."

"We promise," Chase and Maya said together. Xander didn't answer, and since I was choosing not to look at him any more than was necessary, I was cool with that.

Chase stepped forward to the other captain's chair and pressed a button. Powerful engines roared to life. I hadn't seen an anchor when I'd been below, but somehow the boat hadn't moved at all since it stopped here. Probably Xander's doing; he apparently controlled water. *Daelighter.* Excitement bubbled low in my stomach and I had no idea why. This situation should be scaring me. I had been dropped into a completely new world where I knew none of the rules. Instead, I felt like maybe, for the first time in a long time, I was not quite so alone. There were others like me.

3

*a*t first there was only the noise of the ocean to keep us company, and I relaxed because this was my favorite tune. But, while I wished I could just remain in my cocoon of comforting water sounds, I needed answers, and that required me to ask questions.

Turning in my seat, I focused on Maya. She was the one I felt most comfortable with. "I'm going to need you to tell me everything, in detail. Don't beat around the bush, just get to the point. What are Daelighters? How am I involved? What are the four?"

That covered the most pertinent points at this time.

Maya smiled, looking happier than I'd seen since I'd been shot into the boat. "You're already so much cooler than I expected. I love honest, straight-up people." I did also, so it was nice to know we had that in common. "Okay," she started, "Daelighters are aliens. Pretty much."

What in the.... Well, I definitely had not seen that one coming. I'd thought mutants. Aliens just seemed so much more ... out of this world.

I managed to keep my expression neutral while images of little green creatures and ray guns ran through my head. I mean, clearly Xander and Chase were not even remotely little ... or green, but maybe these were like human suits they wore or something.

Maya cracked up then. "If you're anything like me, you're trying to work out how they aren't bulbous-headed mutants. The planet they're from is called Overworld, and they actually have a lot in common with humans. This is what they look like, no disguises. They need the same basic fundamentals as us to survive. Water, oxygen, and the rest."

We might have a little in common with these aliens, but I'd seen Xander in the water—there were also a ton of differences. And since I had a small amount of their abilities, that meant...

"Am I half alien? Is that why I can swim in the water the way I do?"

I didn't mean to sound so horrified, and judging by the way Xander leveled his narrowed eyes on me, he wasn't very impressed with my tone of voice.

"You'd be lucky to be half-Daelighter," he said bluntly. "We are superior to humans in a lot of ways."

"Especially your ego," I shot back before I dismissed him completely, turning back to Maya.

She wore a soft look on her face. I was really hoping it wasn't pity. "You're not half-Daelighter," she said. "You're the same as me. We're humans who were born in their land. Some of their energy infiltrated into ours. This is why you have a semblance of the Royale abilities."

If I wasn't sitting down, I might have fallen over at those words. "I wasn't born on Earth?"

There was no way.... They were wrong. This was some weird, messed-up joke.

I half-lurched out of my chair. I needed to swim. I needed to forget everything I'd just learned. Xander got to me so fast that I barely even had a chance to step forward.

"No, wait." He held me tight and I struggled against him, hating that I felt so out of control. "Listen to me," he demanded, his arms like steel bands that I was uselessly smashing against. "You are important to both worlds. Without your help, millions, if not billions, of people and Daelighters will die."

A sob choked from me before I could pull it back, but I stopped struggling because it was futile. "I have nothing," I said to him. "No family. No future. And now you're all telling me that I don't even have my past, that everything I believed about myself is wrong, a lie told by my parents, who bailed as soon as they got me to the age of eighteen."

No wonder they bailed on me. Their human freak of a child.

A familiar feeling of despair washed through me. Some days I just felt like nothing. I knew my self-worth shouldn't be tied to anyone else, to their actions, but I believed that humans needed a tribe. And I didn't have one. I was adrift in this world, trying to find my tide pool.

"You don't have nothing," Xander told me firmly, loosening his grip just enough to lean back. "You have a destiny far greater than you could have imagined. You have a family you don't even know about, and if you bail on us now, you'll never know about them."

He released me completely, and I lifted my hands to wipe away the stray tears that had escaped. I was an emotional crier. The last time I'd shed tears was when I woke up to the note from my parents. In this moment, my chest hurt almost as much, and I couldn't quite figure out why.

Maya pushed Xander to the side, shooting him a glare. "Stop manhandling her, you big jerk. This is a huge shock. I remember how it felt and I had my parents—who I trusted—tell me about it."

Xander just crossed his arms, leaning back against the side of the boat railing, not at all off-balance even though we were still flying through the water. Maya returned her focus to me.

"I'm sorry, Ava. I really wish there was an easier way to tell you it all."

I waved my hand at her, clearing my throat. "No, I told you to just hit me with it. I'm standing by that. I ... I won't run until you've finished."

She moved, almost like she was going to hug me, but stopped at the last moment. I was both grateful and kinda sad that she did.

"Okay, so Daelighters and humans have a treaty," she continued. "This is the reason you were born in Overworld. You're part of the treaty."

I managed not to comment on this, wanting her to finish.

"Basically, there are four houses in Overworld: Darken, Imperial, Leights, and Royale. These four houses have a wormhole transporter thing set up between Earth and Overworld. It's permanent and the government knows about it. In exchange for this transporter—which helps to power the land of Overworld—the humans got a stone. Starslight stone, to be exact. Which is very powerful and was buried somewhere near the equator to stop an out-of-control series of storms that was rocking Earth."

This was insane, but it would certainly make a great sci-fi television show. Reality, not so fun.

"How do I come into this?" I murmured.

She shot me a wry grin. "Well, the stone is so powerful that it's hidden from everyone except for one Daelighter and four humans. The four humans are like a map. Together they lead to the stone if the need ever arises to find it. They're called the secret keepers."

"And I'm one of them," I guessed.

Maya nodded. "You are number four, actually. The final one who can lead us to the stone."

"You were born in Overworld, in the House of Royale." Xander spoke up, his voice low and dangerously rumbly. "My house."

His assertion felt right; not believing would only be pure stubbornness at this stage. Maybe if I hadn't spent most of my life under the water, with abilities far beyond a human's, I would be more skeptical. But truth be told, the story made sense. Especially with the evidence of Xander right in front of me.

Land came into sight then and this spurred Maya on. She hurriedly explained the rest to me. She told me about the four overlord minors—Xander and Chase were apparently royalty in their land, which explained the arrogance. And she went into a little more detail about the four secret keepers, and then finally about Laous.

The one creating all the drama in both worlds.

This Laous was a Daelighter who wanted to find the stone, wanted the power, and would stop at nothing to get it. He'd hurt and killed and kidnapped his way through the first three keepers. All that was left was me. It had been his people who'd shot at us yesterday. I rubbed my arm. The bandage was long gone now, just a thin line of stitches from Doc's handiwork remaining.

"What happened to your arm?" Xander's question was

abrupt. I wasn't sure why he'd bothered to ask when he clearly didn't give a shit.

Not wanting to look at him, but not able to be that rude, I gave him a quick glance and said, "Just a scrape from yesterday. A bullet grazed me."

Before I could avert my eyes, I noticed his darkened from blue to something that resembled a sky about to rain bloody hell down on earth, dark and stormy.

Swallowing hard, I turned away and hurried to say, "I have no idea at all where this stone is ... like, not a freakin' clue. If I'm the final, and I'm the one who is supposed to hold the knowledge of this location, then shouldn't I ... know?"

Chase turned, hands still on the wheel holding us steady in the ocean. "I have a theory about that, actually. We can talk more about it when we get back to our home."

"Secret lair," Maya cut in, shooting her *mate* a cheeky grin. "Home would be a little ... homier."

Ugh, they were just too darn cute. Couldn't they take that somewhere else so us lonely people didn't have to hate them through envy? Deciding it would be easier if I just turned away, I swiveled around again to face forward. Xander stayed on the side, just in the periphery of my vision. Annoying squid.

We were closing in fast on land now, and I was somewhat excited by the prospect of meeting the others. I'd heard a bit about Emma and Callie, the first and second of the secret keepers. Apparently the four of us had a special sort of bond. They'd been waiting for me to see if we would feel a stronger connection together.

Someone had been waiting for me. Pretty sure that was a first.

Chase took the boat around familiar headland. We were no longer on Lanai but I knew a lot of these islands well. He slowed and docked on a private mooring. "The others are still out searching for you," Maya explained as we moved to get off. "You were moving around so much every time we tried to track you using the crystal."

The crystal part was a little extra weird. Apparently when dipped in the blood of the previous keeper, it would track the next one. Daelighters really needed to come up with a better system for hiding their things.

"I was moving across the island last night," I confirmed. "Walking to reach my friend. He's a doctor. He patched me up. And then this morning I was swimming all over."

Maya's face fell. "I'm so sorry you got hurt because of me. Laous is.... He needs to die. Nothing else will suffice."

My very brief and limited experience with Laous had me agreeing with her. He'd been power-spraying bullets into the ocean like a madman, trying to pick us off like we were nothing more than animals. In fact, he might have actually hit some of the sea creatures, and that was not okay with me.

Oh, and there was also the small thing of him wanting to steal a stone that was keeping both worlds alive and functioning. Worlds he lived on. He had to be completely insane. "What is Laous's plan once he gets this stone? Does he think the threats to both worlds are no longer there? That the treaty is obsolete?"

Maya shrugged. "I'm not sure he's thinking clearly at all anymore. He had a very traumatic childhood. He let some of it slip to me when he thought I was in his custody and not going to be released. All he sees is the power. He's determined to never be vulnerable again."

Xander and Chase both shook their heads then, almost in sync. "There was never any indication that Laous had an abusive upbringing," Chase said. "From what my parents said, he was top of his classes, succeeded in all areas, had a close tie to his brother, Lucas."

Xander made a sound of agreement. "And Daniel's father, Lucas, never mentioned anything about his parents being that horrible. He would have said something, right? The only thing he ever told Daniel was that his parents were killed in an accident just before Daniel was born."

Daniel.... I was trying to remember who he was. Pretty sure he was the mate of another secret keeper. Callie, maybe.

We all just stood on the dock, and since security was an issue, I found myself looking around, trying to make sure there was no attack on the way. "You're safe right now," Xander said, brushing by me so he could take the lead.

I tried not to react, but his skin sliding across mine, even for that brief second, created a strange sensation in my body. I had momentarily forgotten I was standing there in just a wet shirt and underwear, but Xander definitely created an awareness in my body. My blood was bubbling ... fizzing. Like water when it was disturbed.

Shaking that off, I hurried after the small group. Maya fell into step with me. Before I could stop her, she reached out and linked our arms together. Somehow, despite her tiny stature, it worked comfortably. "I'm so glad we found you before Laous." She flashed those kind blue eyes at me and I couldn't bring myself to pull away.

It kind of felt nice, actually. Like I had a friend. I remembered how it was done. I hadn't been a loner my entire life, but it had been a while.

"I'm glad as well, as long as you all aren't leading me to my death now."

Maya just chuckled and squeezed my arm. I had to laugh too. I mean ... their story was so far-fetched that it had to be true. No one would make up something that crazy. Plus ... it explained so many things about me. My water abilities. The reason my parents always called me a burden and a responsibility. They needed to make sure the secret keeper was kept alive until I turned eighteen. After that, I was on my own. My own responsibility.

It would have been nice if they'd told me more about Daelighters before they just bailed. I almost walked right into a huge situation involving aliens. Freaking aliens!

"Why do you think my parents never said anything to me? I mean, if they work for the government and this was their job, surely they shouldn't just take off?"

Maya let out a tiny huff, almost like annoyance. "They will be in big trouble when the government catches up to them. Not to mention, you're not just a job, you're their child."

I shrugged. "I thought I was, but maybe they had to adopt me? Maybe my actual parents were killed?"

For some reason, that made me feel better, an explanation I could go with rather than that the very people who should have loved me most thought of me as nothing more than a job to get through.

"I will check with my parents as soon as we're back in contact," Maya said. "We're off the radar now, in case Laous figures out how to track us."

Her face fell, and I could only guess that if you had a loving family, it would be really tough to not be able to talk to them.

Our conversation was cut off when we arrived at a very fancy black car parked just around the corner from the moored boat. "This is our ride," Chase said, holding the door open for us. "Time to get back to the secret lair."

He winked at his girl, and she shook her head, a soft smile spreading across her face.

Meanwhile I was trying to control my breathing because it was all getting real for me now. Secret lair. Aliens. Fancy cars. None of this was my life.

I had no choice. I needed to see this through. So I was getting in the car.

4

"I'm soaking wet," I reminded them, staring at the seats. "I will destroy the leather."

"Here is a towel to keep you warm." Xander surprised me by handing across a huge, warm, white beach towel. "Don't worry about the seats, you won't hurt them."

Maya shot me a grin. "These guys have more cars than brain cells. Don't stress about it. They really don't care."

I shrugged. "Okay, then, I can only offer."

My hair was mostly dry from the boat ride, so I just quickly rubbed the towel over the ends.

"Your hair is amazing," Maya said, her gaze running along the strands. "It's silver and rainbow. Unicorn hair."

More like mermaid hair. "This is a House of Royale thing, right?" I asked Xander, wanting it confirmed. I'd seen it in his hair, so I was pretty sure.

He nodded. "Yes, this is a feature from my house. The pigments in our hair open up under the water, which creates a rainbow effect. Like when rain and sun mix together in the sky."

Such a cool fact. It was nice to finally know why some of these things happened to me.

Once I'd wrapped the towel around myself, I climbed into the back. Xander ended up taking the seat on the other side of me. Chase drove, with Maya sitting shotgun. I spent most of the trip staring out the window. Maya shot me worried looks every now and then, but mostly she just held hands with her mate and sat quietly. After some time, I felt Xander's eyes on me, and had to shift around in my seat toward him. He had answers I'd sought my entire life. I wanted to know about the world under the sea, about my abilities. I wanted to know if I would eventually be able to stay under there, in the world of my heart.

"Do you live under the sea?" I asked softly.

His eyes were too beautiful; it was hard to concentrate when they were focused so intently on me. Luckily he had such a rotten personality. That helped me not look at him as anything more than a means to an end.

"Yes," he said. "House of Royale is a world under the water."

"They call it legreto," Maya chimed in from the front. "Not water."

I didn't turn to her. Xander held my attention too strongly. "You sleep under there?" I hated the note of hope in my voice. I wasn't a Royale. I was a human with a little Daelighter energy within me, but I wanted so badly to live under the sea.

He nodded. "Our ability to breathe below and above the water is what makes us unique on our world. So, when I'm in my house, I'm always beneath the water."

My eyes burned as I tried to clear my throat. "I have to come up for air," I whispered. "I can stay under for a long time, but not forever. I always—"

I broke off because he didn't care about my hopes and dreams. It was better for me to keep it to myself.

Xander didn't say anything more, but his gaze wasn't quite so dismissive the next time he met my eyes. Eventually I turned back to the window, watching the island flash by. They had taken their boat out quite a way from their safe house, which was probably to hide the trail if anyone was following.

Chase eventually turned off, taking us inland, toward a small patch of rainforest. He had to use the four-wheel drive capabilities of the car to get over some of the rougher areas. I noticed through the trees there was an estate of huge beach houses, and when we pulled up and all got out, that was the direction they led me in.

Their secret lair wasn't really secret or lair-like. It looked like an upmarket beach shack, one of those new builds trying to mimic the original island shacks in design and materials, only everything was too fancy and new to actually fit in.

My misgivings about this "safe house" were smashed when we took the side entrance and walked down into a basement of sorts. Okay, definitely not common in Hawaii. I didn't know anyone with a basement. Xander led us toward an elevator ... in their house. He had to use his handprint to open the silver doors. I was pretty sure this was the first elevator I'd ever been on, but, of course, I'd also thought I was born on Earth, so what did I know?

As I was about to step into the metal box, unexpected nerves had me hesitating. I had to take a deep, calming breath to overcome them, before I stepped inside. My hands remained tightly clenched as the doors closed, and when it lurched to the side, I had to swallow my shriek. I reached out and grasped a nearby rail to steady myself.

"Are you okay?" Maya asked.

I bobbed my head up and down. "Yep. Just … first time in an elevator."

Thankfully we came to a halt not ten seconds later. It was a huge relief to step out, and I blinked at the large room filled with computers and huge screens up on the walls. It looked like those surveillance rooms in cop drama TV shows. I recognized a lot of the images that were flashing by in black and white. Lanai and Oahu were prominent.

"We're tracking Laous's movements," Chase explained, crossing over to a set of three huge screens. He reached out and pressed an image, making it larger. It looked like a traffic camera, which had to be privately owned because outside of the main tourist hubs there was no need for cameras here.

"Facial recognition has picked him up a few times," Maya told me as she joined her mate. "He's definitely still looking for us, but so far has remained on Lanai."

It was probably lucky they got to me when they did. Lanai was not huge; it would have been a miracle not to run into him. A sudden terrifying thought hit me. "My friend, the one I stayed with last night, is he safe? Will Laous somehow track me?"

What if he tortured Doc to try and find my location?

I was already heading for the door. Swimming from Oahu to Lanai would be no problem for me, especially if Doc's life was at stake.

"Wait, it'll be quicker if I get Lexen to check on him," Chase said, pulling a cell phone from his pocket. "They're on Lanai. What's the address?"

I quickly told them how to get to Doc's place, and then turned to the surveillance. "Can we get any images over that area?" I asked.

Chase was on the phone, so Xander stepped up, his hand

moving superfast, tapping a sequence into a keyboard. It almost looked like coordinates, and then I jumped as Doc's porch and roof came into sight.

"It's a satellite image," Xander explained, "so I'm limited, but it looks like everything is quiet there."

"Is there any way to see the porch clearly?" I pressed in closer, not even caring that I'd have to touch the prickly Daelighter. I just needed to see Doc.

Xander didn't say anything. He pressed a few more buttons and the angle of the image changed. All my breath whooshed out of me as Doc's familiar grizzled face came into view. He was staring out across the ocean, looking somewhat peaceful.

I only realized I'd slumped forward in relief when Xander shifted his arm slightly—I'd fallen right against him.

"Sorry," I muttered, stepping back. "Thanks for checking on him for me."

Chase finished talking to Lexen, dropping his phone to the table. "He said they're going to head straight back. He wanted to know if you want him to bring Doc back to this safe house?"

I shook my head. "He won't leave, trust me. He's a very stubborn old man, and he hardly ever leaves his house. If Laous hasn't found him yet, it should be fine." It had to be fine, because if I cost Doc his life—even if the old dude was ready to die—I would never forgive myself. Never.

Chase nodded, keyed in a message, and sent it off.

"We can check on him through this satellite as well," Xander reminded me. "At least until we head back to Overworld. After that, I'll have some of the House of Royale members stationed close by check on him."

Wow, that was so much more thoughtful than I had expected. Especially from Xander. "Thank you," I said, focusing on the fact that Doc should be safe. I wasn't quite ready to think about leaving Earth for an alien world. I was just going to pretend he didn't say that.

"How many Daelighters are here at the moment?" Maya asked, dropping into Chase's lap. He wrapped an arm around her.

"We have a few hundred from the different houses," Xander said. "More arrived last night. They're here in case Laous got his hands on Avalon first. We would have had to fight him and his army then."

"Army?" I asked.

Xander let out a short laugh. "Yeah, he's managed to get the Gonzo on his side. Black ops military group, very big into war and rebirth of the world."

Well, great. This story just got better and better. It did explain why there were so many guns shooting at us yesterday.

"I'm going to program Ava into the security system," Chase said, and then he turned to me. "If you get locked out or separated from us for any reason, you can always get back here and hide out."

I nodded, feeling somewhat happy that they were including me. They had said I was a huge part of this, that we were a family. But people said a lot of things that they didn't follow through with. This was a small step toward building trust between us.

Chase was typing away. "I'm going to need handprints, and you'll get a code as well."

My left hand curled in even further than normal, and I wondered how it would work for this sort of security system.

"Will one hand work?" I asked, not embarrassed exactly, but wanting to put it out there. I waved my left hand at them, showing the ropy scar tissue on my palm and wrist and the way my fingers curled in. "I was attacked by a shark years ago.

My hand is pretty shot now. I won't be able to get it straight enough to press flat."

It took a lot of guts for me to just throw my flaws out in the world like that, and in the moment of silence that followed, my heartbeat pounded in my ears.

Maya was the first to react. She jumped up off Chase's lap and wrapped her arms around me. "That is so freaking scary, but also amazing. You were attacked by a shark and survived!"

I didn't know how to react to her hug. It had been months since anyone had even attempted to hug me, aside from those few people I saved from drowning. And they were more about keeping themselves above the water.

I patted Maya's back. "Yeah, it was scary, but I still love sharks. He didn't mean to hurt me, I just got in the way of the fish he was going after."

Luckily it had only been a baby great white. Any bigger and I'd have lost my entire arm.

"We don't have the same marine life in Overworld," Xander said, relaxing back in his chair. "The *meglam* would be the closest, a cross between an alligator and a shark. Outside of Royales, they rule the waters."

I froze, just a little, because the mental image of what he described was scary. "Sharks are the kings in our waters, and I respect them."

"I'm glad to hear that," Xander replied. "Humans are notorious for thinking they are the only creatures that matter. Everything else is expendable."

I was no normal human, but there was no point telling him that. Xander clearly had a thing against my kind, and I really didn't have time to care.

Chase went back to the previous subject. "In regard to the security, I can definitely just use one hand."

Nothing more was said, and no one seemed grossed out by my mangled hand. That made me feel another level of comfort with them.

Once all the security stuff was done, Maya twisted around so she was facing Chase. "So, I think you should tell us now what your theory is about Ava and the map to the stone."

"I think we need to take Ava back to the waters of Royale," Chase said. "Back to wherever she was born. I assume that's the place that will reveal the map. Somehow."

"Like the knowledge will appear in her mind? Or the network will kick in and show us the way?" Maya pressed.

Chase shrugged. "No way to tell, and I could be completely off track, but I've always wondered how exactly the network managed to tie four humans together who were all born at different times. I know your births had to be within the same year, but that doesn't seem like a close enough connection."

Xander crossed his arms, leaning back into the wall. "My understanding of it is that the secret keepers are a chain. With each birth, another link was added. The final link is Avalon, and she is the one with the lock attached to her. The lock and the key. Staying in the same year of birth was probably just so the chain was completed relatively quickly to satisfy the treaty terms."

His intelligence didn't surprise me, and I liked the way he called me by my full name. For some stupid reason.

Chase nodded. "That makes sense. When the others get back, we can decide on the best route home. We need to figure out the map straight away."

I cleared my throat, because it almost felt like they'd forgotten I was here. "I'm not sure how I feel about leaving Earth...."

I trailed off because that statement pretty much said it all.

Before anyone could reply, the elevator behind us whirred, followed by a clunk. I took a step back when a new group filed through the metal doors. There was no way for me to tell who they were. I didn't recognize any of them, and I felt uneasy again.

An auburn-haired girl broke away from the crowd and pretty much sprinted for me. Well, she took two steps, tripped over something on the floor, and sprawled across the ground.

"Shit!" she cursed as she pushed herself up with two hands. "This is why I don't run," she moaned. Before she could pull herself all the way up, a huge dude scooped her into his arms.

I let my eyes rest on the guy. He was definitely a Daelighter. Dark-haired, flashing dark eyes, symbols on his head just like Chase and Xander. One of the overlord minors, I would guess.

He was gorgeous and intimidating, but he held the girl in his arms with great care.

"Emma, babe, you really have to stop falling down. You're giving me anxiety."

Emma and this overlord were clearly in love. He held her like she was precious, cradling her close, his gaze locked on hers. She had one hand resting against his face as he moved closer to us.

Behind them was another pair. The chick was tall and blond, the guy shaved-headed and menacing, and they too were in love. He had a hand on her back; she was leaning into him.

I took another step back, my eyes darting between the three secret keepers and their mates.

"Ava?" Maya was off Chase's lap now. She took a step closer to me. "Is everything okay? Come and meet Emma and Lexen, and Callie and Daniel."

She waved me over, but I took another step back.

"You're all couples?" I asked, trying to keep the upset from my tone. "How?" Why hadn't they told me that part before now?

The love in the room was overflowing everywhere, but I didn't understand how it could be possible. It made me question the strong warmth in my chest whenever I looked at Xander. What was going on here?

Emma, back on her feet now, crossed the last few steps to stand before me. She was smiling brightly, although there looked to be a flash of worry in her eyes as well. "It's so nice to meet you," she started. "I've been waiting such a long time for the four of us to be together."

I swallowed roughly, trying to find some moisture. "I...." God, what the hell was I going to say? This was just getting too weird for me. "It's nice to meet you as well."

Because I was hyperaware of Xander, I noticed him stand. He was out of his chair and before me in a heartbeat.

"Stop panicking," he said bluntly. "Yes, the secret keepers and the overlords are connected. The eight of us are part of fate's plan, but that doesn't mean you and I have to follow the trend. My world is not for you. There would be no way for you to survive. All you have to focus on is finding the stone. Once we do that, the council is going to figure out another way to hide it. They're going to try and break the link you four have to it. This should all be over then."

Callie, the blond secret keeper, gasped. "I didn't know that was the plan."

"We got word last night," Daniel said. "The new treaty is in the works now. The humans have agreed that this way of hiding the stone does not work. There will be no more secret keepers once this is all over."

They continued to talk over each other, discussing everything that was going on, but I could not get past what Xander
had just said. There was a fated bond between the secret
keepers and the overlords, one that had created these strong
relationships I was seeing. But he didn't want to even acknowledge that with me. I was not for him. Not for his world.

Not for his world.

He hadn't moved, still standing before me, those ocean
eyes locked on me.

"Excuse me," I said coldly, pushing past him. I needed to
get out of here before I screamed or cried. The emotional
crying thing was a real bitch when I was trying to hide how
much his dismissive words had hurt me.

Why the hell had they hurt me? I didn't know him or care
about him, but rejection was always a bitch.

He didn't move. "Get the fuck out of my way," I said,
keeping my voice toneless. The curse word should be enough
for him. "I need some space."

He took a step back and I sucked in a quiet breath.
"Where's the bathroom?" I asked Maya, who was close by.

"Just down the hall," she said, pointing. "There are a few
bathrooms back there. Feel free to use whatever one
you want."

I nodded. "Thank you."

I could feel eyes on me as I hurried off, but I didn't
look back.

5

My breathing was ragged as I moved quickly toward the bathroom; my face felt very flushed. When I got inside the first generic white, tiled space, I closed the door and leaned back against it.

Eventually I made my way across to the sink and mirror, letting the towel drop to the ground. My hair fanned out around me, dry and wavy from the ocean. Other than that, I was a mess: barely clothed, salt and sand across my skin, eyes wild and greener than usual.

It was hard for me to believe that I had woken up this morning with the same life as always, and within a matter of hours everything had changed. I didn't even know who I was anymore.

I stood there for a long time, trying to calm myself. Hiding in the bathroom all day sounded like the best idea ever, but I knew it wasn't going to happen. They wanted to get back to Overworld. They wanted to find this map I possessed. Basically, all of their family talk could be construed as "we need you, so we'll keep you around for a bit."

There was a light knock on the door then and I swung around. "Yes?" I said shortly.

"Hey, it's Emma."

"And Callie," another voice added.

"And Maya," she finished.

"We'd just really like to introduce ourselves, explain every-thing," Emma chimed in again.

Knowing I couldn't avoid them forever, I decided it was better to get it out of the way.

"Sure, come in," I called, leaning back against the sink.

I couldn't get comfortable of course, so when the three girls trooped in, I was shifting left to right like there was a sea urchin on my ass. I forced myself to stop fidgeting because they didn't need to know how awkward I was.

The room wasn't huge, and with the four of us in there it felt downright small. Emma was the closest; she stopped right before me. I didn't feel uncomfortable, though; she main-tained just enough personal space.

"Hi," she said softly, her blue eyes soft and kind-looking. "I'm so happy to finally meet you."

She held her hand out and I didn't hesitate in reaching forward to grasp it in greeting.

"Sorry for bailing," I said quietly. "It's just been a really weird day. Usually when that happens I escape to the ocean. Being stuck inside ... it makes me a little insane."

She squeezed my hand briefly, and in the same moment Callie touched her shoulder, and Maya moved in close enough for her arm to brush against Emma's.

The four of us gasped. Mine was because a buzz of what felt like electricity had just zapped through me and was still running up and down my arm.

"You all felt that, right?" Callie asked. I immediately

pegged her as being a little reserved. Her eyes were gray and guarded, but not unkind.

"Yep," Maya said as she nodded. "Holy crap, that was stronger than when we all went into the network."

The buzz seemed to be increasing, and I was about to mention something to Emma when she wrenched her hand out of mine. "Sorry," she said breathlessly, "but I was afraid we were going to blow up or something. That was intense."

My chest heaved up and down as I tried to breathe and process what had just happened. "What was that?"

Before anyone could answer, a heavy knock on the door had us all jumping. "Everything okay in there?" asked a deep voice. I was pretty sure it was Lexen, but I couldn't be sure. "We heard you all gasp."

Emma cleared her throat before answering. "We're all fine. We'll be out in a minute, Lex."

There was no sound for a moment, and then I heard his footsteps leaving. Emma straightened and said, "I knew there was going to be a strong connection between the four of us." She looked between us. "The secret keepers are connected on a basic level, the same way we are connected to the four overlords."

"I noticed that," I cut in dryly. "It's actually one of the reasons I 'needed some air.'"

Maya chuckled. "Been there, done that. I was running off for 'air' far too frequently when I was first initiated into this world. When I realized that there seemed to be a common theme of secret keepers being soul mates with Daelighters ... I didn't really handle that information too well."

"So, the three of you are all...?" I trailed off.

All of them nodded.

"Lexen's dragon soul chose me as a mate. They only have one in a lifetime," Emma said.

"Daniel tied our souls together when Laous killed me," Callie added. "So now I have to stay around him and the House of Imperial land or my soul starts to fade."

I blinked at her. "Uh, killed ... what?"

She smiled, which turned her face from pretty into breath-taking. "Yeah, it's a fun story, but suffice it to say I'm doing great now. I'm very happy with my fate."

She looked like she was doing great, definitely not like someone who had been killed recently. Her platinum blond hair was thick, her skin was glowing, and she looked healthy and fit.

"I'm really glad Laous didn't succeed," I told her sincerely. I wasn't sure if it was the electrical shock we all generated, or whatever bond they were talking about kicking in, but the kinship I suddenly felt was very real ... and a little scary.

"I'm glad too. Missing out on knowing Daniel is something I don't even want to think about," Callie told me. "Not to mention finally finding a family with all of you."

It warmed my heart to be included like that. I could tell she meant it as well, and my stupid emotional tears were trying to surface. Forcing them down, I turned to Maya. "You and Chase ... you're bonded as well?"

She nodded, her long, wavy, purple-streaked hair tumbling across her shoulders. "Yes, he is from a land where the trees are gods, pretty much. They tethered our souls together. It's a forever sort of bond."

My throat felt full, my chest felt tight, and I was trying to figure out if I was about to have a full-on breakdown. "Xander," I spluttered, shaking my head. I couldn't get any more words out, and suddenly Emma was wrapping me up in a hug.

"Don't worry about Xander," she whispered to me. "He is part of our group, the same as you are, but it doesn't mean that you two have to be together. That's not how it works. You're free to make your own choices."

I sort of snorted, and when she pulled away I quirked an eyebrow at her. "You three had a choice?"

"Yes," Callie said without hesitation. "The connection to our guys was there from the start, especially for me and our soul-bond. But I chose to be with Daniel. We could have just stayed friends. Or allies."

Maya distracted us then when she attempted to jump up to sit on the sink. She was so tiny that her butt just skimmed the edge and she tumbled down. Callie managed to grab her before she hit the floor.

"Dammit," Maya groused. "This is why being short sucks. Especially when I'm surrounded by all you supermodel types."

I couldn't help but smile. "Girl, I'm so far from a supermodel." I waved my hand at her, letting them all see the scars. For some reason I knew they wouldn't judge me. That was rare, and I really hoped I wasn't wrong.

"That's from the shark?" Emma asked, wide-eyed as she reached for my hand.

I nodded. "Yep, just a baby one, thankfully."

Maya and Callie both leaned over for a closer look.

"The scars show how badass you are," Emma said as she stepped back. "Don't ever doubt how gorgeous you are. You're probably the closest thing I've ever seen to a supermodel. No one cares about a few marks on your hand. You are perfect."

"How tall are you?" Callie asked. "I rarely meet women taller than me. It's a nice change."

"You're definitely beautiful," Maya put in quietly. "Honestly, you didn't see Xander in the boat because I could tell you

47

were trying not to look his way, but he didn't take his eyes off you the entire time."

My heart swelled, and I realized the strength in a group of strong, confident women who weren't trying to tear each other down. Support and encouragement. They were straightening my crown rather than trying to steal it, because they all wore crowns as well.

Until this moment I would have been that chick who said they preferred to have male friends. Dudes were chill; we'd surf together, drink together, and be mostly drama free. But I knew now that I'd been missing out by not having girlfriends.

"You three are ... so nice," I said, sounding like the biggest loser, but wanting to express my feelings anyway. "I don't think I've ever felt so accepted before."

"We're a team ... a family," Maya said, her voice wavering. "A bond that is beyond any normal human friendship. The four of us might not have been physically together for that much time, but our souls have been connected since birth."

"When we all touched," I told them, "I felt that. Whatever nerves I had about being in this world ... they've almost completely faded away. I never would have believed it could happen like this ... but here we are."

The next knock on the door was not quite as heavy. I still jumped of course, because it felt like I was in a bubble in this room. A warm, sweet bubble.

"We have food out here," Chase said. His voice I would recognize anywhere, it was so damn smooth. "Whenever you're ready."

My stomach growled in response, reminding me that I hadn't eaten at all today. I had no idea what time it was, but it felt like hours since I woke for my swim.

"I could eat," Callie admitted, laughing. "This soul-bond

thing is kind of draining on me, especially when I've been away from House of Imperial for an extended amount of time." She met my eyes then. "Are you okay to come out now? Because we can totally stay in here longer if you need more time."

"I'm hungry too," I decided. "Let's eat."

Emma clapped her hands and the other two threw indulgent smiles at her. "Emma is our cheer squad," Maya told me with a huge grin. "Even though I'm the one who was the actual cheerleader, Emma is the one who rallies us all together."

"She's the best," Callie added.

Emma's cheeks went very pink and she waved them away. "I'm just all about showing people how much I care about them. I lost my family—I felt lower than I ever had. I didn't think I'd ever be happy again. But I am." Some of the joy filtered out of her eyes. "Even though I miss my mom and dad so much. God ... so damn much. It still hurts to even think about them. I know they'd be so happy if they could see my new family, and that makes it a lot easier. Every day it gets easier."

Maya let out a strangled sob. "We need to leave before I start bawling. It's going to happen. I promise."

I was right there with Maya; my eyes felt damp and hot. Thankfully as we all started to file out of the room, I managed to get my emotions under control. I also felt ... better. Truly calm and content for the first time in a long time. Of course, the moment I came face-to-face with Xander—leaning against a nearby wall, staring in our direction—all the confused emotions from before smashed right back into me.

I need the ocean. It was the best thing to clear my head.

When he walked over to us, my chest got tight. I tried to figure out what he wanted. *Wait, are those sweats in his hands?*

"They're going to be way too big for you, but I figured you might want some ... pants," he said, holding them out.

His eyes were filled with humor, and I was pretty sure he was checking out the long length of my bare legs. Reaching out, I worked very hard not to snatch the clothes out of his hands. I seriously didn't want to wear his pants, but I also didn't want to keep walking around in my underwear.

I quickly shimmied into them, tightening the drawstring as much as I could so they stayed up. "I have clothes," I told him as I rolled the legs up a few times. "They're at the lifeguard tower back in Lanai. They keep my bag for me when I go swimming."

Xander shrugged. "You're going to have to say goodbye to that bag for now. We can't risk going to any of your normal hangouts."

When I was clothed and upright, Callie reached out and linked her arm with mine. "It's okay, we're practically the same height. I'll share until we can get you your own."

Thankful for her intervention, I turned my attention in her direction. Together we moved over to the table. I could feel Xander's eyes on me, but I was determined not to look back.

When we reached the food, Callie released me and I mouthed a thank-you to her. She just smiled. Trying not to act like a starving weirdo, I took my time looking everything over, when all I really wanted to do was grab as many things as I could and stuff them into my mouth.

"Swimming at the speeds we do burns a lot of calories."

I knew it was Xander; I could feel the energy running between us. It had been there from the first moment in the water together. When he touched me it increased greatly, but I would be stronger than it. I knew now this was just a byproduct of the secret keeper thing. Nothing more. Wearing his clothes was literally the only time I was getting into his pants. End of story.

"I already know that," I told him. "Generally I have to eat five or six full-size meals a day. Otherwise I lose a lot of weight." Not to mention I was six feet tall—I had a lot of body to fill up.

"Take as much as you want," Emma said, shooting everyone a look. "Let Avalon go first," she told them.

"It's okay," I cut in. "Seriously, don't worry about me. I don't need any special treatment ... and it's just Ava," I added.

"I'm Lexen, it's nice to meet you," the dragon lord dude said. The gorgeous, intimidating, scary overlord.

"Nice to meet you, too," I managed to chirp back.

"Daniel," the shaved-headed one said. "Overlord of House of Imperial."

He was blunt. He suited Callie, who I felt had the same honest bluntness to her—from what I had seen in the ten minutes I'd known them all, of course.

All eight of us were standing around the table now; no one had moved toward the food. It almost felt like ... we needed this moment. The eight of us together.

"It feels different now." Maya broke the silence. "The energy between us. It's stronger. More complete."

Emma quickly jumped in then and told the boys what had happened when the four of us touched. No one spoke, even when she was finished. I wondered if they were unhappy about it, but I wasn't quite confident enough in this group to ask.

"That's what I was talking about before," Chase said finally. "About how we'll find the map Ava possesses. It's something to do with the connection that the secret keepers have to not only

Overworld, but also to each other. I think we need to go to the legreto of Royale, all of us together."

Lexen shifted forward, his eyes intense and focused. "This is a good theory. We should head out tomorrow."

Chase nodded. "Yes, we have no time to waste. The only reason Laous hasn't ordered his human army to level Hawaii to the ground is he doesn't realize we have Ava yet. The second he does...."

"We'll leave first thing in the morning," Daniel said, sounding very boss-like. I remembered from Maya's update in the boat that he was the only one to step into the overlord major role, and I could see the authority written all over him. "The plane is ready to go. I suggest we leave here about 3:00 A.M. Let the dark cover our tracks."

"I'll make sure the helicopter is ready," Xander said, closing off the conversation.

Holy crap. They have a plane and a helicopter?

Then I remembered they were royalty in their land, and it all made sense.

Everyone focused on the food then, grabbing a paper plate each. I waited my turn, perusing the large selection. It consisted mostly of salads, sandwiches, fruit, and very little meat. Which was fine with me. On occasion I would eat raw seafood, but other than that, I wasn't a huge fan of land-dwelling animals. Not for food anyway.

I grabbed a garden salad with a creamy mustard dressing, two salad sandwiches, and a fruit cup and small tub of yogurt. Pretty much all of my favorite foods. Fresh salmon would have topped my salad off, but I was definitely not going to complain.

This place seemed to be only partially set up for living; there was no table to eat at, so I just slid down against a nearby wall and put my plate beside me. Everyone sat on the floor, spreading out across the wall, and ate with me. I tried not to get excited about something that was not a big deal. Probably not to anyone else, anyway.

While I was eating, I took some time to observe them all.

Emma and Lexen sat close together. She picked at his food and he just shook his head with a brooding but indulgent expression on his face. Eventually he handed her his entire pasta, and she leaned up to kiss him on the cheek. Callie and Daniel were a little different; they sat close as well, but each ate their own food quickly and without fuss. Maya and Chase were so sweet. She had her legs draped across his and he had an arm wrapped around her. They seemed far more interested in each other than food. Actually, all three couples were far more interested in each other. Food appeared to be a secondary need.

I tried really hard not to look at Xander, even though there was a bit of a third-wheel feel in the group, and it would make sense for me to gravitate toward him. Thankfully, there were four people between us, so I didn't even appear rude by not talking to him.

Why do I keep thinking about Xander?

I forced myself not to do anything except focus on each bite and enjoy the fact that I wasn't alone. Outside of eating with Doc last night, I hadn't had dinner with people for days, so this was a huge deal for me. I wouldn't let any guy, even one who pretty much looked like a water god, ruin it for me.

6

"Tell us about your life, Ava?" Emma asked, leaning over Lexen to see me. "Have you always lived in Hawaii?"

I swallowed the last of my sandwich, pushing the plate to the side. "Yep." I nodded. "Pretty much. For as long as I can remember, anyway."

"What happened with your parents?" Callie asked.

I pursed my lips together, trying to think of a way to explain my family's dynamics without making myself sound utterly pathetic. "They're not terrible people, just ... uninterested. In me, mostly. They're scientists, all about the stars and way less about their kid here on Earth. Seemed the moment their responsibility to keep me alive was over, they decided to head out on a long holiday. Some sort of expedition cruise that will take them stargazing across the world. I have no idea if they're planning on coming back or not. All they said was the full circumnavigation would take a year."

"How long have you been on your own?" Callie's eyes were dark, her expression filled with understanding.

"Since June, so almost six months."

It felt longer, and yet at the same time I could barely even remember my parents. They'd checked out long before they actually left me.

"How did you survive on your own?"

That question came from the end of the row. I turned toward him because I just had to look. No matter how much I tried to ignore Xander, something kept tugging me back in his direction. "They left me a little money, and I have two jobs. When they first took off I ended up living with a few friends, but then we had a falling out. So, from then I've just been sleeping on the beach. You know ... surfer life."

Homeless surfer life. His eyes narrowed on the "falling out" part and I prayed he wouldn't ask me to elaborate. There was no way I wanted to go into the almost rape I'd experienced at the hands of one very drunk roommate. Joseph had given me the creeps from the start with the way he stared and brushed against me. At the time I decided it was fine to put up with, because at least I had a roof over my head. I just went out of my way to avoid him as much as I could. Unfortunately, one night he got wasted, and the lock on my door had not been enough to keep him out.

I'd bailed that night and never looked back.

"You'll never be alone again," Emma promised me, and with relief I turned away from the intense, probing gaze of the blond Daelighter at the end. "Despite everything Laous has taken from us, and the loss of ... Marsil...." She choked on his name before recovering. "There is one good thing to come from all of the bad. Us. The eight of us are a team."

Maya and Chase had touched briefly on Lexen's brother, who had been killed in a battle with the resistance. The catch in their voices told me it was a very hard loss. It scared me to think that maybe one of the people in this room could be hurt while we tried to wrap this entire Laous mess up. I'd only known them for a short time, but already I knew I would mourn their loss.

"I'm really overwhelmed," I admitted, unable to keep the truth inside any longer. "Despite the Laous situation, meeting the rest of you feels like one of those 'too good to be true' situations, and that makes me want to keep pushing you all away. But ... I'm tired of always having to fight."

Letting them see me vulnerable was scary, but I felt like the only way to know their true intentions was to put myself out there fully and see what happened.

Emma was draped completely across Lexen now. She crawled over his legs so she was close enough to hug me.

"There was probably an easier way to do that," Lexen said with a shake of his head.

Emma tilted her head around to stick her tongue out at him, then shimmied back to her spot beside him. When she was there, she leaned out and said, "We have your back, Ava. Fighting is not so bad when we share the load."

Callie snorted from my other side. "Dibs not sharing my section with Emma. Girl can trip over literally anything." She softened those words by blowing Emma an exaggerated kiss.

Emma just laughed, seemingly completely unoffended. "So true. I feel sorry for anyone who has to be next to my uncoordinated self, but I promise you won't be alone. Or have any feeling in your toes."

"I'll stand with you," I said in a rush. "I can handle it."

Before she could reply, Lexen made an intense rumbling sound and then Emma was in his lap. He moved her so quickly I literally didn't even see it happen. "I have enough coordination for the both of us," he told her, and she practically melted into him. His eyes met mine then, and for the first time the endless darkness in them didn't freak me out. "Em is right, you're not hefting the load on your own anymore. No longer will any of us walk this road alone. The eight of us are meant to be together. We're meant to rule Overworld together."

"You're insane if you think our parents are going to let us unite the houses like that," Xander said, his voice flat, but the mild undertones of disbelief were there. "Sitting together at lunch is one thing, but you're talking about trying to overcome decades of hate and prejudice."

Daniel cut in. "No one said it would be easy, but there has been too much dissension in our world. The fact that Laous managed to recruit members of all four houses to his cause should tell us that we can all work together."

"It'd be nice if we all worked together for a cause to better our people," Callie said. "Not one that could kill everyone."

From my position, Xander looked to be staring out into the wall opposite where we sat, his expression unreadable. He finally said, "I think that you're all looking at this from a naïve, simple perspective. Hundreds of years of hatred and rivalry is not going to be undone just because the four of us are best friends. Or because the three of you have found your mates. But I will go with the majority ... I'm willing to try."

He got up then and walked away, and I almost went after him. Mostly because I wanted to yell at him. I really loved the dynamics of this group. For the first time in months I didn't feel alone, and he was making things awkward and uncomfortable—even if I did think that he made some decent points.

"My mom always said that the first step to any change is simple ... just take a step in the direction you want to go," Maya said in her soft voice. "Be the change you want to see. We can talk about hoping and wishing for a difference all we want, but we're the only ones in a position to actually do something about it. I think seeing the four overlords, major and minor, coming together, is that *change* that your people need to start seeing."

"Our people," Chase reminded her.

She shot him a rueful smile. "Right, still wrapping my head around that."

"I know I can get my parents in," Lexen said.

"Same," Chase added.

Daniel chuckled. "I'm already overlord major, so you know I'm in."

There was a beat of silence and we were all thinking the same thing. Xander said he would go with the majority, so hopefully he'd convince his parents as well.

"We can't do anything until we figure out the map and find the stone, though, right?" I asked.

For some reason, knowing that this map was contained within me, I really needed to figure out how to do that part first.

"Right," Lexen said, getting to his feet with Emma somehow still in his arms. He dropped her gently down and they remained close together. "First thing is to figure out where the stone is and prevent a war and the possible destruction of two worlds. Then we can figure out the best way to move our world forward. As a team. The fates didn't bring us all together for nothing."

Speaking of fate in a literal manner gave me chills. I wasn't religious, but I believed in powers bigger than me. I communed with Mother Nature a lot. You couldn't surf the massive swell, feel the power of the ocean, and not believe that there was a greater power out there.

Everyone else got to their feet then and the three overlords quickly discussed their next steps.

"We need to inform our people here about what is happening now," Chase said. "I think most of them should return to Overworld. We'll keep a few here for backup security."

"I agree," Lexen said, then turned to me. "We'll make sure your friend is safe."

I nodded gratefully. "Thank you. Doc is a good man who's already been through a lot of tragedy. Nothing can happen to him."

"It won't," Emma promised. "The Daelighters are strong. They will protect him if needed."

Lexen nodded. "Okay, so it's late afternoon now, and we have to be at the helicopter by 3:00 A.M. Might be best if everyone rests now."

I was tired, for no other reason than my entire world had been turned upside down today.

"Aliens are real," I murmured, chuckling to myself.

"Insane, right?" Maya chuckled with me. "When my parents first told me, I seriously wondered if I'd heard them correctly or if maybe I was losing my mind."

Emma, who was midway through a yawn, rubbed at her eyes. "I was pretty sure it was a dream. That maybe I'd died in the fire with my parents and everything after that was some weird afterlife." Lexen's face went scary when she mentioned dying, and it was very clear he did not want to even think about that possibility.

Callie broke the heavy air of Emma's sad confession. "I've known since I was small. It was lucky my mom didn't let me go anywhere except fight class, because it wasn't until I was like ten that I learned that not everyone was aware of the aliens walking amongst us. I'd have probably started blabbing about it to anyone who would listen if I'd been in school."

I waved my hand at her. "All little kids believe in aliens and ghosts and monsters. No one would have thought anything of it."

She shook her head. "I find that so weird. It shows how little I know about kids and friendships. I never had any friends until I met Daniel. He's my first best friend, and now there are all the rest of you guys as well. It's helping me understand human nature a lot more."

She probably didn't know then that a true friendship, unconditional in its love and loyalty, was one of the rarest things to find. And the most precious.

MY ROOM CONSISTED OF A BED, two side tables, and two lamps. The lamps were nice, with pale blue covers and dangling gems all around, but otherwise there was nothing distinct or interesting to look at. I was supposed to be sleeping. The early morning start would be here before I knew it. But I couldn't shut my mind off. No matter what I tried, there was no way to stop thinking about everything I'd learned today.

Especially Xander.

He was like me. I had finally found another person—alien —who felt the same way about the water that I did. His people actually lived under there. I expected envy to hit me hard, bitterness that I wasn't Royale enough to be able to live under the water. But there was only overwhelming gratitude. Because of Daelighters, I got to be more than human, experience more than regular humans could dream of. I'd always loved my differences.

The voice of hope inside of me would not shut up. *You can*

fit in with them. Whatever had happened when the four of us secret keepers touched was cemented deep inside of me. The connection. The bond.

I must have drifted off at some point, my sleep solid but short. The clock read 1:30 A.M. when I opened my eyes again, and I knew there was no way I was going back to sleep anytime soon.

Since I needed to pee, I got out of bed and silently moved about the quiet house, using the closest bathroom. When I was done, I wandered into the "surveillance" area. No one else was awake yet, and I decided it would be easiest to just wait for everyone here. Settling back, I watched the different images flash by. It was hard to make things out clearly with the dark and grainy night vision of the cameras, but I just searched until I found one near the beach. Seeing my water would have to be enough for now.

"What are you doing up?"

I jumped at least a foot, landing rather ungracefully in the chair and spinning around to Xander. "Couldn't sleep," I said, pressing a hand to my chest. I could feel my heart beating against it. "Why are you up?"

I hadn't turned any lights on, and it was only when he stepped closer and the illumination of the screens washed over him that I realized he was wearing nothing but a pair of board shorts. "Need to swim," he said, sounding less like his usual belligerent self. "Too long out of the water and I start to go a little stir-crazy."

Oh yeah, I got that.

He turned then, like he was just going to walk out, and I tried hard to ignore the bereft feeling inside of me.

He paused, his voice gruff as he said, "Do you want to swim as well?"

I was up and at his side so quickly that my head actually spun. "Yes, thank you," I said somewhat breathlessly. "I need to swim."

His face was mysterious, shadows washing over the hard planes. I couldn't tell what he was thinking, but it felt like there was less animosity between us. It was almost comfortable standing here with him. Not waiting for him to change his mind, I ditched the sweats he'd lent me, draping them over a nearby chair, and then clad just in the underwear and midriff shirt again, followed him out of the room and into the elevator.

When we got outside, Xander took a few moments checking around the front of the house before he'd let me leave, and I waited, hopping from foot to foot. When we finally started to move, the low, warm breeze brought the scent of salt and water, and whatever tension I'd been holding inside eased as soon as my feet hit the sand.

"We don't have sand in Overworld," Xander said quietly, both of us staring out across the dark water. "It's one of my favorite human things."

I didn't know what to say to that. It was one of my favorite *human* things as well, which no doubt would only annoy him. I chose to stay silent. The water called us down, and I let out a low breath as it swirled around my feet. It was a few degrees cooler than the air; the perfect temperature in my opinion.

"Stay close to me," Xander said when I was shoulder deep. "Laous is still out there. It's a huge risk having you exposed like this."

"I promise," I said. "Unless we see a shark. It's the one thing which has me wary in the ocean, and I usually bail."

Xander's eyes flicked down to my hand, which was curled in slightly at my side, the scar tissue tight tonight.

"You don't have to worry about anything in the water while you're with me. I'll keep you safe."

Then his face shuttered and he dived below before I could reply. As I followed, I really wished I knew what he was thinking, because for a moment there it almost looked like he cared.

7

The moment the water closed over my head, waves pushing me back toward the shore, my night vision kicked in. Out of the water I saw maybe five percent better than most people, but under the water ... everything was clear.

Spikes of moonlight lit up the landscape below. Xander took off, going deeper, and I followed as close as I could. Actually, I was pretty sure he was pacing himself, because I would never have been able to keep up with him at full speed. He'd already proven that by chasing me down yesterday.

The further we got out, the more marine life was around and the lighter my heart felt. As my body relaxed, I started to swim more freely. I didn't call for the dolphins—they wouldn't hear me from this distance anyway. I sent out my love for them though, hoping they'd sense the vibrations in the water. Water carried emotions and messages. I truly believed that.

A water bubble smashed into my face unexpectedly, and I would have screamed except I recognized the sensation from yesterday. This was one of Xander's communication bubbles. The exprendo channel.

"Don't be alarmed," his deep voice echoed across the space around my head. "But there is a shark close by. Two, actually."

The moment someone told me to "not be alarmed" was the exact moment I usually freaked out. A firm hand gripped my scarred one, and because I'd been expecting a shark attack, I let out a shriek and yanked myself free. In doing so, I broke the exprendo channel around my head.

Since I needed to breathe, I used the moment to power up to the surface, sucking in a deep breath before diving back below. My legs dangling while sharks patrolled underneath was one of my only irrational fears. Sharks did not usually attack humans; it was really rare actually, but ... I couldn't help myself.

As soon as I was below again, I scanned the water, searching for the predator of the ocean, and saw nothing except a few butterfly fish, which I took as a good sign. They wouldn't be hanging around if a great white was close by, so either the sharks were one of the less dangerous species, or they weren't close anymore.

After another minute I calmed completely and started searching for Xander. He'd told me not to leave his side, and only ten minutes into the swim I'd already lost him.

Something grabbed my injured hand again, but this time I didn't freak. There was no pain, and I recognized the feel of skin.

Xander.

He held my hand tightly, seemingly not put off by the scars and marks that defined the underside of my palm and wrist. I'd only dated a few times in my life, but more than once I'd had guys deliberately maneuver themselves so they were on the side to hold my "good" hand. I'd even had one say during dinner that I was "really hot, but the hand wigged him out."

His implication was that if I just got it fixed, I'd be perfect, and then he'd be interested.

I kicked his ass to the curb. My hand was not a goddamn flaw, it was a battle scar. I had to believe that, otherwise whatever shaky confidence I'd built would be lost and I'd succumb to the soul-sucking pressure humans felt to always look perfect.

I was not perfect. And that was okay.

Bubbles wrapped around my face again and the water drained out quickly. "I scared them away," Xander told me, his husky voice bringing my body to attention in more ways than one. He might be a bastard, but he was a damn sexy bastard. Who clearly didn't care about holding my hand. Because he still was.

"We should head back soon," he added. "The others will be waiting for us."

I wanted to protest. I wasn't ready to leave the comfort of my ocean. Of my Hawaii.

I didn't say that though, I just murmured, "Yeah, okay. Let's head back."

He hesitated, just briefly, then he pulled me a little closer, his features still distorted by the exprendo channels. "I promise I'll take you swimming in the legreto of House of Royale. You'll feel right at home. And ... when this is all over, you can have one of my houses in Hawaii. You can come back here and live in your own place."

That was so unexpected that I kind of gasped before slamming my lips together. "Why would you do that?" I choked out. "You don't even like me."

Xander pulled me closer again, our bodies only inches apart, drifting in the water together. "You're part of our team," he finally said. "I have more houses than I need. And ...

House of Royale looks after their members. You are one of us."

A small sliver of disappointment hit me, and for the life of me I couldn't figure out why. Xander had just offered me everything I'd ever wanted. My own place in Hawaii, freedom to surf and swim and live in my ocean, and yet ... his reasoning bothered me.

"Thank you," I told him, trying not to let that emotion into my words. "That's probably the nicest thing anyone has ever said or done for me, but I wouldn't feel right taking it from you."

I pulled my hand from his, and turning around, broke my bubble and took off for the shore. We'd gone out further than I thought, and I had to surface twice for air before I made it back to the sandy beach. It was still very dark, but the air had the slight crispness to it that only came when nearing dawn.

I dragged myself up the sand, resting against it for a beat. I always did this, centering myself before returning to walking on legs. It was a hard transition. A warm body landed next to me and I turned my head to Xander, amazed to see the bubbles of water around his legs dissipate. He leaned back on the sand, his broad shoulders nudging against mine as he stretched. I felt energy trickle across his skin and into mine. The last of the bubbles faded away—

"Wait," I whispered. "Your legs...."

They were joined, a fine webbing across the top, binding them all the way down to the feet.

"We're like your merpeople," he said, leaning up so he was sitting, or more like resting his weight back on both hands behind him. "I can switch between a 'tail' and legs." I sensed the air quotes around the word tail and realized they probably didn't call it that.

Before I could stop myself, I reached out to touch it. The bubbles were completely gone now, so I could see everything clearly. Just before I made contact, I realized what I was about to do, and jerked my hand back.

Xander actually chuckled, the sound low and heady, sliding across my senses. "You can touch me."

Those words shot heat through every part of my body. His laughter cut off then and I wondered if he sensed my need—I was goddamn turned on right now and it was pissing me off, because he was an asshole. I was not one of those girls who thought she could change a man. That was too big a job for me. I preferred not to raise a man-child to try to turn him into a decent human.

Still....

A mermaid tail. It was my dream to be able to live in the ocean, and he was six and a half feet of sexy merman. Of course this would be an aphrodisiac for me.

Xander also seemed to have recovered from whatever softer emotions he'd been experiencing after our swim, and with his tail completely gone, and board shorts somehow back in place, he was on his feet and moving.

I reached his side pretty fast and he shot me a dark look—like he was pissed I'd caught him so quickly. I shrugged. "I have long legs, sue me."

His gaze dragged up the length of my bare legs, his eyes darkening along with his expression.

"I have no idea what you're babbling about, human."

And we were back to the human thing. Before he could say another word, I reached out and wrapped my hand around his wrist, yanking as hard as I could. That move was about as effective as trying to stop a truck with my hands, but it did get his attention. He halted, swiveling around to face me.

Before he could spit out whatever angry tirade was on the tip of his tongue, I poked him in the chest. He blinked a few times, looking down to where I'd poked. The look of pure astonishment on his face was almost comical. Clearly no one had ever jabbed him like that before.

"Firstly, I don't babble," I told him with barely contained loathing. "Secondly, you were glaring at me because I caught up to you so quickly. For whatever reason, you don't like me. Which is fine." I pulled my finger back, crossing my arms over my chest. "Not everyone likes everyone else, but you don't have to be such a fucking asshole about it."

His lips twitched. Minutely. So minutely I wondered if I'd imagined it. He took a step closer and I swallowed the sudden nerves filling my throat. I wasn't used to people towering over me the way he did. Our bodies were almost touching; the heat coming from him was like an inferno. Was the heat an alien thing? Or a Xander thing?

"I don't need any complications in my life..., human." He deliberately dragged the human part out this time. "The rest of the secret keepers and overlords might have found their soulmate and perfect match in each other. But you and me, we are never going to be anything."

I laughed. In his face. I couldn't help it. Who did this arrogant piece of shit think he was?

Again he looked astonished, like I was just shocking him all over the place. The second my laughter cut off, I tilted my head back so that our eyes met. "If you were the last human on earth, I would not touch you." I enunciated each word with care. "And considering you're not even human, alien man, then I guess we have nothing to worry about. I'd prefer my kids don't come out as little green mutants."

Then, with one final eyebrow raise in his direction, I spun on my foot and hightailed it back to the house. My face was flaming. I was so angry that I wasn't sure I could contain it. I had this insane urge to punch a wall or something, which was totally not my usual way of handling things. People who lived by the ocean and surfed, especially Hawaiians, tended to just go with the flow. I always thought that was my personality type as well ... but I could have stabbed Xander to death and not lost a minute of sleep over it.

Not one minute.

By the time I stomped to the house, my anger had only increased. It might have set in permanently at this stage. Of course, when I got up there, I couldn't remember the code I had been given last night, so I had to wait for the dumbshit to open the door. Xander breezed by like he didn't have a care in the world. Meanwhile, I was trying to decide which part of his body looked the easiest to stick the knife in.

Probably the throat. I could just slam it right in and he'd be dead.

Holy shit. I was losing my mind.

No dude was worth going to prison over, even an alien dude. So I would just have to suck this anger down and deal with him until the crisis was over. Back in the main section of the safe house, I could hear the others moving around. I quickly gathered up my borrowed pants again and hurried toward the bathroom. Emma popped out of her room just before I shut the door.

She was dressed in jeans and a white shirt, Converse on her feet. She blinked at the wet state of me; a small smile lifted her cheeks. "Do you need some clothes?" she asked.

I let out a sigh of relief that she hadn't pressed me on where I'd been. No doubt she could put the clues together and figure it out.

"That would be great, if you have something that might fit me?"

"Callie should have something," Emma said. "You can start your shower. I'll drop them at the door."

Just as I shifted back to shut the door, she added, "There is a new toothbrush and some makeup and other bits and pieces for you in the top drawer. They have these safe houses stocked up."

Gratitude hit me hard. "Thank you," I murmured. "I'm really happy to have met you and the other girls."

Her eyes lit up. "Same. I feel complete now," she said with a breathtaking grin. "Our family is complete."

With a wink, she spun and hurried off in the direction of Callie's room. I took the quickest shower in history, and when I stepped out I wrapped the towel around me and brushed my teeth first. I never used makeup; no point when I was in the ocean so much. Luckily my skin was tanned, my eyelashes and brows really dark, and no one really cared what you looked like when you had sparkly gray hair.

So this was as good as I was getting.

Emma was true to her word, leaving a small pile of clothes on the other side of the door. There was new underwear—with tags—along with black leggings and a white shirt. I shrugged them on, and while the pants and shirt were a little short, baring my ankles and stomach, they fit well enough. I didn't have shoes, and there was no time for me to grab my Converse, left at the lifeguard station in my bag, so I'd just have to go barefoot.

Going barefoot didn't bother me. Shoes were useless for someone who was mostly in the ocean. But I did find it amusing that the only pair of shoes I had ever owned were

Chucks, and that they also appeared to be the shoe of choice for the secret keepers.

Everyone was in the surveillance room again. Xander, Daniel, Chase, and Lexen appeared to be in the middle of a serious conversation.

"They're figuring out the best way to get the helicopter out to take us to the airport," Maya whispered to me when I sidled closer. "It's noisy, and if Laous is monitoring the airways for traffic, then it's going to be very obvious."

She had a point. "He's probably staking out the airports as well," I suggested, thinking that's exactly what I would have done. Why bother hunting us down; eventually we'd come to him.

"We're not using the same airport as last time," Daniel said, turning from where he was speed-typing into one of the computers. "We're taking the boat out first, then a helicopter, then the private plane. We're going to do everything we can to confuse the trail."

"He's going to know we're heading for Overworld, though, isn't he?" Callie asked, leaning back against a nearby wall. I hadn't had a chance to see her this morning until now, and she was very pale. Her lips were almost colorless.

She looked ill, like a bad case of the flu had hit her. Before I could say anything though, Daniel rose from his spot at the table and in two long strides moved to her side. His arms were around her in a flash and Callie sagged against him. She dropped her head onto his chest, and as she closed her eyes some pink came back into her face.

"He will know, which is good because we don't want him to attack Hawaii," he said. "But we want to make sure we can get away without any bloodshed as well. This is the dilemma." He dropped a kiss on Callie's head, before turning to us. "We can't waste any more time. Callie has been away from House of Imperial for too long. Her energy is fading."

"Your energy is keeping her steady, right?" Emma asked with urgency. "Because the plane ride is at least six hours back."

Daniel nodded, although the worry in his gaze did not lessen. "She will make it. I'm sharing energy with her right now, but ... we don't have time to waste."

That really shook everyone into action. Lexen got off the phone, as did Xander, both of them declaring that everything was set up for all of our transports.

Then we were off.

I wasn't sure it was a conscious thing or not, but the overlords kind of shuffled the four girls into the center, spreading out around us. Callie ended up between me and Emma. We both reached out to wrap an arm around her because she still looked wobbly. She leaned on me more than I expected she was comfortable with. As we moved Daniel kept shooting worried eyes at his mate, but she just waved him away when he tried to take her back into his arms.

"I'm fine, you do your overprotective thing keeping all of us safe. My girls have me."

My chest hurt then, emotion so strong it was painful. This was what a family felt like. This was what it felt like to be relied on. Being relied on might not sound that brilliant, but it came with the stipulation that I could rely on others as well. Now that ... that was my idea of amazing.

The boat was not where we left it yesterday; someone had moved it to a nearby marina. I helped Callie, practically carrying her, until she collapsed against Daniel's chest. He wrapped his arms around her, and again this seemed to send some relief and energy through her.

Xander was the driver, comfortable behind the wheel of the marine craft. The engines seemed extra loud in the early morning silence, and in no time we were moving across the water.

Step one was complete. Hopefully the next two legs of the journey would go as smoothly.

8

$\mathcal{T}$he helicopter was not waiting in a nice, open, easy to access sort of area. Once we were off the boat, we had to cross about two miles through a pocket of forest. I worried about Callie, but she kept up without fuss. I wasn't the only one shooting her concerned glances; she just wrinkled her nose at us.

"I'm fine," she repeated more than once.

I was distracted when we reached the helicopter. I'd never been close to anything like it—it was like a large beast, sending plumes of leaves and dust flying as the blades rotated. I didn't know who the pilot was, but clearly he worked for one of the overlords. Xander maybe, because he greeted him like an old friend.

"Tommy, thanks for getting this all set up so quickly for us," I heard him say over the racket.

We were all given protective headwear and then buckled into seats. The pilot wasted no time getting us into the air, and I was enthralled by the sight of the land growing smaller below us—while also trying not to vomit since I wasn't exactly used to flying.

I wasn't sure how the headsets worked, so I didn't try to talk. I just let the million thoughts in my head go free. A lot had happened in the last two days, starting with my rescue of Maya in the water. But for some unexplained reason none of it felt weird.

It felt right.

That in itself should have had me flipping out, but I just ... went with the flow. Wherever this new path took me, something told me it would be better than the path I'd been on. Loneliness ... displacement ... isolation. Silent killers, slowly leeching away my will to live, turning the world dark and depressing.

The moment I'd seen Maya, my vision filled with so much ... hope. I didn't understand it at the time, but now I did. These seven people—aliens—were what I've been searching for. Even if I didn't know that's what I was doing at the time.

The helicopter ride was uneventful—I'd been tense the entire time waiting for an ambush. When we landed at an airport, Lexen got out first, and after he had a quick look around, helped Emma, Callie, Maya, and me out.

No one slowed, rushing across a large open expanse of asphalt toward a very shiny white plane.

"Xander's plane," Emma explained to me in a low voice. "He had one of them moved to this small airport. Luckily it has a just-long enough runway for this size of aircraft."

I'd probably be an arrogant bastard like Xander if I had a private plane as well. *Wanna go shopping? Sure, let's take my plane.*

I must have been grinning to myself, because Emma

chuckled. "I can guess what you're thinking. All of them have private planes. It takes some getting used to."

That hadn't been what I was thinking, but now that she pointed it out, I had to ask, "How can they all have a private plane? I mean, how do aliens make money here on Earth?"

They were royalty, sure, and maybe the government gave them lots of money to integrate into our world. Still, private planes were not cheap, even for royalty.

"They've been coming to Earth for a long time," Maya said, picking up the conversation, her shorter legs pumping hard as she tried to keep up with us. "They own tons of companies, have their fingers in all the major industries, and basically control a lot of the world's wealth."

Number two reason to be arrogant. Still, Xander was a being of the water, like me. Money could not buy the true beauty in life. He should know better.

As if he'd heard that—or maybe it was the narrow-eyed glare I leveled on him—he tilted his head in my direction. "I own PlastoDestruction. Our company designed the machine that is stripping the oceans of plastics, pollutants, and other trash. I'm using my money to preserve this world for as long as possible."

That placated me somewhat, so I gave him a nod and tucked my bitch face away. No doubt I'd have to bring it out again soon; Xander was very good at pushing my buttons. But I had heard of his company, and I'd long admired the work they did. The smallest of grins tilted up the corner of his lips as he reached the steps to his plane. He had a quick chat with the pilots who were standing there before they boarded the aircraft.

He turned to us. "Everything is good to go. Final safety checks are complete." He then stepped aside and let everyone board first. I ended up being at the back of the group, which meant Xander was eye level with my ass as he followed me up. I wanted to turn and see if he was staring, but part of me was worried he wouldn't be, and that would upset me.

Because I was an idiot who stupidly cared if an alien found me attractive.

When I reached the landing, I stepped into the opulent entrance of his plane. There were large, plush chairs everywhere, and I chose one at random. Emma and Lexen were across from me. Maya and Chase to my right. Callie and Daniel were two seats back.

Xander chose to sit in a single seat near the front. I wasn't sure if I was grateful or not that he was putting some distance between us. It was certainly easier to ignore someone when you couldn't see their stupidly handsome face.

"Seat belt."

My head snapped up at that command, and I realized it was the man himself. He had leaned out so that he could level that stoic glare on me. "What?" I asked him, my eyebrows slamming together.

"Put your damn seat belt on. We're about to take off."

I flipped him off. My finger rose without me even taking a second to think about it. I waved it at him like it was a friendly greeting.

He pressed his lips together and it kind of looked like his right eye was twitching.

"Please put your seats upright and seat belts on. We are about to depart." The pilot's voice echoed around the cabin.

This time I clicked my belt into place and focused on the floor. The nerves in my belly were kicking in hardcore. The helicopter ride had been okay, because I could see clearly out the windows. But the plane felt different.

Please don't let me get airsick. That was my one hope. Nothing worse than barfing in front of four hot princes.

The plane taxied, slowly moving into position. It stopped for a few moments. I wasn't sure why that was, but it did nothing except increase my panic. This was not normal. No one should fly like this. I was meant to be on land ... in the ocean. I was leaving my ocean.

Squeezing my eyes tightly closed, I started taking long, slow breaths, in through my nose, out through my mouth. It didn't seem to be doing anything. A hand gripped mine and I squinted one eye open to find Emma next to me.

"It's okay," she said quietly. "I'm not a huge fan of flying. None of us are."

I swallowed, my chest heaving. "It's too enclosed," I managed to choke out. The helicopter hadn't been the same. "I can't see the sky. I can't feel the breezes. I can't breathe."

A choking feeling was creeping up my throat, and I was about live out my worst nightmare by vomiting everywhere. Emma's eyes grew really wide. I heard her shout something, but in that moment the plane cranked into gear and we were all shot back in our chairs as it took off along the runway.

A low whimper escaped me. I slammed my lips and eyes closed again. I was holding Emma's hand like my life depended on it, and while part of me worried I was literally crushing her hand, I couldn't seem to loosen my grip. There were voices around me, everyone talking, but it all sounded like static to me. My brain was locked in the throes of panic.

I lost my grip on Emma, but her hand was soon replaced with another; larger, more callused, and with a heat that Emma's didn't have.

Xander. Somehow that fact registered in my brain even when nothing else did. I wanted to throw his hand away, to move away from him, but I couldn't. This literally felt like life or death to me, and I was holding on with everything I had.

"It's okay, Avalon," I heard him whisper. "All Royales react badly to flying. Something to do with our dependency on the water. But you're going to be fine. You will make it through this. I promise."

For the first time since I met him, there was no tone in his voice. It was just soothing. Caring. For a second I pretended he did care, that he wasn't just trying to prevent a situation where I freaked out at the start of a six-hour flight. More warmth wrapped around me and I sank into it, my head going fuzzy as the adrenaline started to wane and my body crashed. We were definitely in the air, the plane smoothly gliding skyward. My eyes were still tightly closed, but the static in my head was easing.

As my breathing evened out, I pressed my face closer to the softness of Xander's shirt. He smelled of the ocean. That briny, fresh, perfect scent of home. Damn him for smelling like home.

The captain's voice sounded over the loudspeaker again, advising everyone it was fine to remove seat belts and move about the cabin.

"Is she okay?" I heard Chase ask, his voice close by.

Xander shifted, pulling me closer to him. I was half sprawled across his body now, but I couldn't seem to move away. I needed my ocean.

"She's dealing," Xander said bluntly. "She's a lot more Royale than I expected. We're prepared for this when we travel on aircraft for the first time, but I didn't think Avalon would have the same issues."

"Whatever you're doing appears to be helping," Callie said, sounding exhausted. "Thank you for helping her."

I loved that there was so much concern in their voices. No judgement. Just worry for me. There went those warm fuzzy feelings again. Knowing I needed to stop relying on Xander, who was no doubt hating every second he had to "deal" with my situation, I wiggled my hands up to his hard chest, preparing to push myself away.

He didn't let me go though, not even when I applied more pressure in an attempt to move back. I literally didn't shift at all. "Give yourself a few more minutes." His low voice sounded near my ear. "It's a long flight, and I know you need my energy right now to deal. So ... stop fighting me."

Moisture pricked my eyes and I was glad that my face was still hidden in his chest. "You've been fighting me since I first saw you," I murmured back. "I'm not going to be a burden for you."

I was a burden for my parents. It eventually caused them to resent me. I'd made myself a promise I would never be that for anyone else, ever again.

Xander paused, and when he spoke again his voice was rougher. "You're not a burden. In another life...."

He trailed off, and even though I was desperate to hear the rest of that sentence, I didn't ask. But I did quit fighting him, relaxing against him again. By the time I was calm enough to function on my own again, the flight was half over. Xander didn't say anything more as he left my seat, returning to where he'd originally been sitting. But I did feel his eyes on me.

A middle-aged man dressed in a suit paused at my side. "Would you like anything to eat or drink?" He rattled off an entire selection of food and my stomach rumbled in response.

I decided to order a few things, hoping it would be a good distraction. When the steward hurried off, I leaned back and reached for the headphones, which were wrapped around the armrest. A television popped up with the press of a button and I flipped through the millions of movies. I wasn't one to watch television much; I couldn't remember the last time I even went to the theaters, but ... maybe there'd be something here.

"That one is great!" Emma said, walking back from the bathroom. She dropped into the chair next to mine, picking up a second set of headphones.

"Callie and Daniel are in one of the bedrooms," she explained. "Maya and Chase have another. They'll try and sleep for a few hours. I'm too amped to sleep right now, so let's watch a movie."

"Okay," I said, excited. "You think this one?"

She laughed. "Oh yeah, the remake is better than the original. I laughed so hard."

Funny sounded like the exact remedy for what I needed.

The next few hours were killed watching movies and eating food. Emma was one of the easiest people I'd ever talked with, and when Maya joined us, it was just as relaxed.

"Do you think Callie is okay?" I asked, feeling the loss of one member. "She's slept almost the entire flight."

We'd checked on her a few times. Daniel had assured us she was just asleep. But the look on his face wasn't as reassuring.

"We're due to land in forty minutes," Lexen said. He had Emma in his lap, his arms wrapped tightly around her. Both of them looked content. "She'll make it to House of Imperial, no worry."

"We're about to start our descent. Please return to your seats."

The pilot's voice spurred us all into action, and as I slipped back into my squishy chair, I tried really hard not to think about landing. It had to be better than taking off, right? Ocean washed across my senses and I turned as Xander dropped into

82

the seat next to mine. Our eyes met, and I expected embarrassment to hit me, but there was none.

"Thank you for before," I said, wanting to express my gratitude. "I really appreciate your help. I'm not sure what would have happened if you weren't here."

Xander shrugged. "You seem like a strong, independent sort of person. I have no doubt you'd have managed it on your own. But ... just in case, I'm here if you need me."

If you need me....

I really wished he hadn't said those words, because the mental images that sprang to life had nothing to do with flying and everything to do with sex. I was not a virgin; the surfer community was free and easy with more than just riding the waves, but I did tend to be on the more conservative side. I'd had a few casual relationships. One semiserious one. But nothing for the last six months. Just surviving had been hard enough.

But right now, in this very moment, all I could picture was climbing into Xander's lap. Pressing my lips to the bronze, hard muscles lining his chest. Running my fingers through his perfect strands of blond hair. He turned me on in ways that should be illegal. Especially when he wanted nothing to do with me.

Gold flared in his eyes, and the blue went dark enough to almost be black. "You need to stop looking at me like that," he warned, leaning in close. "You and I might not be the soul mate types, but I am attracted to you. You're extremely beautiful, and right now I can think of nothing except stripping your clothes off and tasting every inch of that stunning body. But that's where it would end, and something tells me that wouldn't be enough for you."

Irritation pricked at me. "You don't know me," I returned,

keeping my voice as low as he had. "I'm perfectly capable of handling a casual affair." Despite my calm word, my mind and body were on fire. I couldn't get the visual he'd painted out of my head ... or the fact that he was feeling the same level of attraction as me.

What the hell is happening?

His jaw tightened. "Something you're familiar with?" he asked.

"Isn't it the Royale way?" I shot back. "Not settling into long-term relationships."

He shook his head. "It's more complicated than that. For starters, overlords are together long-term. The energy of an overlord facilitates a proper bond. And more of our people are starting to build long-term family units. We're changing."

Except Xander clearly wasn't.

"Maybe I would be the one who could walk away and you'd be the one wanting more," I suggested casually. "Maybe that is what has you worried."

He laughed, the sound loud and jolting after our intimate whispering.

"Is that a challenge, Avalon? Because I have to tell you, I never refuse a challenge."

Was it a challenge? Did I want to explore this sexual need I felt for Xander? Would there be a possibility I would fall for him though? I didn't want to get my feelings hurt and somehow destroy the group dynamic...

"Who's scared now?" he taunted, and my spine went straight.

"You're on," I blurted out. "I'm game for a sexual relationship, no strings attached. If you think you can handle it with no hard feelings, then I'm in."

He leaned in closer. "Oh, there is going to be a lot of hard. But it won't be my feelings."

I tried not to laugh. His arrogance was almost endearing.

"We need some ground rules though," he continued.

I agreed with that, so I nodded. "Okay, let's think on the rules and then we can discuss them later."

Somewhere a little more private.

He nodded as well. "Agreed. Although, I can tell you my first one right now. No mentioning this to anyone else. I do not need our friends trying to matchmake us. I had enough of that before we even found you."

I could see why they would. The six of them were so happily teamed up, they would have expected the same from Xander and me. But Royales were different. This sort of deal would suit both of us better.

My pulse was racing as we settled back together, energy dancing along my skin even though I wasn't actually touching Xander. But he was close. And all I could think about was sex.

The cabin dropped a little and I realized Xander had distracted me so well that we were almost landed. Looking around, I noticed that Callie and Daniel were absent, which meant Callie hadn't left the bedroom. Worry replaced the sex thoughts. I mentally started urging the plane on.

She had to be okay. There was no other option. I would not find this new family only to have one of them stolen away from me.

"She's going to be fine," Xander reassured me, facing the same direction I was, staring at the bedroom doors.

"I know," I returned shortly. "She's too tough to give up."

I might not have known her long, but I already knew that about her.

She was a fighter.

9

$\mathcal{I}$t turned out that there was no need for any identification when you flew in an alien spac— I mean a private plane. We were ushered into two dark SUVs, and none of the officials who helped us blinked an eye. Not even when Daniel had to carry his semi-unconscious mate to get her off the plane.

Xander and Lexen were the drivers. I ended up in the back seat with Emma in the car behind Xander's. We flew through the town. I barely even got a glimpse of the ocean and cute little houses, we were going at such speeds. I understood it though, and I wished Callie was in the car with us, because I wanted to check on her.

Panic was hovering at the edge of my mind. Emma was very pale, her eyes locked forward through the windshield. No one spoke. It was like we couldn't until we knew that Callie was going to be fine. Lexen practically drifted around the corner, flying between two huge, ornate gates. We then raced along a fancy street. Near the end, we screeched to a halt and everyone was out in seconds.

"I'm taking her right through," Daniel said without preamble. "When she's recovered her energy, we'll meet you at Darken."

Callie's body was limp, her head lolling against Daniel's chest.

Lexen, Xander, and Chase just nodded and slapped their friend on the back. Daniel swiveled and ran, moving superfast. Within a few of my rapid heartbeats he was completely out of sight, disappearing down some green-covered lane.

"Holy shit," Emma burst out, holding a hand to her chest. "I didn't think we'd make it in time. But she's fine, right? Unconscious is not dead...." Her eyes darted between us. "Right"

Lexen stepped to her, both of his hands cupping her face. She calmed as she stared up into his eyes. "She's fine. Daniel will get her there in time. He will not let his mate go without a massive fight. Don't forget he controls the underworld."

Emma nodded as she swallowed roughly. "I know. But ... he can't control everything. Marsil still died. There is only so much Daniel can do."

Lexen's jaw tightened, his eyes almost glowing at the mention of his brother. "He could have saved Marsil, but nothing like that comes without a price. The same way he had to tie his soul to Callie's to save her life, there would have been a price for Marsil as well. I know, without any doubt, my brother would not have wanted anyone to pay that for him."

Lexen's thumbs wiped away the tears trailing down Emma's cheeks. I had to turn away because that moment was so intimate and sad. Holy shit. I actually felt like I might cry myself, and I never knew Marsil. Drifting a little further from them, I examined the beautiful street we were on. Surprisingly enough, I could still smell the ocean, so we had to be near water. It was probably behind all the mega mansions that lined one side of the street. Huge blocks of land. High privacy fences. This was definitely a street for rich aliens.

I walked along the asphalt until I reached the path. On the opposite side to the mansions, it looked like there were some small houses, and I was curious to see what they were like. It took me longer than I expected to reach their little section. They were grouped close together, their land a fraction of the size of the homes across the street from them.

I didn't realize that the others had caught up to me until Emma startled me. "That's mine." She pointed toward one of the little houses in the middle. She then paused for a beat, her brow furrowing. "It kind of looks different," she murmured, moving closer. "They all look different."

The bright red door of her place flew open then and two people stepped out, a dark-haired African-American woman, and a red-headed, very fair-skinned man.

"Emma!" the woman exclaimed, racing down the stairs and throwing her arms around Emma. "We haven't seen you for days," she scolded as she pulled back. "You need to keep us updated."

Joy replaced the sadness that had been etched across Emma's face. "Sorry, Sara. We ended up in a safe house and it wasn't that easy to call out in case it was traced."

"But you're all fine?"

Emma nodded. "Yes, we did have a run in with Laous, but we found Ava and got the stone back, so I'd say we came out in front."

Sara's eyes were on me then. She released Emma and took a step closer to me. "Ava ... oh my, you're absolutely stunning." She flicked a glance at Xander. "Lucky guy, Xander."

He just crossed his arms and shook his head, but he didn't

say anything. I expected him to deny it, but he didn't. Which, of course, immediately had Maya and Emma shooting him knowing grins.

The red-headed man distracted everyone when he took a few steps forward and wrapped his arms around Emma. "Missed you, sweetheart."

"I missed you too, Michael," Emma said, her voice muffled.

When they pulled apart, Michael moved to stand beside Sara, draping one of his arms around her. "So, what is the next part of your plan?" he asked, looking between all of us.

Lexen answered. "We're heading to Overworld. First step is to uncover the map Ava holds, so we can figure out where the starslight stone is."

"We have to get the stone before Laous and give it back to the humans," Chase added. "They're going to figure out a better way to hide it this time."

Michael nodded, face serious. "Yes, we've been in touch with Maya's parents. They said there is a new agreement all ready now—they're just waiting on Daniel's signature as the last overlord. They're not going to let something like this happen again."

Maya cleared her throat, drawing our attention. "Clearly someone is going to have to break the bond between us and the stone. Will that also break the connection the eight of us have?"

There were a few beats of uncomfortable silence.

"We have no idea," Michael admitted, shrugging.

"I don't think it can," Lexen told her. "There are multiple bonds between all of us. This would just be one specific one that connects you all to the stone."

Emma nodded, turning back to examine her house again.

"Did you paint our door?" she asked suddenly. "Actually, are all of the doors painted now?"

Sara clapped her hands, her face transforming into one of delight. Michael just shook his head, watching his wife with a soft stare.

"We've been overseeing the renovations of the street," Sara said with a chuckle. "It has been so much fun."

Emma turned back to her family. "Renovations?"

Sara nodded. "Yep, my job for the past few weeks. You haven't noticed because you've barely been here."

"Lexen, Daniel, Chase, and Xander organized it all," Michael added. 'We've just been overseeing the work."

Emma let out a low breath of air, turning to the man at her side. "You ... you did this?"

Lexen laughed. "You don't have to sound so surprised. I can, on occasion, think about helping others."

Emma shook her head, sniffling. "It's not that. You are very involved when it comes to Daelighters. You're an amazing leader. But humans ... you don't often think about humans."

He wrapped her up before she could blink, hauling her into his body so her feet were dangling off the ground. Emma didn't seem to mind; she flung her arms around his neck and clung tightly to him. "I think about you every second of every day," he said softly. "I know it bothered you that these shacks were for humans."

"So we fixed them up," Chase added. Maya let out a little sound of happiness, and then she was throwing herself into his arms.

I wrinkled my nose at Xander. "While I think this is a nice gesture, don't expect a hug from me."

He quirked an eyebrow in my direction. "Bad form not to show your gratitude."

"I said it was a nice gesture." I shrugged. "That's as much as I'm giving you."

Oh, and me, naked beneath you. Because we were going to do that.

Turning away, I pretended to be very interested in the scenery. "That's my house there," Xander said. I jumped when his voice was much closer than I expected. I glared at him.

"Back up, dude. You're way too close."

He actually laughed at me, and somehow I managed not to throat punch him. "You definitely embrace the surfer vibe. I like it."

Placing one hand against his chest, I attempted to shove him back. He barely moved, which was freaking annoying. Why were men always so much bigger and stronger? Okay, human men usually weren't. I held my own with a lot of them, but Xander was built like a fucking tank.

"Stop flirting with me," I said. "This is not what we're doing, okay?"

His gaze flicked down to my hand, to where my fingers were almost bunching in his shirt. I yanked it back quickly, realizing what I was doing, and hurried away from him to stand with Maya and Emma. I didn't even care that I'd have to put up with the PDA.

Emma was saying goodbye to her family. "...see you all really soon," she said as she pulled back. "We have to go now though."

Sara and Michael's faces fell. "Please be careful," Sara begged, hurrying in for one more hug. "We love you so much."

"I love you, too." Emma blew them a kiss, straightening. "I'll be back before you know it."

She sucked in a deep breath, turning to walk along the street. The rest of us hurried to follow. Emma was on a mission. I tried not to look Xander's way, but I was far too aware of him to be able to completely ignore him. It didn't help that I had a million questions I wanted to ask. Not just about us, but also about his world.

Deciding it was better not to get too friendly with him, lest we blur these lines we were trying to establish, I asked Maya, "How are we getting to Overworld?" The word *spaceship* had been floating around in the back of my mind, but it just seemed so far-fetched.

"A transporter," she said with a soft smile. "It's like this ... ball of light that Daelighters created using their network."

Ah, yes, they had mentioned that to me before. "The permanent transporter set up in the treaty...?" I confirmed.

"Yep," she said.

"The lights connect our worlds," Chase added. "So, if we hold on to a beam here, we can use it to bring us to Overworld. It takes a little while to get used to it—"

"Especially if you get lost inside of one," Maya interrupted. "But you'll be fine. Xander won't let you go."

I tripped, startled enough that I almost hit the deck. I recovered easily, but it was odd for me to be clumsy. Freaking Xander, he was impacting me in more ways than one.

"Why will Xander be helping me?" I asked, ignoring the snort from the man himself.

"You need a Daelighter to guide you through," Maya said, her eyes sparkling as her lips half-tilted up like she was trying not to smile. She looked between Xander and me. "It's safer if it's one Daelighter per human. That way you have no chance of getting lost inside the transporter."

The annoyance I was feeling must have shown on my face. She let out a laugh. "If you want to go with Chase, I'm happy to go with Xander. I can share my mate for the trip back."

For a split second, I considered taking her up on that offer, even though I felt like an absolute fucking moron making a big deal about this. The problem, I was coming to realize, was that I hadn't thought this "sexual relationship only" thing through. It was a great idea in theory, but Xander and I were not like most casual hookups. We were stuck together in a situation that required a lot of "helping" and "togetherness." Which, as far as I could tell, was only going to create problems.

Maya was still waiting for my answer. I had just opened my mouth to tell her I'd go with Xander, when he reached out and grabbed my arm, pulling me to a halt. "I'm more than capable of getting you there safely, Avalon." His grip wasn't tight, but his expression had drawn into hard lines, eyes flashing at me. "Do not doubt my ability to keep you safe."

I resisted the urge to step into him, because there was something about the concept of "safe" that I craved. Instead, I gently shook his hand off me. "You're right," I said, and his eyes widened. "But be aware, I don't generally rely on others to protect me. I'm out of my depth here with all the alien stuff, and that is the only reason I will concede to your help."

Turning, I found that the others had kept walking, disappearing past the parked cars. Xander made no move to hurry after them; he just stood there, watching me.

He did at least look a little less angry.

Before I could ask him if we were cool now—I had agreed to his help—he stepped forward and wrapped his arm around the middle of my back. My body bent to his will, curving into Xander, pressing against his hard lines.

When his lips landed on mine, my breath whooshed out of me in a rush and I had to swallow down the moan that wanted to follow. I lost all control of myself, my lips parting so our tongues could move together.

The taste of Xander just about dropped me to my knees. He even tasted like the ocean.

It was too much. My heart was thundering in my chest. It was only his hold on my body that kept me from dissolving into a puddle at his feet. His kiss was hard ... demanding ... and I loved every second of it. He was taking what he wanted, and I did the same right back. Bubbles tingled in my blood, the way they did when I was swimming at top speed through the ocean.

"You taste like home," he said as our lips parted. His eyes looked troubled, but there was no doubt he was into it. I could feel the evidence of that pressed against my body, and I actually wished we weren't right in the middle of the street.

"Sex only," I reminded him. He tasted like home to me as well, but we had to ignore that for now. "Otherwise it's going to get complicated."

That seemed to knock some sense into him. His arm loosened and I wobbled, my knees still weak. He did keep a hand on me for an extra moment, making sure I was stable, before he stepped back. "I don't do complicated," he said, a tinge of surprise in his voice. "I can't." He shook his head then. "We should go, the others will be waiting for us."

No more words were spoken as we hurried to follow the path to the transporter, but something had shifted between us. Things felt ... different. Charged. Intense.

I could not wait to get to the sex part. Holy hell.

10

A transporter, it turned out, was literally a ball of light. It also turned out that Xander was able to reach out and grab hold of one of those strands, after which we were jerked into a weird, soundless wormhole. It felt like the sort of situation that would cause me to freak out again—there was probably no place further removed from my ocean—but instead I was fascinated.

This was a once in a lifetime experience.

Xander kept a tight hold on me, and at no point was I worried that I would slip out of his hand. When the light got brighter at the end, I did close my eyes, stumbling forward. Xander used his strength to keep me standing. The moment I felt reality and gravity return, I opened my eyes and pulled my hands from his. I wanted to see everything at once.

"Oh my God," I gasped, turning in a circle to take it all in. "This is Overworld?"

Xander chuckled. "Well, this is one part of Overworld. There are lots of sectors, but we don't interact with each other."

That was interesting. Everyone on Earth traveled between countries. "Why don't you interact?" I decided to ask.

He shrugged. "There's no easy way to travel to other sectors. It's actually easier and less dangerous for us to travel to Earth. Some of the other lands have creatures that are not compatible to us. Very dangerous creatures. The Draygo people are thought to be originally from another land."

It was all so fascinating. I wanted to know everything. Hopefully I'd have years to learn it all.

The large disc we had landed on had a light transporter right in the center, and there were three lands surrounding it. "What is that place called?" I pointed to the section that was packed full of trees.

"House of Leights," Chase said, wandering over to us. "That's Maya's and my land."

House of Leights ... tree people. I remembered from their explanations, but it was still hard to imagine what it all truly meant. How did a tree and a person combine? Like ... how?

"And that one?" I moved on to the land of mountains and green valleys.

"House of Darken," Lexen told me, staring out across his land.

I'd saved the best for last of course, turning my eyes to the vast stretch of water. There were no waves like in Hawaii, but it still called to me in a way that made it difficult not to just run over and throw myself at it. "House of Royale," I whispered.

Xander made a low rumbling noise at my side. It sounded like it came from deep in his chest. "Yes, that's our home."

He said *our* so causally. It hit me like a ton of bricks. *Our home.*

To stop myself from crying all the happy tears, I quickly

searched for a distraction. "Where is House of Imperial? Has anyone heard from Daniel and Callie?"

"She's fine," Emma said immediately. "Daniel contacted Lexen a minute ago. Callie just needs a few more hours of rest —they'll meet us at Lexen's soon."

Relief hit me hard. I'd been stressing about her health the entire time. "That's such good news, but ... you still didn't tell me where their land is?"

Xander answered this time. "They're the underworld, so it's..." He trailed off and pointed down to the disc. "Under the main land."

Right. Okay. Really hoping I didn't end up going there for any reason.

"How are we getting to House of Darken?" Emma asked Lexen.

"Transporter," he replied immediately. "It will save us time. Father wants me to hurry back. He said he has something important to discuss with us all."

Emma lurched forward. "It's not about Jero or Star, right? Or Ambra?"

I didn't know who these people were, but they were clearly important to Emma. Which then, for some stupid reason, made them feel important to me.

"Or my parents?" Maya added, her voice rising in pitch.

Lexen shook his head, hands reaching out to steady Emma and Maya. "No, it's not about my siblings or Mother. Or your parents, Maya. I'm almost certain nothing is wrong. Father said not to panic, but he might have some information to help us."

Emma and Maya both relaxed. As did I.

"Okay, well, we should hurry, then," Emma added. "It's not like Roland to call us back unless it's something important."

Lexen didn't say anything more.

The next transporter was shorter, taking us directly into Lexen's home. Or ... a small dark room in his home. When we entered the main part of the house, I got the whole "prince" thing. Everything was light and open, with lots of very expensive, handmade-looking furnishings. We passed so many rooms, I knew I'd be completely lost if I had to navigate this place on my own.

"Father is waiting in the main dining room," Lexen explained as we took a set of stairs up to the next level. "It's just through here."

The first thing I noticed through the double set of doors was the table. It could easily seat fifty people, maybe more. Made from what looked like one long sheet of wood, it was stained dark with carved legs, the chairs all matching and high-backed with carved wood accents.

This looked like the sort of room I'd expect in the Queen of England's home. I immediately felt intimidated, my feet slowing as we all entered. I felt out of place everywhere except the ocean, but this was mammoth out of place.

Xander, who had entered a little ahead of me, noticed me hovering in the doorway. He backtracked in my direction, his expression unreadable. "Everything okay?" he asked, tilting his head to the side.

I nodded. "Yeah, it's just ... not my usual scene."

Understatement of the year.

"I'm not even wearing shoes," I added, swallowing hard.

"I can help with that!"

That enthusiastic voice belonged to a beautiful girl with long dark hair. She was dressed impeccably in a knee-length black dress and heels. Her clothes looked designer, the boat neckline showing off her slender shoulders.

"Come with me. I'll find you something to wear. I've been collecting clothes for the secret keepers," she added, holding her hand out to me.

"Uh." I hesitated, my eyes moving to Xander's even as my brain screamed at me not to rely on him for anything.

"This is Star," he said, his smile lighting the dark planes of his face. "Lexen's sister. She's in charge of our fashion."

Star slapped her hand over her mouth. "Oh, gosh, I am so sorry. I've heard so much about you through the network, I feel like I already know you."

I had to chuckle. Star had a way about her that put me right at ease immediately, a skill I wish I possessed. "It's lovely to meet you. I'm Ava."

Star nodded, her eyes sparkling as she ran them from the top of my head to my toes. "You're much taller than I expected," she mused, not really talking to anyone. "Slim and toned. You probably prefer lighter outfits that are easy to ditch in the water."

"I do," I said with another chuckle, interrupting her.

"What size are your shoes?" she asked.

My lips twitched, but this time I managed not to laugh out loud. "I'm usually a nine. Sometimes nine and a half, depending on brand."

She reached for my hand again, but Xander intercepted her, sidling his body between us. "Roland has some news. Avalon can't leave until she hears it."

Star nodded a few times, that pondering look back on her face. "Yep. Yep, no worries. I will grab the clothes and be right back."

She was gone as fast as she appeared. "She's got a ... lot of energy," I said, blinking at the spot she'd just occupied.

Xander made a noise of agreement. "Yep, Star has a heart

that is pure. A rare find in any world. Since Marsil, all of the Darkens have been grieving. It's good to see a fraction of her spark return."

The thought of that beautiful, sweet, kind woman grieving made my chest ache. Some people should never have to face the darkness in the world; they were too gentle for it. Lexen, he was more resilient. I expected he did his grieving in private, maybe with Emma. Star wore her emotions out there for all to see.

I hadn't noticed until we moved further in the room, but there was more than just one stranger standing at the far end of the long table. The first one I saw was a man who looked a lot like Lexen, right down to the dark hair and overlord marks on his head. I was going to guess this was his father. He wore authority like it was part of his outfit.

As we got closer, I examined the two other people at the table, a man and woman, quietly staring down at the wood. Emma and Maya looked confused, standing a little to the side while Lexen and Chase spoke to Roland.

"What's happening?" I whispered to Emma when I reached her side.

She turned to me, shrugging as she said, "I have no idea. I'm just waiting for Lexen to fill me in."

As if he'd heard her, he turned and addressed all of us. "I'd like you all to meet Shirley and Jet."

Shirley was a curvy woman, looking not much older than us. She had long red ringlets, large green eyes, and a fair complexion. She smiled and waved, some animation coming back into her face. Jet was tall, with blinding white teeth that stood out starkly against his dark skin. He didn't wave, but he gave us a smile that was somewhat friendly.

"It's nice to meet you," Maya said, reaching out to shake both of their hands. She was so confident. I was a little envious; social interaction didn't come as easily to me. I was surprised to find Emma acting standoffish as well though. She was usually so friendly.

"She is comfortable with the secret keepers. Considers you all family. But strangers, not so much," Xander whispered in my ear.

I didn't question how he knew what I was thinking. I often couldn't hide my emotions. And I'd been staring right at Emma as she shied back toward Lexen.

"Jet and Shirley are former secret keepers," Roland said, his deep, accented voice vibrating around the room. "We managed to track them down, hoping they might be able to give us some additional information."

I paid closer attention to them now. All of us did. Emma especially, leaving the background, stepping right up to take a seat across from them. She leaned forward, eyes wide.

"You both look so young," she exclaimed. "But you're almost a hundred years old?"

Jet nodded, a wry grin tilting up his lips. "I aged normally to twenty, but from then on I have barely changed," he said, his voice a rich timbre.

Unbelievable. I mean, they'd told me about the aging thing —very briefly—but being confronted with it like this ... it was a lot to take in. Life could be really hard at times. I wasn't sure I was ready for hundreds of years of that. Maybe if I found that home I was searching for though, it wouldn't seem so bad.

"Which house were you born in?" Maya asked, taking the seat next to Emma.

"House of Leights," Shirley said.

"House of Imperial for me," Jet added.

Maya's face lit up. "Do you feel connected to nature?" she asked the woman, leaning much closer. "Since the moment I learned to communicate with the trees, I've been so energized and rejuvenated by nature."

Shirley's eyebrows drew slowly together, and she shook her head. "No, I've honestly never felt anything like that. Outside of aging slowly, there have been no other effects from being born in Overworld."

The silence felt heavy then, and I wasn't sure what everyone else was thinking, but I was surprised. I was very different to the average human. It was the reason I'd always thought I was a mutant.

Everyone turned to Jet, and he shrugged. "I'm with Shirley. I've never shown any signs of being different to a regular human, outside of the aging."

"Do you feel a connection to each other?" I asked, because I would never forget that moment the four of us girls touched.

Shirley and Jet exchanged a look and my mouth almost fell open when they both shook their heads. "No, not really," Shirley said, sounding unsure. "I've never met Jet before today, and I have to say, so far there is no special bond springing up for me."

"Same," he agreed.

Emma lurched half out of her chair, eyes locked on Roland and Lexen. "Why are we different?" she demanded to know. "The original secret keepers are nothing like us. We have a bond to each other. It's a tangible thing. And ... the way we are all soul-mated with overlords of the four houses—"

"Except me," I cut in.

Xander grumbled under his breath, and Emma paused before shooting me a half grin.

"Yes, except Ava and Xander ... allegedly." She winked at me and I stuck my tongue out but didn't say another word. I couldn't deny there was an attraction between me and the Royale asshole, so her theory did stand.

"So why are we different?" Maya finished.

Shirley and Jet shrugged. "I have no idea," he said.

Chase let out a low breath, and we all turned to find a contemplative look on his face. "I've always thought that the energy of the secret keepers had an ancient feel to it. It reminds me of the ancient overlords."

"How do you even know what these overlords' energy feels like?" Maya asked. "Are they still around? I mean, I assumed that some of them ... died off."

Chase nodded. "The ancients died long ago. Most of our people eventually choose to end the longevity. No one wants to live forever."

I didn't even want to know how they ended it. Hopefully it wasn't like sacrificing themselves on their blades or something similar.

"So ... how do you know the energy?" Emma pushed.

"All overlords are blessed at birth with crystals from the ancients," Roland said in his quiet, commanding voice. "It is said that in the beginning there was only one house. House of Daelighter. Four overlords ruled the lands together and controlled the full network. Each of them had a crystal excavated from their favorite part of Overworld. They molded them onto the top of long staffs, and each piece was infused with their energy."

"This worked for a long time, and there was peace," Chase added quietly. "But, over time, different Daelighters started to take different gifts from the lands ... the network. Nature segregated them. And then they segregated themselves."

"There was jealousy and fighting," Roland said. "Everyone wanted something that another had. The ones with the same gifts banded together and formed their own little groups. Eventually, they had to split the four lands, the four peoples, each going to where their gifts were strongest."

"We've been divided ever since," Xander added, sounding less cynical than he usually did. "A land divided will eventually fall."

"We're working together now," Roland declared. "For the first time in many, many years, we are putting all differences aside. All four houses working together as one."

Something didn't make sense to me though. "How did the four overlord minors manage to become such good friends?" I asked, hoping this question wasn't a huge faux pas. "I mean, if the four houses have an inbuilt standoffishness with each other, then how are Lexen, Daniel, Chase, and Xander besties?"

Xander snorted under his breath. "Besties? Seriously, human ... never refer to us as besties again."

I tilted my head to the side and faked a broad smile. "Seriously, alien ... would you prefer BFFs?"

His lips tilted up, and I worked really hard to push down the memories of our kiss. Of how soft his full lips were. Of the way my body was craving our first moments together. His grin grew and I had to turn away. I was already in too deep.

Focus on the physical. I could not let emotions enter the equation.

Lexen, ignoring Xander, answered my question. "We have been friends from a very young age. There was just this ... bond between us from the start."

"It was instant," Chase agreed.

Roland let out a low chuckle. "They thought they hid it from us, but we all knew they snuck around to meet each other. With the exception of previous Imperial overlords, we all agreed it was a great way to start returning unity to our land."

Lexen made a rough sound of disbelief. "You knew?" he asked, shifting forward. "And approved?"

Roland nodded at his son. "I've always known, but it was safer for you all to keep it hidden. So ... even though it pained us as parents, we never advised you to bring it out into the world. Not until you were all capable of defending yourselves. Defending this brotherhood."

I could see that the three overlord minors in the room were honestly astonished by this. Emma and Maya looked surprised as well. I had no opinion on it, because I'd never really known any of this information until now. The original secret keepers were quietly observing and didn't say anything. It kind of felt like they knew even less than me about the politics of this world. I was going to assume they'd always just lived as humans, with no reason to know about Overworld outside of the basics.

Xander stood a little straighter, understanding crossing his face. "I dismissed a lot of Emma's theories about our 'fated" existence simply because it's not in my nature to accept the thought of being controlled, even by a higher power. But ... only an idiot would deny it any longer. Even the simple fact that I feel protective toward Avalon tells me that this is beyond a simple right-time, right-place circumstance. The overlords and secret keepers are bonded, and now ... now I want to know how they managed this. Because..." He gestured to Jet and Shirley at the table. "The previous secret keepers did not have any sort of bond. They were not closely connected to the houses. So why now?"

My breath had caught in my throat the moment he said he felt protective toward me. I didn't really know how to process that. Attracted was one thing. That was purely hormonal. But protective ... that spoke of something deeper.

Dammit. Damn him to hell. He was not allowed to bring anything deeper into it. I didn't want to feel anything for him. Because the ending was always going to be the same: Xander and me separate.

"We have to find the Draygo who blessed each of the secret keepers' births," Lexen said, speaking almost to himself. "He's the one who also hid the starslight stone. I don't think anyone but that Draygo can give us answers."

"How will you find him?" Emma asked. "You said no one has heard from that particular Draygo for eighteen years."

Eighteen years? That was a long time to fall completely off the radar.

"How is this Draygo avoiding the network?" Maya asked, resting her face on her hands. "Wouldn't someone that powerful be easy enough to find?"

Chase reached out and rubbed her back, his movements gentle and rhythmic. Her eyes got all blissed out and she probably missed it when he said, "There are ways to hide yourself if you don't want to be found. Sort of like a do not disturb on a cell phone. This particular Draygo is on a permanent DND."

Lexen studied the table in front of him, his darkly handsome face contemplative. Finally he said, "I wonder if Qenita could find him. The draygones are able to tap into energy beyond anything Daelighters can touch. The Draygo are somewhere between the two—Qenita has a lot more power than I do."

Emma was on her feet in a heartbeat. "Ask her! Now! We have no time to waste."

I swallowed hard. "When you say draygone ... you mean...?"

Because it had sounded a lot like *dragon-with-an-accent.* I knew this was an alien world ... but....

Maya and Emma both turned sparkling eyes and broad smiles on me. "Oh yeah, you know it, girl. Dragons!" Emma chirped.

"Motha-freaking-dragons," Maya added.

Well, I'd be damned. They had dragons here. "Is the myth on Earth taken from Overworld?"

Emma and Maya both nodded. Chase answered. "We're not totally sure, but there is a high possibility it was from stories passed on by Daelighters that crossed to Earth in the early days. Long before there was any treaty."

"That's cool," I said softly. "It's kind of nice to know there is an extensive history between our people. And no wars."

I had no problem with peaceful invasions by aliens, that was for sure.

Lexen rose to his feet and reached down to lift Emma from her chair. "Em and I will speak with Qenita. If she thinks she knows the location of the Draygo, then we'll take off to find him straight away." He turned to Chase and Xander. "I'll let you both know through the network. Keep an eye on the girls. Keep them safe. We'll be back soon."

Emma rushed to give Maya a hug first, then she threw her arms around me. "You'll be safe with Xander and Chase," she murmured in my ear. "See you soon."

I squeezed her a little tighter, lowering my head so that no one saw the pain in my eyes. I didn't like her going off without me. It was bad enough that Callie was not with us. I had this insane urge to keep our group together; splitting up felt like a bad idea. Maybe it was the fact that I'd only just found them. More than that, it was a feeling deep in my soul.

Splitting up would be the destruction of us all. Only together could we defeat Laous.

11

*T*here was a moment of silence when Emma and Lexen left. Then Jet said, "I think it's time we returned as well. Sorry we weren't more help to you all."

Shirley nodded, getting to her feet. "Outside of the fact that I've barely aged since I was twenty, there isn't much about Overworld I'm familiar with. Once the line of secret keepers was broken and I didn't even have to check in, I didn't have any other contact."

Roland shook both of their hands. "Thank you for giving us the information you did. You helped more than you think. I'll escort you both back to Earth now."

We all shook their hands, then they started toward the main door. Roland stopped and turned back to us. "You're all welcome to stay here as long as you want. My wife.... She's not dealing very well with our son's death. But Star can show you to a room. Might be a good idea to wash up and get some sleep while you can. We know Laous will be planning his next move. It's not in his nature to give up." He walked away, before pausing at the door and turning back once more. "Oh, and

Maya, your family and Brad are in the west wing. Star is pretty familiar with their suite. She'll take you there as well."

Maya's face lit up like a kid at Christmas. "I have missed them so much," she almost cried, her eyes shiny.

Roland nodded. "They have missed you terribly as well." With a final wave, he was gone, ushering Jet and Shirley with him.

Doors banged open then on the opposite side of the room to where Roland had just left. "I'm back," Star cried, rushing through. "Sorry for taking so long. I got stuck helping Jero go through some new security measures he's implementing."

Her hands were filled with bags, jumping about haphazardly as she crossed to us. She dumped all of them into Xander's hands. "Can you take care of Ava for me? Your normal room is ready to go." She swung around to Maya. "Brad is annoying the ever-living hell out of me. He knows you're back and is demanding you visit him ASAP."

Maya smirked. "Same old arrogant best friend. I've actually missed his bossy ass."

Star shook her head, a smile breaking out even as she fought to contain it. "He's certainly entertaining."

There was the slightest of pink tinges to her cheeks, and I hazarded a guess that Star might find Brad annoying for more than one reason. Just like I did Xander.

"Will you be okay?" Maya asked, turning to me. "I know you've just entered an alien world, and this is all probably very overwhelming."

"And everyone has bailed on you," Chase finished for her.

I nodded in jagged, rapid movements. "Oh, totally. I'm fine. Xander knows what's going on. You go and catch up with your family. Take as much time with them as you can."

She let out a happy squeak, gave me a tight hug, and pointed a finger at Xander. "Don't be an asshole," she told him shortly before turning and nudging Chase and Star out of the room.

"Come on," Xander said, heading in the opposite direction. He didn't look back to see if I was following, and I spent most of my time glaring at his broad shoulders, almost missing the stunning house we were moving through. I had no idea what the city was like outside of this castle, but I imagined it was lush and rich, with green rolling hills like those I'd seen on the platform.

The inside—I noticed when I tore my eyes from Xander—was very light and open, with pale cream walls and lots of thick rugs and plants. The air was warm; it was light and breezy, almost like spring on Earth.

"How big is the city outside of this castle?" I asked Xander, wanting to fill the silence. "Are we out in one of the valleys between the mountains?"

He looked over his shoulder. "We're inside a mountain. Everything in this city is carved from stone. I believe there are tens of thousands of Darkens in this particular city."

I blinked; a chuckle escaped. "You're messing with me, right? Inside of a mountain? Like dwarves?"

All I could think of was a fantasy movie I had seen years ago where the dwarves lived deep in the mountains, carving everything out of the stone. It made me feel claustrophobic. All of that mountain above us.

Xander didn't chuckle at my statement though, and my feet ground to a halt.

"A m-mountain?" I stuttered. I was an outside, water person. I couldn't be in a mountain or cave or anything that like. It was like the plane all over again. I felt embarrassed to keep having these moments, but I couldn't seem to help my body's responses.

Salt water and sunshine flitted across my senses and I closed my eyes. "It's okay," he whispered, his voice very close to my ear. I could smell him. Feel his energy. The tendrils of panic started to lessen. "My room here has a very deep bathing pool. You will feel better when you're in the water."

He continued to talk to me, his voice remaining in that same low, soothing tempo, and eventually I was able to open my eyes and straighten. I bumped into him, not realizing just how close he was. Our eyes met and I sucked in a breath. His were the darkest blue I'd ever seen. They almost looked black.

"Thank you," I breathed, not moving away because I physically couldn't force myself to.

He nodded a few times. "You're going to have to learn to deal with the sensory deprivation better."

He didn't say it meanly, but it still sparked annoyance within me. "It's been like a day, maybe two, since you plucked me out of the ocean. I'm currently standing on an alien world. I think I'm dealing about as well as one could be expected to in the circumstances."

He tilted his head to the side then, like I had reminded him of something. "Right," he finally said, focusing on me again. "You are right. You're actually handling this better than the majority of Royales would. I forget ... that you're mostly human."

He swung away from me and I almost sagged.

Just attraction. It's just attraction.

The mantra ran through my head as I started to move again, following Xander the rest of the way along the hall. We ended up on a floor of bedrooms, from what I could see through their open doors. Xander stopped at one about halfway along. "This is where I usually stay." He gestured for me to step forward. "You should stick with me, Avalon. As I said, I have the largest bath, and I'm also the only one who can calm you down. You respond to Royale energy."

Another spark of annoyance, but I didn't disagree.

Xander dropped the bags Star had put in his arms on the bed, and I saw a few different items, along with some Converse, tumble out.

There was only one bed in here, but it was huge—like two king-sized beds put together. I tried to focus on that so I didn't have to focus on the one thing really drawing my attention ... the male across from me.

It didn't help that my body was on fire, my skin so sensitive that just my clothing moving across it was almost painful. Painful but good. I was trying to think of what I should say when hands wrapped around my waist, picking me up and pulling me back against a hard chest. Xander's lips were on my neck before I caught my breath, and then I forgot everything except him.

He held me like that for many long moments, my back plastered to him, his lips exploring whatever bare skin he could find. I was a blissed-out, turned-on mess by the time he spun me around and lifted me higher. Through instinct and need, my legs wrapped around his waist, my body arching into his. I wanted to be closer. I wanted to be naked.

I really wanted him to be naked.

Lifting my head, I kissed him hard. He let out a low groan as our tongues tangled together. The taste of him was so fucking good ... better than I ever anticipated.

"You're still sure," he murmured against my mouth, "that you can handle a sex-only relationship?"

If I hadn't been able to see the softness in his eyes and hear the true concern in his voice, I might have been pissed at his question. But it was clear that he was genuinely checking in with me.

'I'm sure," I whispered back, wondering if maybe, just maybe, I was lying to everyone in this room. Because Xander was an enigma begging to be unraveled. And I shouldn't be this curious about someone who was only a booty call.

I couldn't stop, though, even if I wanted to. I'd just have to be strong enough to let him go when he walked away. I'd lost things I cared about before. I could do it again.

"I'm sure," I repeated, stronger this time because he was still watching me closely, dissecting my expression.

Before he could pry further, I tilted my upper body back and ripped my shirt off, leaving just my bra and a lot of bare skin. Xander's throat moved as he let his eyes trail across my body. "I'm ready, Xander Royale," I said. My voice had a distinct purr in it, which was not like me, but I had pretty much lost control of myself at this point.

Whatever concern he'd been holding faded then and he took control again. Kissing me hard, he walked us back toward the bed, dropping down with me still in his arms. He lowered himself back, slowly, using some sort of impressive core strength. I mean, how freaking strong was this guy? I was thin, but not exactly light. You couldn't be six feet tall with swim-mers' muscles and weigh nothing. But Xander lifted me and moved me around like I was featherlight.

There were just too many attractive things about him, which was no doubt why my needy hormones had kicked in. *Except his personality.* Couldn't forget what an asshole he could be. Hopefully that would be enough to stop me ever really falling for him.

When he was flat on his back, I shifted so I was straddling

him, clenching at the hard length of him under me. "Shirt off," I ordered. "And pants."

Xander grinned, a wicked sort of smile, and I forced myself not to react. "I like a bossy woman in the bedroom."

Sweet. Baby. Jesus.

He lifted himself half up and reached back to pull his shirt over his head. My breath caught as his chest came into clear view. I'd seen him in the water before, but at the time I'd been trying not to pay too much attention to the broad, bronze, ripped lines of his body. He was so well-muscled; bulky only where he should be, and lean carved lines in other areas. I had to swallow hard to clear my throat. *I repeat: sweet baby Jesus.*

The overlord marks extended down his neck just a little, but his chest was bare, and I took my time running both hands across the smooth skin. He was like me, not a lot of body hair, but there was still enough for me to trace.

I'd been so consumed with his amazing chest—what could I say, I was definitely a pecs and abs sort of girl—that I'd missed the fact he'd managed to get his pants off without dislodging me. He wore boxer briefs underneath, and as I let my eyes roam across the muscled length of his thighs, I wondered if I might have been a little hasty in choosing my favorite parts.

Xander was fucking incredible. Damn him.

He distracted me when he lifted me up with one hand, somehow removing my pants with the other so I was now clad only in bra and underwear. Xander took his time, just as I had done, to explore my body.

"You're perfect," he said under his breath. And then he added, so low I almost didn't hear him, "Of course you are."

I wasn't sure what he meant by that, but I did like that he was as attracted to me as I was to him. When he reached out and linked his fingers through mine on my scarred hand, I started to think I was in way over my head. There was no way to remain impartial to someone like Xander.

In desperate need, I leaned forward. Xander rose up to meet me in a searing kiss. I opened my mouth, allowing his tongue to sweep against mine, and we moved frantically together, underwear the only thing keeping our bodies from joining.

When Xander pulled away from me, my breathing was heavy. "Please tell me you have condoms," I huffed, as I pulled my hand from his so I could thread my fingers through his hair.

He groaned as I pulled his head closer to mine. "Xander?" I asked, more demand in my tone. "Protection ... do you have some?"

He shook his head. "Fuck. No, I don't. We don't require the same sort of birth control that humans use."

I stilled against him, my body aching. The last thing either of us needed was a child to deal with. That would really hurt the "friends with benefits" arrangement. We stared at each other for an extended moment, unsure what to do next, then his expression brightened. "Wait, Lexen might. I'll check his room. Don't go anywhere."

In a flash, he lifted me up and then he was gone. With a groan, I rolled facedown, closed my eyes, and screamed into the bed, the sound almost completely muffled. I was so damn turned on right then I couldn't think straight.

Strong arms lifting and turning me had my eyes flying open again. Xander wore a satisfied look on his face as he settled me back onto his lap. "We good?" I asked him.

His smiled broadened. "We're good for five rounds. Do you think that'll be enough?"

I laughed, wondering where this bold, sexy side of me had come from. I'd never been this way in the past, but something about Xander....

"For now," I replied.

His eyes went dark and hooded. He dropped the foil packets on the bed, reached out, and cupped my face. My lips parted and all breath rushed out of me as he leaned forward and kissed me again. This time it was controlled, slow. I could feel the softness of his full lips and taste the slight saltiness.

"I'm predicting that sex with you might just kill me," he said, when he pulled away.

I lifted an eyebrow. "Only one way to find out."

In a flash he flipped me over, dropping me back on the bed so he could crawl over the top of me. His lips pressed into my stomach, and my muscles there tensed as I started to move on the bed. I couldn't seem to stay still. I needed ... everything.

"God," I gasped, fisting the bedsheets as he moved lower.

Using his teeth, he slowly pulled my underwear down, his hands under my butt to lift me higher. My head was spinning. I wondered if you could actually die from pleasure overload. Every part of my skin was on fire, sensitive to the point where the bed felt like it was sparking energy across my body.

When my underwear was gone, Xander returned to exploring my body, taking his time as he touched me, moving his tongue over me. "I need...," I begged.

"You need...," he repeated, lifting his head up.

"More," I gasped out. "I need more. Now."

He tilted his head to the side and his beautiful eyes shone. "All you had to do was ask, Avalon."

He reached for the protection, and somehow got naked and put the condom on in the same single movement. For someone who didn't normally need to use protection, he was skilled at getting it on. He moved over the top of me again, and I reached out to wrap my arms around him. As he lowered down toward me, my legs wrapped around him too.

"I'm really liking the 'benefits' part of this arrangement," I murmured as he slowly entered me. So slowly that it was almost like torture. The sort of torture I would sign myself up for anyday.

"I got you, Avalon," he murmured, his lips already moving across my throat as his body moved inside of mine. "You will never leave my bed unsatisfied."

As another gasp left me, I knew that every word he spoke was the truth. As long as I could continue to protect my heart, I was in safe hands with Xander.

12

*I*t turned out that five was the exact right number of condoms needed to satisfy Xander. And ... if I was being truly honest, me as well. By the end I was exhausted and fulfilled in a way I'd never been before. Daelighters had a lot more stamina than human males, that I could attest to. I'd only been with a few guys before Xander, of course. The ocean was a much bigger priority to me than sex, but the difference was very clear.

"Come on," Xander said, after we'd finished session five— both of us crashed out on the bed, covered in sweat, breathing heavy. "I think it's time for us to clean up."

I groaned, trying to lift my hand up to cover my eyes, but not having the strength to move it. "Too tired," I mumbled at him. "Dead."

He laughed, this low intoxicating rumble, and my insides tightened. Holy shit. It was like my body had been trained. In half a damn day. Trained to respond to his husky voice.

Before I could hurt myself with all that thinking, I was

lifted up and thrown over his shoulder. Gently. But my breath still whooshed out because I wasn't ready for it.

Xander slapped a hand on my ass, holding me in place as he walked toward the bathroom. "You need water," he said, moving with graceful strides.

From my current position, I was staring at his perfect ass. Firm, with the long lines of his thighs flashing beneath as he walked. Jesus. Maybe I'd just stay here for a few hours.

His hand on my butt started to move slowly up and down. I groaned. "No more. We don't have any more condoms. So ... control yourself."

He laughed again. "Easier said than done when you're naked across me like this."

I huffed. "You threw me across you, and ... just shut up."

His entire body shook as his laughter rocked through us. I realized that up until this point I'd barely heard him even chuckle. He had been so closed off when I first saw him ... so angry. I wondered if his attitude problem back then had been about me, an expression of his annoyance at being "forced" into a relationship by the fates, or if there was more going on in his life, more that weighed on his mind.

I wanted to ask him. I was a naturally curious person, but something told me that question might destroy the very fragile peace we were currently experiencing together. I was not ready to go back to Asshole Xander yet.

Xander paused, then there was a light jolt as he stepped down. I couldn't see anything, but warm water washed over my legs. My body went even more blissed out as warmth surrounded me.

"Arghhh, *sofreakinggood*," I mumbled, when he lowered us. My words cut off as our heads went under the water.

The bath had to be massive, because as he released me I

could spread myself out and still not touch the sides. It was also at least six feet deep from what I could see below.

As I floated on the top, facedown, Xander's face came into clear view underneath. He was lying back on the bottom of the bath. I let my eyes rove down the length of him, greedily drinking in every naked inch. He pursed his lips, and I knew what was coming now. The exprendo channel. The bubble crashed into my face.

"You need to stop looking at me like that," he growled, the moment the water drained from around my face. "Otherwise, we're going to play the pull-out game."

I snort-laughed, because he was so damn confident. "I don't play games when it comes to diseases and babies," I shot back at him.

I moved closer to him and the bubble around my head popped. As I brushed against him, he reached out and pulled me down, blowing another bubble out at the same time.

"I would never put you at risk" was the first thing he said. "There are no diseases you need to worry about from me."

"What about pregnancy?" I asked, trying not to think about what else he'd said. "Never put you at risk" was a very caring sort of statement.

He moved under me and I groaned, my legs winding around his waist. "Pregnancy ... still a possibility. A very small possibility because we don't know if we're that compatible. In truth, Royales do not view offspring the same way as a lot of other houses, but overlord children are different. Because of the royal bloodline, they stay with their family. I would not object to having a child with you, if you'd like to share that responsibility with me."

I froze then, trying to see his expression through the

bubbles. That was the only thing I disliked about the exprendo channels—they distorted my underwater vision.

"I was created by two parents who didn't really love me," I said slowly. "Or each other, from what I could tell. If I ever have a child, I want it to be with someone I plan to love for the rest of my life. And considering my life now looks like it might be indefinite, that would be a rare find indeed."

I hadn't, until this moment, stopped to think about the real consequences of living forever. I could love a human. But even if I found someone I could trust with this secret, I'd only be able to love them for a short speck of my life before they grew old and died. I wasn't sure my heart could handle that.

"What are you thinking?" Xander asked, sounding somber.

"I'm not a Daelighter," I whispered, "but I'm also not human. I don't fit in anywhere. I've been alone most of my life ... and I can't see how that is going to change for the rest of eternity."

He was silent for a beat. I liked that he didn't just rush in to offer me false platitudes. My situation was unique—well, not completely unique. All secret keepers were in the same position. It was okay for Emma, Maya, and Callie, though. They had their soulmates who would live forever as well.

But not for me.

In my panic, words tumbled out of my mouth. "I want a family. I want that sort of bond and life. In this regard, I'm much more human than Royale, because you said Royales don't do that. I can't be with a human because I can't watch someone I love age and die." One more thing occurred to me. "I suppose ... I suppose I could try to find a partner in one of the other Houses."

There was a long pause before he said, "Firstly, if you found a human that you wanted to marry, you could give them some of our food. This could extend their life many hundreds of years, if eaten regularly."

Say what? That information should have made me feel a lot better, but it didn't.

"And secondly, why are you stressing about this right now? You just told me you don't want to settle down. You're all in for this casual partnership." Xander almost sounded like he was angry. "The physical without the emotional."

"I am all in," I said, trying not to get upset at his tone. I was sharing something real with him and he was acting like his old dickish self. "But I'm only eighteen. Eventually I'll want more. I will want to have it all."

I didn't think he was going to answer, and I was about to push myself away from him when he spoke, resigned, "Humans aren't your only option. Most Royales might not, in general, form long-term bonded relationships ... but we are starting to change. So, never say never on that front. Or, as you said, there are the other houses. There's usually no cross-mated relationships between the houses, but if that's something you need to be happy, I will make sure no one questions you."

He was the one to break away and rise to the surface, and for the life of me I couldn't figure out why my chest hurt when he did. When I surfaced next to him, I spun so I could see his face. A neutral expression met mine.

"Sorry if I upset you," I said slowly. "I shouldn't have unloaded my personal stuff on you."

He shook his head, water droplets flying off him. "It's fine. It's good to make sure we're on the same page still. For now, you and I are doing this no-strings-attached thing. The only stipulation from me is that you're not with any other

Daelighters or humans while we're together. Royales are possessive during the time we're together."

I nodded. "I can agree to that, as long as you also don't stray."

"Deal." The heaviness of his expression lifted, and he drifted back to rest against the side of the massive bath. I followed, but instead of moving to sit right by him, like I might have when we first entered, I dropped back on the opposite side.

Xander looked amused. "They're going to come looking for us soon," he said. "This was a nice little interlude. I have a feeling life is going to get very hectic for the next few days."

I nodded. "I'm thinking the same thing. I can feel this ... energy almost, running along my skin. Something big is about to happen. It's like being in the ocean just before the huge storms. I can feel the electricity in the air. I always know when the storm is coming."

Xander nodded. "It's one of the things I love the most about Hawaii, when the storm clouds roll across the sky. We don't have clouds here. Our water is from beneath the land."

"I'd miss never seeing a storm again," I told him. "So maybe living under the water isn't quite everything I want in life."

Xander chuckled. "Sometimes the water isn't greener on the other side. Earth has a lot of wonders that Daelighters dream of experiencing, but very few of us make it through the transporter. The ones that do, most of them return home."

From what I'd seen, it seemed like there were tons of Daelighters moving between the two worlds, but in reality it was probably only a small percentage of their total numbers.

"Can anyone cross to Earth?" I asked, wondering if there were rules about it.

Xander shook his head as he leaned back further, his long arms resting across the top of the bath on either side of him. "No, you need to receive permission from your overlord. There are long wait lists, some longer than others depending if you want to go for a vacation or to live. We closely monitor all Daelighters on Earth, which is something your government insisted on. There's also a limit to the numbers of us allowed to cross. Lots of rules and red tape involved."

It made sense. If an alien race was trying to set up shop in my world, I'd want to know what they were up to as well. "I'm still surprised that my government is so compliant with you all crossing to Earth," I said honestly. "The stone must be something seriously important to the human race."

"It is," he said. "Before the stone, you were heading for a cataclysmic event. Nature was set to wipe you out."

Before the true horror of that could sink in, there was a loud knock on the bedroom door. Xander's head fell back and he groaned. "For a moment there, reality was far away," he murmured.

It didn't sound like he was talking to me, so I didn't reply. I stood, sending a silent goodbye to the water as it trailed down me. Xander's head snapped forward again, his eyes locked on me. The blue darkened—a sign I already recognized.

"No time, Romeo," I teased him, taking my time as I walked up the steps and out of the bath. I didn't feel one ounce of unease at being naked in front of him like this, which was really unexpected. Maybe it was the simple fact that I didn't have to try and impress him. We'd already established the rules of this relationship, and now we were just enjoying it.

As I reached for a neatly folded towel in a set of dark gray shelves near the entrance to the tiled bathroom, hands landed on my hips. I hadn't even heard him move, but I sure as hell felt him when he spun me around, his lips capturing mine.

I forgot everything in that moment. I'd always thought it was a cliché when chicks in books and movies said that, but Xander literally had the ability to wipe everything from my mind. I became nothing more than reaction and need.

I'd had sex more times in the past few hours than I had in the past year, and yet I wanted him again. A loud noise echoed at the edge of my brain, but I managed to ignore it.

"Xander, are you in there?"

The shout had him pulling back, and as he did I managed to regain some clarity.

He turned away slightly. "Hang on, we'll be right out. Avalon was sleeping."

I snorted, pressing my face into his right bicep. I hadn't slept for a second, and now I was going to have to pretend to be well rested. I was well satisfied though, which was close enough.

"You have five minutes," the male voice at the door said, before footsteps echoed away.

"Come on, we'd better get dressed," Xander said, reaching for the towel and wrapping it around me. He must have used his power as well, because by the time I rubbed it across my body and hair, I was dry.

Xander's hand landed firmly on my ass, just short of a slap. I narrowed my eyes on him playfully and he laughed. "Put some damn clothes on," he finally muttered. "Or they will have to break the door down."

With a shake of my head, I hurried across to the clothes Star had gathered for me. The underwear fit, which was almost unbelievable. How the hell had Star guessed my sizes? I was going to call that Daelighter magic. The rest fit as well: a simple white shirt, tan cotton shorts, and Converse in the exact right size.

"Where do all of these clothes come from?" I asked Xander when we were both dressed.

He shrugged. "Star has always dressed us. She loves it. Lexen said she makes some of the clothing herself."

That would be a very useful skill indeed.

I started running my fingers through my long hair, silky and untangled from whatever Xander did to remove the water. That and the natural magic of my Royale hair. "Do you use toothbrushes here?" I asked.

"Yep, there's a spare in the top drawer," he said, pointing toward the bathroom.

I hurried, deliberately not looking at the huge, steaming bath. Water was almost as enticing as naked Xander, and I had no time for either right now.

There were a ton of spare toiletry items in that drawer, so I grabbed the few things I needed. Within two minutes I had my teeth brushed and my hair pulled back into a loose braid.

"You ready?" Xander said, appearing in the doorway.

"Yep." I smiled, snapping the band around the ends. "I'm ready to go."

We didn't touch as we walked toward the bedroom door, but there was so much energy between us it almost felt like we were. Or maybe that was my nerves. For some stupid reason, I could be naked as the day I was born around him and not feel any unease, but now that our clothes were back on....

I had no idea where we stood when we weren't sexing.

Before I had time for an existential crisis, Xander opened the door and we were out in the hallway. A group was standing near the end—our friends. As we got closer, I tried really hard to keep my expression neutral. "Sorry," I blurted out, not sure where to look. "I must have been more tired than I thought. I really crashed after Xander let me use his amazing bath."

There, that was normal, right? No one would be suspicious.

"No problem!" Maya said, smiling. "Chase had to drag me away from my family. It was so hard leaving them again, especially knowing that this part of our journey might be the most dangerous of all."

That sobered everyone up.

I took a step closer to Callie. "You look great," I said. "Are you feeling much better?"

She nodded. "Yep. So much better. Dan got me back in time, thankfully. I had to sleep for a few hours, but now I'm ready to go."

She looked amazing, her skin golden and flushed with health. She wore all black, with a silver-studded belt holding her boyfriend jeans up. She ran her eyes across me. "I see Star put you in the secret keepers uniform."

I chuckled because I'd thought the same thing. "It suits me perfectly. I prefer clothes that are lightweight and easy to remove for swimming. Shorts and T-shirt dresses are my favs."

Maya's eyes got really wide as she clapped her hands. "One day we're all going shopping together. I love my casual clothes, don't get me wrong, but I also love dressing up. Girls' night!"

Callie grimaced, but she didn't say anything. Something told me she wasn't that big a fan of shopping.

"Are Emma and Lexen not back yet?" I heard Xander ask Daniel and Chase. His question drew our attention back to the boys.

Daniel shook his head. "No, but Lexen sent word that they were going to meet us in about ten minutes. So we should start moving."

Everyone began to walk then, and I waited to fall in at the back of the group. Xander paused, settling in at my side. I didn't miss the knowing looks Maya and Callie shot us. Xander was right, matchmaking was totally on their agenda, but they were fighting a losing battle. Xander was a Royale, and even though he said the overlord family had a stable family to ensure their bloodline remained clearly identified, he'd also told me on more than one occasion that that was not the future for us.

No long-term commitment.

We ended up back in the room with the huge dining table. It was empty when we arrived, so everyone took a seat to wait. "So, the next step of the plan is to go to House of Royale?" Callie asked, holding one finger up like she was counting down. "Figure out the map?" A second finger came up. "Then go and get the stone before Laous tracks us down?"

The guys all nodded. I started to feel really nervous that I was going to let them all down. That maybe the map wasn't on my body like they hoped.

"I've never seen anything on my skin which could be used as a map or coordinates," I told them. My eyes flashed to Xander's for a split second and he gave a minute head shake. He hadn't seen anything either, and he probably knew some parts of my body better than me at this point.

"She doesn't even have any freckles," Maya added.

I literally didn't have a single freckle. The only marks that marred my skin were a few faded stretch marks on my thighs —thank you, puberty—and the scars on my hand.

Chase replied immediately. "I think it's going to have something to do with the legreto you were born in, Ava. Likely you have to go back there again."

Daniel nodded. "That would be the place the map was first placed on Ava, so it makes sense."

Xander straightened, his eyes going faraway for a moment. I was about to ask him what was wrong when he said, "Lexen is almost back. He found out something about the Draygo."

We all turned toward the main door, waiting for them to enter. But, instead of the two familiar faces we were expecting, a silver-haired woman burst through the door.

Daniel shot to his feet. "Colita! What are you doing here?"

I blinked as the woman—*Colita,* apparently—hurried forward, her long dress trailing after her. She wore something that looked like a combination of a summer dress and robes, layers of wispy material fluttering around her as she moved.

"I had a vision," she cried, and collapsed.

13

*X*ander caught Colita just before she hit the table, lowering her down into the chair he had just vacated. Her eyes were half rolled back in her head, and I found myself rushing to her side. I lifted her hand and felt for a pulse, relief hitting me when there was a strong buzz under my fingers. It seemed a little fast, but for all I knew that was the normal speed here.

It was beating at least, and that was the most important part.

"Who is she?" I whispered to Xander. "Is this the Draygo?"

She didn't look the same as Lexen, all of that scary energy. But maybe the females were different.

He shook his head, face drawn with worry. "No, Colita is a normal Daelighter. Kind of. She's a seer, able to discern future events through dreams and visions."

"She's also my *drenita*," Lexen rumbled as he hurried into the room.

Emma was right behind him and she caught my confused

look. "His godmother," she murmured, giving my arm a quick squeeze when she reached my side.

Xander moved back to allow Lexen to stand at his drenita's side. The Darken overlord reached out and grasped Colita's hand. Realizing I was still holding her other one, I gently set it down.

Lexen's eyes shot to me, and I quickly mumbled, "Just feeling for a pulse—it's strong but fast."

Something white flitted across the dark of his eyes and I swallowed roughly. It disappeared just as quickly though, and most of the tension left the room when he gave me a slow head dip. "Thank you," he said, voice octaves lower than normal.

He turned back to Colita. Her eyes were open and focused again. She sat up slowly, shaking her head. It took her only a moment to notice the multiple sets of eyes locked on her. She stumbled to her feet.

"Lexen," she cried as he steadied her. "I saw Laous. In a dream. He is amassing an army. Astoria is filling with Gonzo and Daelighters as we speak."

Xander slammed his fist against the table, and when he pulled his hand away I could have sworn there was an indent in the thick wood. "He's smart. He knows he can wait us out. Eventually we'll have to return to Earth, especially if we're trying to find the stone."

"What if we never did?" Callie suggested, crossing her arms over her chest. "He could wait there for hundreds of years. If we stay here, then no one will touch the stone and everything can go back to the way it was."

Colita shook her head violently. "No! No, he won't wait. He has taken the town hostage, all of the humans outside of those safe in Daelight Crescent right now. He's trying to draw you out, and if you don't come back soon, he's going to start killing the humans. By the end of my vision, Astoria was awash in blood."

Emma's eyes immediately filled with tears. "No," she whispered, her hand pressing to her chest. "All of those innocent people. We can't let him do this."

"What else did you see?" Lexen pressed Colita. "You don't normally dream your visions ... how did that happen?"

Her face crumbled as she released Lexen to massage her temples. "I ... I don't actually know. But ... you're right, I don't usually dream my visions in this manner. It also went on for much longer than I can generally hold a vision. If I had to guess, I'd say that someone was helping me see."

Daniel drew our attention. "Rao is a dream seer. Could it be him?"

Colita looked confused for a beat, until recognition cleared that expression. "Rao ... your brother who went missing? Your father declared him dead. I remember the farewell ceremony."

Daniel nodded stiffly. "Yes, apparently he didn't die. He was taken by Laous—he's been using him in his cause ever since."

"But we think he might have switched sides," Callie added. "He has helped more than one of us."

Colita nodded a few times, her eyes misty. "There was a man in my dream. He kept his face in the shadows, so I couldn't see him clearly, but he was very big, with a dark aura."

"That could be him," Daniel said shortly. "He's even bigger than me, and his face is burned. He was caught in the fires of the justices, and Laous was the one to find him, faking his death so that we would stop looking for him."

There was an extended silence; I didn't know most of the people they were talking about, but I could sense how serious this information was.

"How long do we have?" Callie asked, her voice devoid of emotion.

Colita squeezed her eyes closed tightly. "I can't tell," she said with a wavering voice. "The vision is not clear. It's not ... it's not giving me enough information!"

Lexen pulled her close, hugging her tightly. "You've helped immensely," he said, as he pulled back. "We know where Laous is now ... we're prepared."

Colita straightened, purpose and determination filling her. The fear and panic that had been defining her features faded. "You won't do it alone either." Her voice thundered. "The council will rally the houses, and all of our warriors. While you're off finding the location of the stone, we'll be making sure that you can make it through Astoria."

She kissed Lexen on both cheeks, as well as Emma, bade the rest of us farewell, and rushed from the room as quickly as she had arrived.

"Before we discuss this possible battle situation," Maya cut in when Colita was gone. "What did you learn from the Draygo? Did you find him?"

Lexen and Emma moved closer, tightening our circle. When Lexen started to speak, it was in a hushed voice. "We didn't find him, the one who was there when the secret keepers were born, the one who hid the stone. But we did chat with a relative of his."

"Lexen had to go full-on dragon hybrid mode before any of them would talk to him," Emma cut in, her voice wavering. "I mean, I thought Lex was scary when he dragoned out, but this group was ... very animalistic."

Lexen rumbled, acting very animalistic himself right then. "I shouldn't have taken Emma. There was probably more information I could have gotten from them, but my instinct was to get Emma away from their threat. So I didn't stick around. Thankfully, Qenita was there, keeping an eye on her for me."

Emma pursed her lips, and we could all tell she had not been happy about being swept to the side by his dragon.

"There were a few there who knew of the Draygo I sought," Lexen continued. "They said he moved to another sector in Overworld. I'm not sure I believe that, because it's never been done before, but it would explain why no one has ever crossed paths with him."

Chase let out a low breath. "So, dead lead, basically?"

Lexen shrugged. "Yes … and no. While we didn't get the information about the starslight stone's location, I did find out a little about the reason for our bond, which was one of the main questions I had for him. Turns out that when the first secret keepers were born here, the bond was done just through a basic energy sharing technique through the network. This connected the four in the chain, and they received Daelighter energy for longevity. The Draygo thought this would be enough. But they didn't have as close a connection to Overworld as he hoped."

"Why did they want them to have a close connection to Overworld?" I asked. "Was it important in the location of the stone?"

Lexen nodded. "Yes. While they had a connection to each other, and they had some of our energy, none of them would have actually led to the stone. They weren't bonded to it. Or to Overworld. This wasn't discovered until Callie's father died."

"So … what happened?" Daniel asked. "Why are our girls different?"

Emma picked up the story. "The Draygo used the actual stone with us, and this time, when he performed the birth ceremonies for the four of us, he did things differently. He not only placed the stone in the legreto we were born in—"

"But also the crystals of the ancient overlords," Lexen added quickly. "He believed this was the way to tie the girls not only to the stone, but also to the four houses."

Chase let out a surprised huff. "That's why their energy feels like the ancients'. The Draygo basically tied each of the girls to the overlord family. To our energy."

"And our bonds were formed," Callie breathed. "Could it be as simple as that? The overlord energy you all possess recognizes the overlord energy we possess?"

Daniel pulled her into him, his eyes burning. "It makes you our perfect matches, and I have to say, fate chose very well."

Callie snorted. "Always with the fate thing."

I noticed she didn't argue about the perfect match part, and I tried really hard not to look at Xander. It definitely explained why I felt so closely tied to the water, why I had the extra abilities that allowed me to be like House of Royale members.

We had ancient overlord energy from the crystals that had originally blessed each house. Our DNA, which at one point had been fully human, was now mutated.

"As much as this additional information is helpful," Xander said. "It doesn't change our current task. We need to continue on. As Colita said, we don't have much time."

"My parents already have our warriors ready," Chase said smoothly. "The council will find no issue there."

"A few of the leaders in House of Imperial have requested to not be involved," Daniel said shortly. "Mostly because we never concern ourselves with anything other than our own issues. I informed them that this was going to change from now on. We will be united with the other four houses. So,

Imperial will be there or they will find out how much power an overlord wields."

Energy thundered from him, sounding like the roar of flames. The room also got a lot hotter until Callie placed a hand on his arm. She whispered something I couldn't hear, and he immediately started to calm.

"Darken is definitely in," Lexen said when the tension was gone. He shifted his focus to Xander. "Royale?"

Xander nodded. "Yep, you know we'd never leave our allies to fight without us. Colita will be able to quickly gather numbers. We've all been prepping for this for months now."

"We just need to find the map first," I reminded them, very aware that somewhere on my body—if Chase was right—there was a map of the starslight stone's location. We weren't going anywhere until we got that.

Xander lifted himself up from where he was resting against the long table. "Let's get back to the center platform. That's the best place for me to help you all be able to survive in Royale."

Callie clapped her hands together. It was so unlike her normal calm demeanor that I stared at her for a moment, trying to figure out what happened.

"I have always wanted to be a mermaid," she said, almost breathless. "This is a dream come true."

You and me both, sister. You and me both.

Xander met my gaze then and I couldn't help the broad smile that spread across my face.

"Are you ready to go home?" he asked, and I would be a liar if I didn't admit that my chest tightened at his question. It felt ... intimate. Maybe it was just that we'd been naked an hour ago, but home was such a huge concept, especially for someone who'd never really had one.

"I'm so ready," I finally said. "I've been dreaming about a

world where I could live under the water since I was old enough to swim."

He held out a hand for me and I blinked at it. So much for keeping the relationship a secret. No one said anything though, and I didn't hesitate to place my palm against his. We were going on an adventure and I had literally never been more ready.

BY THE TIME we took the transporter back to the main platform, I was jittering on the spot like I'd had ten energy drinks. The eight of us stood across the edge of the platform. Below us were the waters of Royale. It wasn't like the ocean in Hawaii. There were no waves outside of the small movements from whatever was going on below. Far out, it looked like something broke the water line, rocks maybe—I couldn't tell what it was from this distance.

My skin felt tight, like I'd been out of the water too long and it was starting to dry out. "The legreto here is a little different to water," Xander explained as we all ditched our shoes and any extra pieces of clothing. "It has tiny bubbles throughout it that allows us to stay under indefinitely—we can filter the water and oxygen through our lungs. For the rest of you, though, you're going to need a little extra help."

He lowered his hands, and with barely a flick of his wrist, an entire plume of water shot up into the air, hovering at Xander's side. He stepped up to Lexen, who remained relaxed, despite a torrent of water circling around him. Something told me the Darken overlord knew exactly what the extra help entailed.

"The key is to relax. Don't fight it," Xander said as he lifted his hands, placing them close to either side of Lexen's head.

He didn't touch his friend, but there was not much space between them.

The water slowly trickled up in the gap between Lexen's face and Xander's hands, forming a bubble covering Lexen's head entirely. When Xander stepped back, I realized I couldn't see Lexen at all, his face obscured by the water swirling around his head.

"It's like the exprendo channel," Xander said as he moved toward Emma. "But this is an exo-exprendo bubble. They filter the oxygen in the water for you and are superstrong—woven more tightly so you can't break through it easily. I don't want you all to accidentally bust through it when we go deep."

Emma looked nervous, swallowing roughly, but she didn't stop him.

By the time Xander had gone down the row, the water he'd drawn from the House of Royale was almost gone. I was the last one. He paused in front of me, his expression intense. "They can't see or hear us clearly right now," he murmured.

He leaned in closer, and I closed my eyes as his lips gently brushed across mine. "Are you ready?" he murmured against my mouth.

"Yes," I said with urgency. "I've been ready for this since I was born."

He nodded. "Yes, you have."

He stepped back, his hands cupping my face briefly, before he pulled them back to allow the cool water to wash over my cheeks. There was a decent gap between the bubble and my head, and I immediately understood what he meant about limited vision and hearing. When fully covered, I could only make out some shadows and muffled sounds.

I was just wondering how we knew to go in the water, when my feet were swept out from under me and I found myself being tossed into the air. I would have screamed, but it was over too quickly, water closing over my feet as I sank below.

The moment my head went under, the bubble turned translucent. "I've linked the bubbles," Xander said, his voice echoing, "so we can chat to each other. The water takes your message, so it's a little slower than normal speech. Be patient."

"Best freaking day ever," Callie exclaimed a beat later. "This is a dream come true."

Daniel's low chuckle reached us all, and I realized that we would all have far less privacy than normal. We were going to hear everything everyone said, even if it was whispered. I'd have to remember that.

"Is everyone a strong swimmer?" Xander asked abruptly. "I should have asked that earlier. I tend to forget that not everyone is born swimming."

"I'm not," Callie replied.

"I have her," Daniel said a moment later. "I'll keep her safe."

"Everyone else okay?" I asked, prepared to help if needed.

There was a bunch of yeses, and it was hard to differentiate them, but no one had said no, so it didn't really matter.

"Stay close to me," Xander said as he turned in the water, facing away from the platform and the wall that descended into the depths below. "There are predators in these legretos, and while we have an accord with them, they're still hunters."

He'd mentioned the meglam being like a shark, and while I'd love to see one, I also really hoped we didn't. They sounded scarier than the sharks I was used to.

We all moved toward him, my heart doing happy little twirls in my chest as we swam further into the well-lit world. Being back in the water was the best feeling ever. As we got deeper, the light did not wane. It was almost like the water itself was filled with light.

"This is incredible," Callie said, her voice bursting with emotion. "I'm actually swimming."

She sounded like she was going to cry, which made me want to cry. What an incredible experience for her, especially since the molecular structure of the water here appeared to make swimming easier than normal. When I stopped moving, for example, I didn't sink. I could stay in the same spot with little to no effort. These were the best waters for inexperienced swimmers.

"There are multiple pods and villages under here," Xander said as we continued deeper into his world. "The first one we will cross through is Spectra. This is our gateway sector, where the strongest reside. The first barrier to outsiders."

My swimming picked up pace. I was desperate to see the first village in Royale. Xander reached out and captured my hand just as I was about to dash past him. "Slow," he said. "You're not going to miss anything."

I expected him to let me go then, but he didn't. We just swam together, hand in hand.

And it was really freaking nice.

"You kept your legs," I noted, very aware that everyone could hear us.

A moment later his chuckle echoed through my bubble. "Yeah, I don't really need the speed or strength of the tail at the moment."

My next words died on my tongue as the outer boundary of Spectra came into view.

14

The first barrier was literally a barrier. The iron-looking fence with spikes across the top extended out on either side. It went deeper than I could see and ran right up to the top of the water. I was pretty sure this was the break in the smooth water line that I'd seen from above.

"No one enters our villages without permission," Xander explained as he turned to lead us along the bars. "This barrier extends far into the sky, even though you can't see it."

Ah, it must be invisible above or something. Very clever.

I found myself examining it closer as we moved along it. It should have been ugly, such a dark, modern piece clashing with the beautiful fantasy setting. But it wasn't—the iron was mostly covered in what looked like coral and seaweed, creating colorful art. No two panels looked the same.

I was so enthralled by what I was seeing, I missed the gate until we were pretty much right at it. When Xander touched his hands to the center of the panels, they slid back along the lines of the barrier and allowed us entry.

"Overlords get all the special powers," he joked.

It was in that very moment, as he drew me along with him, my hand still firmly encased by his much larger one, that the scope of who he truly was hit me. Sure, the concept of him being a prince and ruling a land was not lost on me. I'd understood it from the first moment I heard of his lineage. And as a human living not-under-a-rock, I'd seen the royal couples on television multiple times. They were important people, I got that, even though they were mostly just figureheads.

But here, Xander had literal power. He could control water. Command metal to open. He had warriors at his disposal, if previous conversations were anything to go on.

No wonder he wasn't interested in anything long-term, despite the fact we might be fated to be together. He was probably looking for his equal ... another Daelighter who would match him. I might be more skilled than a human, but I had nothing close to Xander.

The maudlin turn my thoughts had taken was pushed aside when we entered the village. It was structured much the same way all towns were, except for a few differences. Here, the houses were long and cylindrical, all different sizes. A lot of them were connected, spanning out in street-like formations.

"Think of them like telephone lines," Xander explained, noticing my curiosity. "The lines of communication extend between all the chambers, and if you want to contact anyone, you can."

"There's no water inside the pods?" Emma asked as she swam a little closer to peer inside one of the round, opaque sections. Lexen stopped her before she pressed her face to it.

"You have the choice to drain or fill your pod," Lexen explained, drawing Emma back into the group. "You'll find that some here identify closer with the caramina side, and others with the land dwellers."

I turned to find Emma nodding, her expression contemplative. "That makes sense. Genetics are interesting, the way they can vary so greatly."

I could sleep in one of those. The thought hit me so hard that I actually jolted, knocking my hand out of Xander's. He was right at my side in an instant. "What?" he demanded, his arms wrapping around me, pulling me closer. "What happened?"

I swallowed roughly. "These pods ... I could sleep under the water."

He relaxed, tucking away the fierce warrior that was hidden under the surface of his devil-may-care attitude. "Yes," he said simply. He held me for a beat longer than I expected him to before he let go ... of everything except my hand.

We didn't see our first inhabitant until we were deep into Spectra. A line of warriors swam past us at rapid speed, stopping only to salute and bow to their overlord minor. They bore a multitude of weapons, including razor-sharp spears.

There were a lot of sea creatures dashing about as well.

"We sleep on different schedules to most of Overworld," Xander said when Callie asked where all the civilians were. "Right now, it's very early morning here. The guard shift just changed, which is why they're moving about."

By the time we exited Spectra—it was a mile or so long, filled with hundreds of pods—my body was thrumming with the need to go fast. Xander must have felt the same way, because he said, "I've called for my cousin and sister to help us get to the overlord village. We don't have time to waste."

"That's the waters where Ava was born?" Maya asked.

"Yes," he said immediately. "There's a direct current there

from the mountains of Darken, from the sacred legreto. If anything will reveal the map, it's this location."

With my advanced underwater eyesight, I saw Xander's family coming from a long way away. There were three of them, and the moment they came into sight, his entire demeanor changed. Anger filled his expression; his fists clenched tightly. I jerked my hand back because he was pulling on my scar tissue. That movement seemed to remind him of where he was. *Sorry*, he mouthed to me, and I nodded, because it was fine. It hadn't really hurt.

The first one to reach us was his sister. I guessed that based only on the fact that she was the only chick. She was beautiful, like her brother. Same blond hair, only hers was in a braid to her waist, the strands shimmering with rainbow hues. Her top half was lithe, clad in a tight white wrap around her breasts. Her bottom half was the tail, water bubbling around it, hiding most detail from view.

She greeted her brother with a defeated expression, bowing her head low. He reached out and captured her chin, and in the same instant she had a bubble around her head as well, connecting her to our group.

"You never bow to me," Xander said quietly. There was a pause then. "Why is he here, Dawn?"

I flinched as he said her name, a mixture of love and pain coating each syllable. She shrugged, pulling her face from his hand. "You know I have no choice."

Xander shook his head. "You're wrong. You always have a choice, and I will support you making the right decision."

It was that moment Dawn seemed to realize that we could all hear their private conversation, and she straightened, her movements so graceful in the water that it was easy to forget she was actually swimming. "My apologies, you must all be ready to return to dry land ... my parents have our pod ready for you ... the legreto has been removed. We can be there in no time. If you are agreeable, my mate, Donovan, and cousin, Burton, will help you move faster."

She pointed to each of the men who were hovering a few feet away. Xander greeted Burton with a nod, but it was clear he was pointedly ignoring the heavily-muscled mate of his sister. Donovan had strong features and flashing eyes, the sort of eyes that could give a girl nightmares if they were directed at her. The eyes of a predator. His dark hair was cropped close to his skull, his arms decorated in tatted art, as well as two armbands around each impressive bicep. He looked strong ... arrogant ... very sure of himself. He watched Dawn like she was a possession.

I didn't like it.

He looked at her the same way my old roommate had looked at me.

My skin crawled at the thought of him touching me, but I didn't want to cause a fuss. Hopefully I was a fast enough swimmer to not need help.

Donovan flicked his tail, heading for Dawn, only to veer off at the last second toward me. His mouth opened and bubbles emerged—he was saying something. Xander had not connected him to our channels though, so I couldn't hear anything.

My self-protective instincts roared to life as he got even closer, my hands lifting to a defensive position by the time he reached me. Xander cut him off with one arm thrust between us.

"No!" It was a snap of command from the overlord that had Donovan's very dark eyes flashing.

He said something again, bubbles flying around the water,

and Xander, who was wedging his way between us, driving Donovan back, said with a growl, "Avalon is mine. You're not even supposed to be here. We don't need your kind of help."

Donovan's calm expression faltered for a moment, the monster inside peeking out. I really wished we weren't getting the one-sided conversation. I wanted to know what he was saying to rile Xander up so much. "You're no hero to me," Xander said shortly, before he turned his back. "My family owes you nothing more. You will do well to remember that."

"Leave it," Dawn cried, and when I turned to her, my jaw clenched. She looked ... broken, like she just couldn't give anything more. "We made the deal. Now we must honor it."

Xander squeezed his eyes shut tightly for a moment. "I have been honoring it," he said hoarsely. "I've done nothing but honor it, which is why he's still alive. But ... I have my hard limits, Dawn. You're one of those. I won't let him hurt you any longer."

She crumbled, and I could hear her soft sobs. "If it stops the beast," she whispered, head still down, "then I can endure it. For our people."

Xander let out a roar so guttural that both fear and concern hit me simultaneously. Donovan crossed his arms, leaning back casually. Xander pointed a finger at him. "Leave now, or I will risk the beast. Don't believe me ... fucking try it."

Donovan just smiled, like he already knew he'd won. But he was close enough to me that I could see his eyes, and they held a new emotion, buried under his cockiness. Xander scared him.

He turned, mouthing something over his shoulder before he disappeared into the waters around us. "We need to hurry," Dawn said when he was gone. "He's giving me an hour to get back to our pod, so let's get your friends home."

Xander's fists were opening and closing, over and over, and my craving to comfort him was strong. But ... I was not his mate. He did not want that role filled by me, and I would have to respect his wishes on that.

Lexen moved closer, one of his hands gliding through the water to land on his best friend's shoulder. They had some kind of silent communication—I heard nothing, but their eyes were definitely talking—and Xander calmed slightly. He turned then, capturing my gaze. I tried the same silent conversation ... *Are you okay?*

He gritted his teeth, shaking his head once. I hated that I couldn't ask him more without everyone else knowing. I'd just have to try again later. He got back to business quickly.

"Okay, let's group up. One Royale to two non-caramina. Avalon should be able to keep up on her own."

Xander linked arms with Emma and Lexen. Dawn took Maya and Chase. Burton ended up with Callie and Daniel. I noticed that bubbles were surrounding Xander's legs as they morphed into his tail, and I prepared myself for some speed. Finally.

When they took off, I released my inner water child, following close behind. My blood bubbled, my soul soared, my heart felt lighter as we dashed through the water. Sea creatures joined us in the same way they always did back home, and I marveled at how many were similar. There were gorgeous animals that moved like dolphins, long and sleek. They had very short rostrums and were a bright turquoise in color, blending into the water around them.

A few others were of the scary variety, but I noticed Xander keeping an eye on things, sending out little blasts of red-tinged water if any got too close. We passed by a few more smaller towns as we went, filled with pods and coral gardens. It even looked like there were playgrounds for the young, built from a multitude of materials. It was literally like we'd stumbled into the set of a fantasy movie.

But it was very real.

When the next giant pod came into view, I noticed a definite increase in guards. They lined the entrance, which was again barred with huge gates.

"Home," Xander said simply as half a dozen weapon-wielding Royales rushed to open the gates for us.

Once we were inside that perimeter, our pace slowed down. I was almost disappointed to slow, exhilarated from the race across the waters of Royale. The density should have made it harder to move forward at speed, but I'd adjusted easily. I would even go so far as to say I moved even faster here than back in Hawaii. *Home.* The whisper of that word just wouldn't leave me alone. I would always be torn between two worlds.

On the bright side though, two homes wasn't the worst thing to have in one's life. No home would always win that prize for me.

15

urton left us when we reached the front chamber of the biggest pod I'd seen since we'd dived into the waters of Royale. Dawn and Xander led us through an arched doorway and into the front sectioned-off area. With a whir, the door closed behind us, and there were gurgles as the water slowly drained away. Within a minute we were all standing, dry as we had been before we entered the water.

It felt weird to be back on "land," and my legs shook for a beat before my equilibrium returned. There was no movement in the pod, despite being under the water. If I didn't know better, I would have sworn we were on land.

"Come on," Dawn said, her voice more melodic when it wasn't being filtered through the water. "Our parents are waiting for you."

Doors whooshed open, and we stepped into a long hallway. Art hung along the wood-paneled walls. Carpet covered the floor. "We never go underwater here," she explained, leading the way. "This front section is always dry, but it's best not to open any doors unless you're sure of what is on the other side."

That was good information for the others, but personally I was already missing the water.

The hallway opened up into a huge, gorgeously attired room. Definitely fit for royalty. The carpet was a very pale shade of green, and most of the furniture was white. Huge pieces of art adorned the walls between glass panels that show-cased a view of the water around us. "It's perfect," I breathed.

I'd thought I'd said it low enough that no one would hear, but across the room Xander's head snapped up. His eyes were burning, and it was nearly impossible for me to tell what emotion that was. Arousal, anger, fear, worry ... they were all tangled together.

Before I could combust right there on the spot, a couple appeared, striding in together from the side of the pod we had not explored.

"Xander!" the woman exclaimed, hurrying forward to hug her son. "We have been worried about you."

He returned her hug with force, and then moved on to shake hands with his father. "We found the last keeper, and now we need to find the map," Xander explained after he'd greeted his parents. "Come and meet the girls."

He led them toward us and I tried really hard not to fidget. His mom was stunning, taller than me by a few inches, and looking not much older than us. Her hair was white, and unlike a lot of the Royales I'd seen, it was short, hanging only to her shoulders. Her skin was a creamy brown color, and I could see where Xander got his bronze skin tones. Actually, both of his parents were bronze-skinned.

Xander crossed to me first. "This is Avalon," he said when

he reached my side, both of us facing his parents, who had stepped forward. "She's the Royale secret keeper."

I stood still, waiting for one of them to indicate what sort of protocol was expected of me. Xander waved a hand at his father. "Tristall," he said, before turning to his mother. "And Lettie, overlord major of House of Royale."

Lettie held a hand out to me and I placed mine in her cool grasp. She shook firmly, and I relaxed somewhat. "We're so pleased to finally meet you," she said, sounding as melodic as her daughter.

She dismissed me pretty quickly after that, moving on to the other girls in the room. I really wasn't sure how to take her, because she held herself very formally ... almost coldly. But I had to remember who she was. No doubt it wasn't the easiest task being a ruler. The level of responsibility resting on her would be titanic.

Tristall captured my attention when he captured my hand. "Absolute pleasure to meet you," he said, much more warmly than his mate. "We will assign you a pod so you can come and go from Royale as much as you'd like. Would you prefer it be here, in the overlord village?"

His request was so random and unexpected, I froze up. My eyes darted to Xander's, even though I told myself not to look his way. This decision had nothing to do with him, except for the fact that it would be easier when our "thing" was over if I wasn't living in close proximity to him.

I tore my gaze away before he could influence my decision. "That's a very generous offer," I told Tristall, letting my gratitude seep into my words. "I've dreamed about being able to live under the water ... to sleep under the water, for my entire life. But ... I need to breathe oxygen from above, and I'm not sure I'd be able to make it this deep without some assistance. So a pod is probably not worth wasting on me."

It hurt me to say that, because my own pod would be akin to my own home, and as a double bonus, it was under the water. All of my dreams could come true.

It was probably for the best, though.

"Get her one," Xander's deep voice cut through. "In this village. I will make sure she's able to come and go as needed." He wasn't looking at me, facing his father directly.

"As you wish," Tristall said. He turned away, but not before he threw a wink in my direction. I wasn't quite sure what that wink meant, but it made me feel a little more comfortable.

"Are you sure?" I said, turning to Xander, stepping closer to him. "It might be easier ... you know ... if I don't live so close by."

His shoulder trembled slightly, and I ached to touch him. I just wanted to press my hands against the broad planes of his back.

"This is right," he murmured, and just as I lost the battle with my control, reaching out for him, he walked away. Frozen, I sent out a prayer of relief that at least he hadn't been facing me.

You're a goddamn idiot.

I had been kidding myself that I could stay objective to Xander. I was already in way too deep. *Dammit.* My heart was going to get annihilated, and I'd walked right into the disaster zone thinking I had all my protective gear on.

I had nothing.

"Are you okay?" The soft voice startled me; I let out a little shriek.

Emma chuckled, reaching out to grab my arm. "Sorry, I didn't realize you were quite that far away."

I shook my head, letting out a small, forced laugh. "No, it's my fault. I was thinking hard enough to hurt myself."

"Anything you want to talk about?" Callie asked. She'd also drifted closer after finishing her turn at greeting the Royale overlords.

"Uh...." I wasn't used to sharing secrets with girlfriends. These particular friends, though, felt more like family. Sisters.

"Actually, I could really use some advice," I whispered, leaning in closer to them. "But it's about Xander, so...."

As I trailed off, they both nodded, like they weren't surprised at all. Maya joined us too, the guys remaining on the other side of the pod, talking with Tristall, Lettie, and Dawn.

"They're discussing the warriors and plans for taking back Astoria," Maya offered, leaning against a wall near Emma. "Chase said as soon as they sort through that, we'll head to the sacred waters."

Emma and Callie both whipped around on me. "Go," Callie said, her eyes still bright from the swim through the water. "This is your chance."

I sucked in a deep breath. "Okay, so ... Xander and I ... we had sex and—"

"What?" Emma shouted so loudly that silence fell over the pod, and all heads turned in our direction. I willed my face not to go red, staring at her like everyone else was.

Emma gave her head a quick shake, relaxing then and laughing. "Oh sorry," she said, waving a hand at Lexen, who was already heading in her direction. "I didn't realize that would be so loud. I just found out my favorite movie was at the theaters and I missed it."

All of the Daelighters looked slightly perplexed by this, except for Lexen who just shook his head at her, his concerned expression fading into a smirk. When the overlords turned back to their discussion, the girls crowded around me again.

"Sorry," Emma whispered in a rush. "You shocked the shit out of me with that one."

I snort-laughed; she had made that very clear. "It's fine," I said, waving my hand at her. "I know it's a surprise, especially with the way he acted when you first found me."

"So ... what happened?" Callie asked. Of the three, she looked the most concerned. I lifted one eyebrow in her direction and she let out a long breath. "I'm just worried about you, because I sense that in some ways you had an upbringing like me. Emma and Maya had loving parents, but we were very alone. And ... I know how Daniel makes me feel. I'm scared you'll do anything ... accept anything from Xander, for just a small sliver of *home*." She shook her head fiercely. "You deserve so much more than that. Don't let him use you for sex."

I sucked in a sob, and she softened her tone. "You deserve more, Ava. As your sister, I'm telling you right now that you deserve everything."

I dropped my head and squeezed my eyes shut. Callie had known straight away what my situation was, because she was right—we were much more alike than Emma and Maya.

"Is that what happened?" Emma asked, sounding upset. "Xander is using you for sex?"

My head shot up as I shook it. "No, absolutely not. I mean, okay, yes that is pretty much our deal, but it wasn't all Xander. I thought ... I thought I would be satisfied with it as well. I've never been so attracted to a guy before, and I figured that this would get him out of my system."

"I'm going to guess you're in way deeper than you ever expected," Maya suggested, and I sucked in another sob.

"Pretty much."

Callie crossed her arms, her eyes shiny. "It's okay," I told them. "I knew what I was getting in for when I signed up. I thought I was strong enough to handle it. That the Royale part of me that doesn't like to settle would get sick of Xander. And ... maybe I still will. It is very new, you know."

I was kidding myself, and I could tell by their expressions they also knew that. No one called me out on my bullshit though, and I loved them even more for allowing me to hold on to whatever delusion I had right now.

"I'm going to stop it," I decided, trying to gather up my shaky resolve.

"Stop what?" Xander's deep voice took me completely by surprise. He didn't give me a chance to say anything. "Are you okay? You look a little ... upset."

The other guys were still talking with the overlords, which meant that Xander had crossed back on his own ... because he thought I looked ... upset?

"I'm fine," I told him quietly. "It's just been a crazy few days, you know."

My words didn't appease him; he turned to the others. "Do you mind if I borrow Avalon for a minute? I'd like to show her the styles of pods she can choose from. My father wants to start hers immediately."

It sounded like a weak excuse, but no one called him out on it.

"If it's okay with Ava, it's okay with us," Emma said, smiling in her friendly way.

Maya nodded. Callie just tightened her crossed arms.

"It's fine," I said, promising myself that I'd just take this one last moment with him.

Xander captured my hand pulling me closer. "We'll be

back in about ten minutes, if anyone asks," he said over his shoulder as we walked away.

I expected him to lead me back the way we entered, because that's where the other pods were. But he didn't. He veered to the right, wrapping an arm around me as he dragged me into a nearby room. The door whooshed closed behind us, and when my head stopped spinning, I let out a gasp. The entire far wall of this particular room looked to be made of glass. Just the thinnest of barriers separated us from the water outside.

"This pod," I said, breathless. "I want one just like this."

I pressed my hand against the glass, lost as I stared out at the water world. After some time I realized Xander had remained back near the door, one leg propped up against it. "Weren't we supposed to be looking at pods?" I reminded him.

He straightened, and my stupid heart skipped a beat. "You lied to me outside," he said, voice low and rumbly. "I need you to tell me exactly what's wrong. I can't fix the problem if I don't know what it is."

"Why do you even care?" I shot back, and for a moment it almost looked like that hurt him.

"Just tell me what it is, Avalon," he said, ignoring my childish jibe.

I swallowed hard. "I'm ... I don't think we should continue our agreement. It just feels.... We're already in really close proximity and it's going to get messy."

Half of me expected him to flip out. Or, more truthfully, hoped he would because that would mean he cared. Instead he looked contemplative, taking a step closer to me. "Why do you want to end it so quickly? I'm free for many more years. We don't have to put a short expiration date on it."

Years. The thought of having Xander for years was like a

dream come true.

"What if I care more than you?" I murmured. "I'm not sure I have enough Royale in me to let go, even after a few years. And the longer it goes on, the more it will hurt me when we separate. I just can't do pain anymore."

His hand wrapped around the back of my head and he applied pressure, pulling me forward until our bodies were touching. "I won't hurt you," he said seriously. "I will treat you right."

"But you don't want me forever."

The moment the words were out, I wished I could take them back. Xander stilled, the heat flaring in his eyes, slowly morphing into something dark. "I can't." His expression was heavy. "And you shouldn't want to be in my world." His hand fell back to his side. "My life is ruled by politics. My sister ... she's a prisoner to a piece of shit caramina because of politics."

"Why?" I asked.

Xander ran a hand through his hair, stepping around me, finally moving closer to the glass. "There's a monster that lurks in the deep, one of the only beasts in our water that does not respond to the command of the overlord. We can't control it. Donovan, he grew up in the same waters, and he keeps it under control for us. In return..."

"He got Dawn as a mate."

Xander slammed his hand against the glass, shaking it. "Yes. And he's a domineering, violent bastard. I found out recently that he hits her when she won't do what he wants. She kept it from me because if I kill him, the beast will come and attack us all."

He swung his head to meet my gaze. "I'm almost ready to take our chances with it."

Donovan's vibe made a lot of sense now. Assholes always

had to asshole. It was in their DNA. "We have to help her." Just the thought of his gentle sister being hurt was enough to have my hands clenching.

Xander let out another frustrated sound. "I've been trying to figure out what I can do. I literally found out right before we left to find you. There's been no time, but he's hurting her."

"Tell your parents," I suggested.

Xander let out a bitter laugh. "Dawn made me promise I wouldn't, because she knows there is nothing they can do. Politics tie their hands. Politics rules our world. Forced to go to school on Earth. Forced to mate. This is the life of overlord children."

It all made sense then. Every single thing clicked into place and I understood.

Xander had always confused me, because he'd said one thing, but the way he touched me suggested another. "You've been warning me off because your mother would never allow our bond, right? You're not free to choose your own mate."

Xander closed his eyes for a brief moment, and I had my answer.

"I'm betrothed to a caramina already, one from a very influential family. They control the shell mines to the north seas. This is where we get a lot of our structural material for the pods."

Somehow I managed to control my reactions to his answer, even though the thought of him being with another woman, touching her the way he had me, made me want to go out and find her so I could rip every strand of hair from her head while repeatedly punching her in the face.

The poor chick probably wasn't even at fault. No doubt she was being forced into this as well.

"Guess that's why your mom was such a cold bitch to me," I

said with a harsh laugh. "No doubt this bond between secret keepers and overlords has her a little worried."

Xander captured my hand. "I don't care what my parents want, but I have to think of my people. They need change, and my mom is not going to be the one to bring that about. If I walk away from her control now, I walk away from my future as the ruler."

"I would never ask you to do that," I said sadly. It was too much to take away the very thing that made Xander who he was. He'd resent me one day for sure.

He reached up to cup my chin, brushing a finger across my cheek. "I've bargained for a few more years of freedom. I can offer you that much."

A single tear escaped from my eye. I lowered my head so I could wipe it away without him seeing. "It's not enough for me," I murmured when I had my emotions under control. "I'm sorry, but ... I deserve more than that. I'm not going to be the mistress while you wait for the wife."

Xander shook his head, a rough, angry movement. "It's not like that. This is why I tried to stay away from you, why I told everyone from the start that I was not the Daelighter for you."

"So why are you doing this?" I asked. "Why even start anything with me under the pretense of it being a casual fling?"

He didn't answer straight away, and I was pretty sure that was the end of the conversation. I turned to move toward the door, done with this heartbreaking moment. Xander wasn't free to be with me, not ever. At least I could comfort myself with the fact that I'd found out now, and not years down the track. I'd only known him a short amount of time. My heart was surely strong enough to recover from one afternoon with him.

Right?

"Because you're perfect," he said, voice low and vibrating with emotion. I paused, desperate for him to say more. "I thought I was strong enough to resist you, but ... there was no way." His voice got louder as he moved closer. "I hoped we could have a casual relationship and eventually I'd get you out of my system."

His heat pressed along my spine and I fought the urge to lean back into him.

"But ... one afternoon with you is not even close to being enough. I want so much more ... I crave you."

I squeezed my eyes tightly closed, biting my lips to stop the tears from pouring free. "Why do you call me Avalon?" I asked, because that random question was the only thing I could think of in that moment that wouldn't make me cry.

His breath brushed across my neck. "You don't know this, but an avalon is a revered animal in Royale. Your parents must have learned about them here, or otherwise it's a huge coincidence. This creature is rare and is considered the most beautiful of all. When I first heard your name, it struck me that you are as rare and incredibly breathtaking as our avalons. You'll always be Avalon to me."

So much for that question keeping the tears at bay. Hot streams ran down my cheeks, and we both stayed in that position for many aching minutes. "We have to get back," he murmured. "My mother will come looking for us soon."

In that moment I hated Lettie, overlord of House of Royale.

She might not know it, but she had crushed one of my dreams—it turned out that the home I had been searching for was not a place at all ... it was a person.

And he was out of my reach.

16

I tried not to kill Lettie with my gaze when we returned to the main room. Emma, Callie, and Maya all shot me worried looks, and when I met their eyes, the concern in their faces only increased. I guessed I wasn't doing a very good job of hiding my feelings.

I was stronger than this though. I didn't need Xander or his family. The girls were mine, and I counted myself lucky to have them. I crossed to the other side of the room, settling next to Callie.

"You okay?" she whispered to me.

I gave a quick head shake, but when she opened her mouth to ask more, I shook my head again. It was too soon for me to talk about it. I just wanted to focus on the plan.

"We're heading out now," Lexen said, stepping away from the Royale overlords. "Tristall tells me that the stream we're searching for is just beyond this village. Overlords live closest to the energy. That stream is their connection to the network."

"Great," I told him. "Let's get this show on the road. I have a life to get back to."

Fuck. I was being a bitch because my heart ached. My soul hurt. My mind was tired.

I was tired.

"Sorry," I mumbled. "Just impatient to figure out where this stone is."

"We understand," Emma soothed.

They definitely understood, only they were all waiting to enjoy their eternity of being all loved up with their mates. I was just waiting to be alone in my waters again. But, before that happened, I was ready to take Laous down. I might not be getting the fairy-tale ending, but I would make sure all my friends did. I'd be satisfied if that happened.

Xander was somber when he joined us, and it hurt me to see the pain in his expression. At least I would still have my freedom after this, while his life would forever be one of duty. I hated that for him. We both deserved more.

"My father is opening the portal for us," he said, his right hand casually sliding into his pocket. "Are you all ready to dive back into the legreto?"

Everyone nodded.

"Let's go, then." Xander turned, striding away without looking back. I fell in behind the others, following them out of the huge living area and into another long hallway. This one was darker.

"Where did Dawn go?" I whispered to Maya, who was just in front of me.

Her long dark hair whipped around as she tilted her head toward me. "She had to go home. To Donovan."

My teeth clinked together and I ground them. She'd said she only had an hour, and from what Xander told me, any disobedience....

I refused to even think about it. Unfortunately, Xander's sister didn't have the same option.

There had to be a way to help her, I might not be able to fix my situation, but someone had to fix hers. Surely having parents as powerful as hers.... It was better if they knew. Maybe this one time, politics would not win.

I would have told them right then and there, but I was scared that I might make the situation even worse for her. But I would not forget her need. Sooner or later, something had to change for her.

"Avalon...."

The way he said my name brought me back to reality. I stumbled forward, realizing everyone else had gone. Xander had come back for me. "I need to put the breathing chamber around your face again," he said, watching me closely.

"Oh, right." I stepped closer to him. "I was just thinking ... about Dawn."

That fire flared in his eyes again. "She's never far from my mind lately. I'm going to exhaust every political channel I can to help her, and if all of that fails, well ... I might just have to take my chances with the beast."

"Your parents have to be able to do something!"

Xander shook his head. "Dawn thinks she's strong enough to handle it and has made it very clear to me that she doesn't want anyone choosing between protecting her and protecting our people. The only reason I know is because I randomly stopped by her pod. She thought I was on Earth."

"Please tell me you smacked him in the mouth," I said harshly.

A wry grin tipped up one corner of Xander's lips. "Broke his nose and fractured his jaw in three places. He couldn't eat or speak for weeks, even with accelerated healing." Xander let out a dark laugh. "I was worried at first that he'd take it out on Dawn, but she said he barely even cared. Violence means nothing to him, it's just a normal way of life. He believes that his strength gives him the right to control my sister, to use that against her. And because Dawn is refusing my help, I'm in a shitty position. I don't want to be as bad as him, taking her choices away from her—she's one of the strongest caraminas I know—but she shouldn't have to handle this on her own."

"I'll help you." The words burst from me, filled with fire and conviction. Just like Xander, I couldn't let this go. "Let's deal with the secret keeper stuff first, then we'll figure out what to do for Dawn."

Xander captured my hand. "It's nice to have someone other than my brothers at my back."

I knew he meant the overlords. They were so important to Xander, and it was nice to be grouped with them. Even though I wanted to be so much more.

"Despite everything, I'm always here for you, Xander," I said honestly. "We'll always be friends, have a bond. No one can take that away from us."

He cupped my face. Our eyes met and held for many long seconds before the bubble formed around my head, cutting him off from view.

When my vision was fully obscured, I allowed a single tear to trail down my cheek before I sucked in some deep breaths and got myself under control. Xander led me until we were back in the water.

The world on this side of the overlord pod was colorful, like it had been built on the edge of a reef. There was an abundance of brightly colored creatures as well, and I could imagine swimming through this area for hours. In fact, there were a lot of Royales doing just that as we moved past. They all saluted Xander before going back to their frolicking. I noticed that not all of them used their tails; there were plenty of legs around, kicking in lazy motions.

Callie let out a huge sigh that drew my attention. "I swam with them," she said, "Best. Day. Ever!"

I laughed, because she wasn't usually the chirpy and cute type.

"The stream is this way." Xander said, moving to the front of the group. "You'll know it when you see it."

We sure as hell did.

"Oh my God," I breathed.

My eyes were watering again, and this time it had nothing to do with Xander. This was pure emotion; the beauty before me almost hurt my eyes. The stream ran like a rainbow through the water, swishing and turning, the colors so vibrant that I felt as if I could run my hands through them and they'd be stained in bright hues.

"Xander, why have you never brought us here?" Chase asked. He sounded as awed as I felt. I was sensing that House of Leights, with their tree gods, might be into the more spiritual side of life.

"Because it's sacred, and we are not allowed here except with express permission from the overlord," Xander told him.

No one argued. When a firm hand pressed against my spine, ushering me forward, I sucked in a deep breath. "What should I do?" I whispered.

Xander's palm was warm as it caressed my back. "Go," he whispered. "Swim. The legretos mix perfectly here, and the colors are brightest right in this spot. This is where you were born."

There was no way in hell they got my mother under here without some sort of hardcore drugs. She was not big on sacrifice, that was for sure. I guessed duty forced her hand. No wonder she was so ready to bail on me when I was old enough to look after myself.

My stomach started to roll as I moved forward, gliding because I didn't want to kick and disturb the amazing rainbow. I gave myself a quick pep talk. "It's going to be fine, Ava. You got this. It's just rainbow water, and you need this map to save the world. You've always wanted to save the world, remember. Like ... a masked vigilante."

"You're going to be fine, Avalon."

I snapped back to reality, letting out a groan as I realized they'd all heard me. I'd totally forgotten about that. "Right, I know that."

One day I'd stop making a fool of myself in front of people I cared about.

The brightness started to overwhelm me when I got closer. I shut my eyes for a moment, moving toward the sacred waters.

I didn't expect it to feel different, but it was icy cold, shocking me enough that my eyelids flew open. A kaleidoscope of bright colors filled my vision, and it took longer than I expected for my eyes to adjust. Reaching down, I lifted my shirt up to find just my normal tanned skin.

"Lift it higher, Ava!" Emma shouted, and I winced as her voice echoed around my bubble. I wasn't the only one, either. "Oh, sorry," she said at a much lower decibel. "I just thought I saw something on Ava's back."

Turning, I kept my back to them while I lifted my shirt all the way up and over my head. "Anything?" I asked.

There was an extended pause, and I was just pulling my shirt down again, planning to turn and make sure they hadn't all been eaten by a meglam, when a warm body pressed against my spine, the heat very noticeable against the chill of the waters. "I got you, Avalon," he whispered. And for that instant in time, I let myself believe that he did.

"What does the map look like?" I asked him.

His hand traced across my back, almost reverently. "There isn't a map. It's a circle of eight figures, and there are coordinates right in the center. Spread across the center of your back."

"Eight," Maya repeated. "That's the eight of us. We're joined, and only together will we find the stone. That's what it means, right?"

"Are we all in the stream?" I asked.

"Yes," Xander said. "When we moved closer to you, the coordinates appeared."

Emma let out the hugest of joyful sighs. "God, that makes me so happy. I knew we were eternally bonded. The eight of us. We're the best family anyone could wish for. I promise I will always have your backs. Always."

"Same," Callie said, quietly. "Now let's go save our worlds."

"Does everyone have the coordinates memorized?" Lexen reminded us of the reason I was in a freezing stream with my shirt over my head. "We can't use the network to figure out where it is, so we're going to have to do this the old-fashioned way."

"Google!" Maya and Emma shouted at the same time.

"The first part is easy enough to remember," Daniel said with a laugh. "I volunteer to remember the zero."

Callie actually laughed out loud. "Always lazy at school, Dan. That's the latitude," she told him. "The equator is the center of the earth, so it's always zero. The other coordinates are the important ones."

"Definitely need Google for this," Maya said. "Nobody knows coordinates off the top of their head."

Xander gently pulled my shirt down and I turned to face them. "Got the numbers memorized?"

Lexen nodded. "Don't worry, Daelighters have excellent memories. We won't forget."

Awesome. Time to go.

My emotions were mixed in that moment. Leaving House of Royale was hard. I'd only been here for such a short time. But it wasn't as devastating as I expected, maybe because I had recently learned the most important lesson of all. Home was people, not places. It all made sense to me now.

Xander recruited some Royales to help us back to the round disc between the houses, and in no time at all we were standing on the edge of this water world, lacing up our shoes.

We weren't the only ones on the disc either, preparing to cross to Earth.

The warriors had come.

17

We made our way through the crowds toward the center of the disc. There were two small groups waiting there, one with Lexen's dad and sister, along with another dark-haired male who bore a scar down one side of his face. They were chatting with a pair of regal Daelighters. When Chase and Maya crossed straight to them, I figured they were Chase's parents, the overlords of House of Leights.

Lettie and Tristall were also in that overlord group; they must have come up while we were in the sacred waters. Lettie had changed from her casual attire and now wore a floor-length dress of seaweed green, its lengths trailing across the ground behind her. The crown on her head was coral-like in structure. The protruding sections that weaved between her hair were in shades of purple and blue.

She looked amazing. And intimidating.

And I still hated her.

Royale warriors stood close by, their spears and spikes held aloft, looking all kinds of scary. I wondered, for a moment, if

Xander went against his mother, would she send those warriors after him? Would she force his compliance?

She seemed like the type of leader who would do anything to get her own way. Especially if she thought it was for the good of her people.

Daniel and Callie, holding hands, moved to take their place as the fourth overlord majors. Imperial warriors shifted closer to them as well, backing their leaders. This was the first time I'd seen a large group of Imperials, and I noted that all of them had their hair cropped or shaved just like Daniel's. Even Callie's hair was very short, stopping just below her ears. Maybe it was really hot down there ... the underworld might have gotten its "fires of hell" myth from Overworld as well.

"We have the location," Lexen said to his father, and we all pushed in closer to hear the conversation. "We're ready to find the stone and put an end to all of this. Have we figured out how to remove the secret keepers' link to it?"

Colita stepped away from the nearby group. "The council can do that," she said, gesturing to the half a dozen other Daelighters she'd been standing with. "We have devised a plan that will break the bonds between the four and the stone. The moment you find it, you need to contact us. We're teaming up with the humans. They've decided not to hide the starslight any longer. Instead the location will be known, and a human and Daelighter army will rotate in guarding it."

"They're going to actually tell humans?" Daniel said cynically. "Is that the best plan? Humans are not known for taking news about impending end-of-world disasters well."

Colita shrugged. "The human government assures us that they can spin this information to keep the panic at a minimum. They're not going to break the whole aliens-walk-among-you to them just yet. We all agree that humans—most of them anyway—are not ready for that information."

I'd barely felt ready for it, and I'd lived with being "different" my entire life.

Lexen moved on, his eyes doing that flashing white lights thing. "What's the plan for right now? Should we leave the secret keepers in Overworld until we clear Laous out of Astoria? I don't want Emma or any of them in danger. They must be protected."

Emma elbowed him in the ribs. "Stop trying to leave me behind. We're a team. I've told you that a hundred times. The eight of us ... we're stronger together. It's a fact."

His fierce expression softened, and he nodded. "I agree with you now. I feel it as well—"

"Finally convinced your stubborn ass," Emma cut in.

His chest rumbled. "Yes, you did. But I also know that if anything happens to you, I will not be able to control my Draygo side. I will destroy the worlds, Emma Walters. A missing starslight stone will be the least of the humans' worries."

Roland reached out to comfort his son. "Lex, we won't let anything happen to Emma ... to any of them. Our number-one priority is to keep all of you safe. You're our future leaders after all."

Lexen didn't relax. If anything, there was an even more animalistic look on his face. He reached out and pulled Emma into his side, and she must have seen in him the same thing I had, because she didn't fight him. He was on the edge of losing it; one more thing would push him over the edge. Not that any of us thought for a second he'd hurt Emma, but everyone else was fair game.

"So what is the best way for us to clear Laous and the

Gonzo out of Astoria with minimum casualties?" Daniel asked.

Colita waved over the other councilmembers. "We're coordinating with the human army," she said as the three males and three females joined us. "Any updates?" she asked them.

A dark-haired man answered: "They're telling us that Laous has a lot of hostages. Pretty much the entire town has been taken. The army is surrounding Astoria, but they won't enter until we give them the okay—apparently they have been tracking Gonzo for a long time, and they're ready to take them down. They're just waiting for us to come in from the inside."

"They're not in Daelight Crescent, right?" Emma choked out.

Roland shook his head. "No, I've got a barrier across the street. House of Darken powers it. So far it's holding.

"What about our friends at the high school?" Emma continued, voice wavering. "Are there any casualties?"

Colita shook her head. "Not that we know of, but there was some resistance initially. I'm not sure what happened to those who fought back."

Emma started to suck in deep gulping breaths, in and out, until her panic faded. As it did, anger took over. "We can't wait another second. If he hasn't yet, Laous will start killing them soon."

"Does it have to be a war?" I suggested, for once not nervous to be voicing an opinion. Xander's mother already hated me. How much further could I fall in her esteem? "What if we tried to make a deal with Laous? Get him away from all the innocent people by telling him that we'll lead him to the stone? That he needs the eight of us to find it, so his best chance is to tag along with us?"

"You want to lead him straight to it?" Lettie asked. "How,

pray tell, do you then plan on making sure he doesn't get his hands on the stone? The aim from the very beginning has been to keep him as far as possible from it."

I shook my head. "I'm not sure about you, but I'm not willing to let an entire town be slaughtered if there is something I can do to prevent it. We really don't have a choice. And no one plans on letting him have the stone; we can fight him better when there are fewer casualties around. Fewer innocents he can use as leverage."

"It makes sense." Xander backed me up. "But we can't forget that Laous has Rao. Maybe he's already warned him."

Colita shook her head. "After my dream, I'm pretty sure Rao is not sharing anything with Laous. The entire emotion I felt in that vision was regret, pain, and an overwhelming sense of guilt."

"We should vote on this new plan," a tall, very blond councilwoman suggested. "Majority rules."

Lettie straightened as well, opening her mouth as if to protest, but Colita got in first. "Yes, in times of war, majority rules is the fallback. All those in favor of a fake alliance with Laous. We will lead him to the stone, and then take him out somewhere along the way."

One by one, the eight of us raised our hands. Roland followed, along with Chase's parents, who had been quietly observing until this point. The council had a quick discussion amongst themselves, but in the end, all of them raised their hands as well. Lettie and Tristall were the last two, and for a moment I thought they were going to stubbornly refuse, even though majority ruled. Then with a single nod in my direction, Lettie raised her hand.

My stomach went all fuzzy at that point, because it had been my idea, and my immediate reaction was to freak out about it failing. But the thought of innocents dying was even worse. We had to try something.

"It's settled," a council member declared. "We will discuss a treaty with Laous, allow him to accompany the group to the stone. You will lead him to the country where the stone is located, and all of us will follow shortly afterwards."

Roland cleared his throat. "And while he's with the secret keepers, we can have our warriors sneak into Astoria and start retrieving the humans," he said in a voice filled with fire. "They will be stashed in Daelight Crescent for safety."

"I've informed the human army," Colita cut in, and I realized she'd been doing a faraway stare thing a second before. Could they literally go in their heads and inform the humans of things? A question to ask later. "They agreed that if Daelighters can focus on retrieving the humans, they will crush the Gonzo. If we work together, in a single coordinated move, hopefully we'll take them by surprise and have minimal casualties."

"What if someone informs Laous of what is happening? And he retaliates?" Callie asked. "I mean, surely he's given his people a way to contact him, even if we take him away."

"I can create an electrical storm that will take out all human communications," Roland said. "And hopefully if our attack is swift, there will be no time for anyone to tell him."

Xander explained that to me. "The network is quite weak on Earth, so we use human technology most of the time to travel and communicate."

That was a good thing, then, because human technology was not that hard to disrupt. Hell, cell phones worked only half the time on my island back home, which was why I gave up on having one years ago.

"We should go," Daniel said, staring toward the transporter. "I'm ready for this bullshit to all be over. I have a house to run. My people are starting to fall apart without a leader."

One of the council members dropped a hand on his shoulder. "We'll have your initiation ceremony as soon as the stone is in the hands of the humans again. Once you are fully connected, you'll be able to bring your house together."

Daniel nodded once, his jaw hard. Callie reached out and wrapped her hand around his, and the slightest of dimples appeared in the overlord's cheeks. She was a very calming influence on him.

Chase's parents stepped forward. "More of our warriors are on the way, but we're running out of room on the platform," his father said. "The Galinta tell us they will guard the land here, so if any with violence in their hearts cross back this way, the trees will respond."

That gave me a moment's pause. *The trees will respond?* I turned to where they towered far above our heads, on the edge of House of Leights. "The trees can respond?" I asked, unsure about what that meant.

"Oh yes," Maya told me. "The trees here are sentient. They could even move if they wanted to. Which makes me feel a hell of a lot better knowing my parents and Brad are back in Darken. I'd hate to think that they could be attacked while we are gone with most of the warriors."

"Our people share an energy with the Galinta," Chase's mom said, her voice somehow gentle and booming in energy. "We can change our shape to be more like theirs, giving us increased strength and power. The Galinta are our home ... our family."

I shook my head. "That's incredible. As someone who loves nature more than anything, I completely understand what you're saying."

The ocean had always been my family, and to see it filled with rubbish and pollution ... it killed me. A lot of humans— not all of them, thankfully—took our natural beauties on Earth for granted. It made me furious when they threw their trash and chemicals into the oceans. Or the forests. Or anywhere it should not go.

Another group appeared in the transporter then, shuffling off into the very limited free space now. "We must start crossing to Earth," Lettie stated, her tone suggesting this activity was akin to wading through a sewerage pipe. "Our warriors can congregate in Daelight Crescent."

Everyone nodded, and the council dispersed, running off to talk with the different members of the houses. "The council is supposed to be a neutral, overseeing group," Xander told me as we watched them move about. "Our houses have rarely had reason to come together like this, so it's good to have them here to coordinate it all."

"How can you handle being ... a leader ... having to make decisions like that ... having the responsibility and happiness of your people rest with you? I'm not sure I could handle it. I just like to swim."

Xander grinned. "All Royales like to swim, so as long as you make that a priority, you'll find happiness is easy to achieve."

I shook my head at him. "You know what I mean."

He shrugged then, his expression sobering. "I've never known anything different. I won't lie and say it's not scary thinking about my mother handing the mantle over to me one day, when she's had enough of her role. But ... I guess I'll just handle it how I do everything, one day at a time, work my ass off, and learn from those older and with far more knowledge than me."

"It'll be a long time before you have to worry about that,

son," Lettie said, an almost joking tone in her voice. "I've still got plenty of good years left in me." Her eyes flashed to me for a moment and grew slightly chillier. "I'll make sure you have a good match. Someone to help with the burden. So don't stress about it."

Ouch. Point received, mermaid bitch.

Xander sidled between me and his mother like he thought a chick fight was about to break out. "I've told you multiple times, it would be much easier if I arranged my own mateship based on what I think is the perfect match for me."

The weariness in his voice told me this was an old argument.

Lettie's expression softened. "I promise you, this is the best way. It's tradition. And it's tradition for a reason, because the most secure matches are ones made with your head, not your heart."

"We did away with the old ways years ago," Roland said from the side. Apparently everyone was listening in now. "Our children are capable of making decisions like this on their own."

Tristall stepped up to stand shoulder to shoulder with his mate. "Royales have always done mateship differently, mostly because it's not in our nature to be in long-term bonds. It works for overlords because of the energy we've absorbed from the network. But ... there is less fighting ... less controversy, when the bond is chosen based on mutual benefits to the two families."

"Less love. Less passion," I added bluntly. "Is it really necessary to accentuate our close ties to fish? Maybe we should try and be more like our Daelighter side."

Lettie sneered at me. "You're neither Daelighter nor fish.

You are a human, one who cannot even breathe under the legreto. You get no say here."

Her words cut, just a little ... a deep paper cut. Still, I had challenged their way of life, so it would be expected that she'd retaliate.

"Watch your tone, Mother," Xander said, and I noticed how tense his back muscles were. "Avalon makes some very good points. I see the flaws in our mateship arrangements. I have told you often of those flaws. I have told you about the time I spend in the Darken home, and how it's warm and light and affection is given freely. If I ever have young, that is the life I want them raised in. I also think we should be encouraging our people to change their way of bonding and raising families. A lot of them are not happy about our way of doing things."

"How do you know this?" Tristall asked. "No one has mentioned anything to us."

I edged around Xander so I could see his face. "I talk to them," he said, some of the anger fading from his voice. "They miss their children. They want to know who their children are. Some of them have been in long-term bondings for many years, but they hide it for the shame of not changing partners often. You're not putting the people first. If traditions are failing, we need to readdress them."

"Enough," Lettie barked her command. "This is personal Royale business. Now is not the time. We will pick this conversation up later."

Xander reached out then, wrapping his arm around me, drawing me closer to his body. "That's fine. But you need to apologize to Avalon."

Lettie inhaled sharply. "I'll do no such thing. I spoke only the truth."

Tristall placed a hand on his mate's arm. He didn't say anything, like he knew better than to question her, but that simple gesture seemed to calm Lettie anyway. She pursed her lips, meeting my eye. "I'm sorry if my words offended you."

I tried not to laugh, because I was sure she wouldn't appreciate me telling her that was the worst apology ever. "Your opinion doesn't really matter to me," I replied honestly, since she apparently respected truthfulness. "I'm not hurt or offended."

Her mouth dropped open and Xander let out a low rumble of laughter. With a brief nod, he turned his back on his family and half carried me to the transporter. "No one ever questions my mom," he said, amusement lacing his words. "I should send fate some damn chocolates for bringing you into my life."

It felt like a vise was squeezing my heart. Fate might have brought us together, but that didn't mean we'd be able to stay together. Before I could reply, he was reaching out for one of the light strands, then we were on our way to Earth. With our friends right behind us.

The moment we stepped through the light at the end, every ounce of charm and cheer disappeared from Xander. In its place was a soldier. He planted himself in front of me and did a slow sweep of the area. Luckily, he'd allowed us to move a few feet from the ball of light, because people started pouring through after that.

"You were supposed to let some of the others go through first," Tristall said, shaking his head at his son. "You are an overlord minor. You cannot risk yourself."

Xander ignored his father, speaking directly to Lexen. "It's all clear," he said. "At least in this section."

Tristall just threw his hands up and moved to stand with Lettie. The pair of them speaking in hurried words. They weren't handling the new Xander very well, and I couldn't blame them. If you're used to controlling your child as much as they clearly were, his sudden streak of I-don't-give-a-fuck was probably very disturbing. Another thing for his mother to hate on me about.

Lexen gestured for us to move closer. He was already pulling out a cell phone. "I'm plugging in the coordinates," he said as we started hurrying along the rose-covered path.

By the time we were out on the main street, followed by an actual army, Lexen had found the spot. "Colombia," he said. "Right on the border between Colombia and Ecuador."

"Well, those are some safe countries to just be strolling in around digging holes," Maya said, with a decent level of sarcasm.

Chase laughed. "You questioning my skills, Maya Anne? I can protect you."

She shook her head at him. "Against an army of drug lords? Actually ... you're probably right. They'd think they were high on their own product if you shifted into a tree."

"How are we going to get there?" Callie said. "Your private planes need a decent airstrip to land on, and a helicopter is very noisy and could bring us unwanted attention. We need ... something between the two, with a lot of stealth."

Colita popped up behind us, and as I turned I blinked at the sheer number of Daelighters there. "The human government and Daelighter council have been combining our technology," she said in rushed whispers. "You might have noticed that the helicopter ride you took to Oregon, Maya, was over much faster than normal. Well, that was because we have a few little secrets up our sleeves."

Maya's eyes went very wide. "I'd never been on a helicopter before, but now that I think about it, it did move very fast. And

I didn't get scared like I normally would, because it was so smooth and airy."

"You have an aircraft we can use?" Daniel cut in, impatience in his voice. "Where do we find it?"

A cell phone rang and Colita lifted the one she held, pressing it to her ear. "Yes. We're in place ... okay ... yes, I will tell them."

She hung up then and said, "We have an aircraft. It's ready and waiting for you at the airfield nearby, where your private planes are. Some of our warriors and the council will follow behind in a second aircraft. Not close enough to be detected, but close enough to help you once you find the stone." She let out a low breath. "Now you just need to convince Laous that you're willing to trade the stone for the freedom of all Astoria's people."

She backed up a little, her eyes clouded with worry. "Good luck."

18

The overlord majors remained close to us as we ventured toward the large main gates that blocked off the street. The rest of the warriors stayed back. We didn't want to act like this was straight-out war yet. We had to get word to Laous first. As we got near the gates, I noticed a rippling in the air in front—the barrier Roland had erected to stop them from entering.

We paused for five minutes so Emma could check on her guardians, who were safely inside their house, then we continued on. "Are we just going to shout over the fence and hope Laous hears?" Callie asked when we were a dozen feet away from the shimmering barrier visible above the high wood fence.

"Someone will hear and get in contact with him," Roland replied. "He definitely has his army stationed close to our street. There has been strain on my field."

I loved how calm and confident Lexen's father was. His confidence boosted my own, and God knew I needed all the boosting I could get.

Xander startled me when he took my arm and pulled me back. I wondered what was happening for a moment, until I noticed the white lights around Lexen. His body started to change, literally. It grew larger, those lights crisscrossing all over it, and I almost stumbled when wings sprang out of his back and scales appeared across his much larger face and body.

"Holy shit," I breathed, blinking, and then blinking some more as I tried to wrap my head around what I was seeing. "He's a ... a ... dragon."

So much for me playing it cool. No doubt Lettie was giving me a scathing stupid-human look, but ... dragon.

Lexen turned and winked at me. "Brace yourself, Ava, you're about to see a Draygo in action."

Emma rolled her eyes at him, shooting me a wry grin. Lexen grinned as well, then his wings shot out and started to flap, lifting him into the air with ease.

When he was hovering just above us, he shouted out in a deep rumbling voice. "Laous!"

Storm clouds rolled in, lightning and thunder echoing across the sky that had been blue not one minute earlier. "Is Lexen doing that?" I whispered to Emma.

She shrugged. "Probably. He's pretty good with the storm power. But it could just be Astoria. This place has the most random weather ever. It can be sunny and hot one second, and then freeze-your-butt-off cold ten minutes later."

The thunder got louder, and I was pretty sure we were all thinking this was Lexen now. Scary-dragon-shifter Lexen. I couldn't take my eyes from him, his powerful presence drawing all attention.

"Laous!"

I shivered as another blast of icy wind rushed along the

street. I was still in just a shirt and shorts, and this felt like winter weather. Especially for someone used to Hawaii's warmth.

A warm arm draped over my shoulders and I almost moaned out loud. "Daelighters run a little hotter than humans," Xander said, settling me in close to his side.

Truer words had never been spoken. Just about everyone I'd met from their world—especially in the overlord blood-lines—was hot to the extreme, and that had nothing to do with their temperature.

The wind started really howling, Lexen's face fiercer than I'd ever seen before. He looked like he was getting mighty pissed. "We have a treaty to discuss with you, Laous." His words echoed out into Astoria. "Show your face before I come and find you."

The gates slowly started to open then and I almost panicked, thinking that we were about to be charged. The barrier remained though, so hopefully this was not an attack.

Lexen lowered to the ground, his mammoth wings flapping lazily as he glided to stand at the front of the group. He shifted back into his human-looking form the moment his feet hit the pavement.

We all crowded closer, and when the gate opened further, I swallowed hard. On the other side was a large group, as large as the one we had behind us. At the forefront was a Daelighter. I knew that because of the marks on his head. He looked stouter than I'd expected, with an unmemorable face. If this was Laous, I was going to guess that this all started because he was pissed about being the ugliest duckling in his world.

"You called for me, Lexen," he said, spreading his arms wide. Fire burst to life on either side of his body, racing up into the air in an impressive show. "Here I am, waiting for my stone to be returned to me."

Men moved in closer on either side of him, lots of men, armed with the biggest guns I'd ever seen in my life. What the hell were they? Bazookas? I didn't have much experience with the army or guns, of course, but these looked like they should be on top of a tank, not in a person's arms.

The Daelighters didn't react, so I made sure not to as well. No need to show this guy that we were nervous. Or that they had the upper hand. "I'm waiting," Laous continued. "My men here are getting very frustrated about not being able to kill any humans. They enjoy killing."

His men had hard faces ... mean, narrowed eyes, and ... huge fucking guns. There was legitimacy to his statement.

"We don't want the humans hurt," Daniel said, moving to stand right at Lexen's side. "They are innocents in this entire situation. So, as a good faith gesture, we will allow you to accompany us to the stone. Along the way, we will discuss with you your plans for the stone, and then maybe we can reach some sort of accord that satisfies everyone. This war has gone on long enough. There will be no more casualties."

Laous grinned. "That was easier than I expected, which probably means this is some sort of trap for me. How about ... you give me the location, and the four secret keepers. Then I can go and fetch the stone myself. We are all sure that these four ... humans ... will be required to retrieve the stone. Once I have the stone, I'll return your ladies to you. And all the humans will go free."

"Not a chance," Xander shot back at him. "The power required to find the map took the eight of us. We're all bonded. You're going to need the eight of us to find the stone."

Some of the cocky confidence faded from Laous's expression. He looked between our groups slowly, like he was trying to discern the lie in Xander's words. One of the men closest to him, an older guy with a dark beard-goatee combo, leaned in and whispered something.

Laous listened for a moment before nodding and straightening. "Fine, if you insist on the eight of you accompanying me, I will insist on leaving my men here to watch over this town. They are all in position to act with lethal force. Your little army will not have the time to stop them before there are mass casualties."

Hopefully Laous was thinking that the Daelighters he could see was the entirety of our people. Better he didn't know that a lot more warriors were still coming through the transporter.

We'd already expected to receive these sorts of demands, but we took a moment to pretend we were having a serious discussion about it. "Think he's up to anything else?" Callie whispered, when our heads were close together.

I glanced over my shoulder to find Laous in a relaxed stance, arms crossed over his chest. He was definitely up to something. No one was that confident without a backup plan.

"We're not going to turn our backs on him for one second," Daniel whispered. "We even take shifts for sleeping, if anyone has to do that. Laous murdered my family to gain power. He killed his own damn brother. There's nothing he won't do to achieve his goals."

We all nodded, and Daniel straightened, turning to Laous. "We accept that deal, as long as you promise nothing will happen to the humans if we cooperate."

Laous smiled broadly. "Of course. I am a Daelighter of my word. I've never lied about my intentions. This would have been much easier if you'd just cooperated from the start."

Emma growled, no doubt thinking that this started when he killed her parents. Lexen, reacting to his mate's pain, let out a much louder growl. His eyes went a blinding white as he took a step forward. Laous actually flinched back, just a brief reaction that he quickly covered. But we'd all seen it.

"We have a private plane waiting for us," Chase said.

Laous, once again wearing a confident expression, nodded. "I will be bringing a few of my people with me, so make sure there is room."

We all had no idea what this special government-Daelighter aircraft was like, but we didn't argue. They could squish in somewhere. Laous again murmured something to the man at his side, who then turned and hurried away, reappearing a few moments later with three others. The first was a very tall man, with a scarred face. *Rao.* This had to be Daniel's brother.

Daniel took a step forward. I could already feel the heat pouring off him. "Rao stays here," he declared.

Laous shook his head. "Oh no, my son will be coming with us. He's disappointed me. His betrayal on Hawaii was not expected, and now he cannot be trusted to be away from me."

Rao did not look up. He didn't meet Daniel's eyes—anyone's eyes. The scars on his face looked quite raw. I'd been under the impression that the burns were old, but ... unless the sort of burns he had didn't really heal, his were fresh.

"Rao...?" Callie's voice was low, filled with pain. "Has he been hurting you?"

The big man lifted his head just a touch and my eyes grew hot and damp. He looked shattered. Defeated. And somehow he'd still managed to reach out to Colita. Still tried to warn us so we had a plan in place.

"We have to get him back," Callie said, almost panicked as

she lurched forward. Flames burst to life around her, and only Daniel's hand on her arm stopped her going right through the barrier to Laous.

I blinked a few times, watching the fire dance across her skin without burning her. *Holy shit.* I was pretty sure there were some things about this world I was never getting used to.

"We will save him," Daniel said, his words bit out in quiet rasps. I wasn't sure Laous could hear their conversation, but he looked pleased with himself anyway. Just seeing that he had caused unhappiness was enough for him.

Why were there so many evil people in the world? In all worlds, apparently? I mean, when did it become the norm to expect that your needs trumped millions of others? Who the fuck did this Laous think he was? My hair started to move around my body, like it did sometimes when I lost control of my emotions. Xander noticed straight away, reaching out to brush his hands across the long strands.

"Your hair is definitely a by-product of the ancient energy you carry," he told me. "Very few Royales' hair responds to emotions like that."

If I had been a less mature person, I would have turned and stuck my tongue out at Lettie. *See, not completely useless, powerless, and un-Royale.*

"Time to go," Lexen said, striding forward. He touched the barrier and a small opening appeared, large enough for each of us to exit single file. "The barrier stays in place," he told Laous as we moved closer to him.

The overlord majors pressed close to the other side of the barrier, prepared to help their children if Laous tried anything. There was a heavy layer of tension in the air as we crossed closer, and not just from our side. One of his men started to fumble at his gun, half lifting it, but before he could point it at us, Chase shot out a long branch from his body and snatched it right out of the man's hands.

Yes, a mutha-effing branch. *Tree-shifter.*

Noise broke out and Laous threw both of his arms in the air, fire crackling off his fingertips in long plumes. He was either having a lot of trouble controlling his energy, or he was trying to act tougher than he was, but he had power leaking everywhere.

"Enough," he shouted. "I will be back with the stone very soon. Then the power and money we deserve will be ours. Until then, remain in position. Craig will be in charge while I'm gone. The line of command remains the same after that."

The noise slowly died down. These men were very used to following orders. Craig reached out and grabbed onto Laous's arm as we got closer. "Don't betray us," he said, his voice loud and clear. "We want what you have promised," he said.

Laous nodded as he shook him off. "I'm a Daelighter of my word. I will share the power with you. Together, we will rule Earth."

That surprised me, and I could see I wasn't the only one. "You only want Earth?" Roland asked from where he was standing right behind the barrier.

Laous nodded. "Yes, the stone is extra powerful here, in a world without any network or true power of its own. This is where I will use it."

No one said another word. I was starting to see the cracks in Laous now. Up close, his eyes were feverish, his face flushed with a manic sort of look. Like a junkie coming off a high, or ready for the next one.

"Are you ready?" he gasped, clenching and unclenching his hands.

We all nodded. Chase and Lexen turned and bowed to

their parents. Xander was still angry with his mother apparently and spared her no more than a single glance. She looked pained by the way he was leaving, but there was nothing I could do to fix the situation she'd caused. I still had sympathy for her though; he was her son, and she no doubt believed she was doing the right thing for him.

As we moved forward, sticking close as a group, Laous fell into step beside us. The Gonzo parted for us to move through them. Rao, and a man and woman, remained on either side of Laous—the Daelighters or humans he was bringing along.

Callie seemed to know at least one of them. She growled in the direction of the chick. "Worn anyone's skin lately, bitch?"

Daelighter then. The bitch grinned and said, "It took me weeks to get the stench of your dead mother off me. Humans are truly disgusting."

Callie lunged forward, Lexen and Daniel both catching her before she could land a blow. "You better watch your back," she yelled, "because I'm going to fucking kill you the first chance I get." Callie growled, flames springing up across her arms.

I was surprised when Lexen didn't let her go, even as the fire licked across his hands. Apparently he always rocked the dragon thing, even when he no longer looked like one.

Even though Callie calmed herself quickly, she didn't stop shooting death glares at the chick, who appeared completely unconcerned, turning her back on us and striding ahead. Two black SUVs screeched to a halt on the main road, just outside the huge gates of Daelight Crescent. Laous got into the second SUV with his people, and Lexen strode across to the front vehicle, yanking the driver right out of the seat and tossing him about ten feet away.

The man didn't get up, and none of us bothered to care as

JAYMIN EVE

we piled into the car. Eight people did not fit that easily, but we made it work.

Xander, who was next to me in the very back of the car, turned around as we started to move. "Laous is ready," he said, "let's get out of here."

Lexen took off then in a squeal of tires. He leaned over and whispered to Emma in the passenger seat, and she nodded. I noticed the other two guys do the same thing to their mates.

"Don't say anything important, the car could be bugged," Xander said, close to my ear.

I nodded, sinking back against the chair. Exhaustion was starting to press on me. I'd barely slept last night, and then when we'd supposed to be resting today, I'd been ... really busy with Xander. I had no regrets about that—I'd never forget my afternoon with him. But it did mean I was edging toward needing some sleep.

"The airfield is about forty minutes away," Xander told me. "Why don't you try and get some sleep."

How the hell he knew I was tired was beyond me. I was doing everything in my power to appear like I had my shit together. "It's fine," I said, shaking my head. "I'm perfectly fine right now."

He wrapped an arm around me, pulling me against his chest. "You need sleep. You also need food. I can't remember the last time we all ate."

On the plane, if I recalled correctly. Which was hours ago. It was nearing nightfall now. The storm clouds still hanging low over Astoria had washed the world in darkness. Shifting around in my seat, I gave up fighting my heavy eyes and allowed myself to relax against Xander. I might have been naked with him a few hours ago, but sleeping was a completely new sort of vulnerability. My body apparently

192

trusted him though, because I almost immediately fell asleep, waking only when the car pulled to a stop.

Xander brushed a hand across my cheek. I lifted my head, groggy and disoriented, and it took me a few moments to remember what had happened, to remember that we were on our way to find a stone, and we had a small entourage of evil psychopaths with us.

I didn't even want to know what that chick had meant about wearing Callie's mother. Just no.

Xander lifted me up. I shook my head, trying to wake properly. "You can sleep again on the flight," he told me. "Even with special tech, it's still going to take quite a few hours to get there."

Special tech indeed. When we exited the vehicle, it was to stand before a gleaming black beast. *Nighthawk* was etched into the side of it in large letters, and I noted that it appeared to have twin engines on either wing, plus rotors on the top. I blinked as I stumbled closer, still half asleep.

"What the hell sort of material is that made of?" I asked, trying to see it clearly.

The black metal, constantly shifting color, shimmered silver one second, black the next, even going almost sky blue.

"Looks like it has chameleon technology," Maya noted. "My dad told me that the government has been working on this for our defense systems. The aircraft will mimic its surroundings, blending right in so they can stealthily fly over enemy territories."

That was exactly what this helicopter-plane was doing. If you changed the angle of your head, it looked different. Two pilots were waiting for us at the bottom of the stairs. Laous crowded right up to them, a creepy smile on his face.

"Welcome aboard," the first pilot said in a serious tone of

voice. He looked between all of us. "I'm Major Kenneth Cole, and I'll be guiding this aircraft for you this evening. We will be departing at eighteen-hundred hours. Please make your way on board and secure yourselves into one of the chairs. We move extremely fast, so it's best to remain seated and buckled in at all times."

Major Kenneth Cole was certainly confident. I wondered if he knew that almost all of his passengers tonight were aliens ... of some description.

Laous tilted his head to the side. "How long will our journey be?"

The human met his eyes dead on. No fear at all. "No way for me to estimate that until we're in the air. It will be at least three hours."

Laous just nodded, pushing his way on board, his people right behind him. I almost chuckled out loud. It was like being forced to go on vacation with your most hated family members, knowing you were going to be stuck doing activities with them for days on end.

Chase was the first of our group to step onto the silver stairs, Maya right behind him, followed by Daniel and Callie, then Lexen and Emma. Xander ushered me in front of him, and then he brought up the back of our group. We stayed close together, and I hated it when Chase entered the black beast, disappearing from sight.

Thankfully we weren't far behind. When I stepped in through the front section, it was to find a huge round open area, seats backed onto either wall. Nothing fancy like Xander's private plane; this was bare basics. I quickly crossed to the seat beside Emma and dropped into it. The straps were harness style, but easy enough to buckle up, with a single clip over my chest. I tightened each side of the shoulder straps, pressing myself back into the chair.

It wasn't the most comfortable way to travel, but it was probably safest. Xander took the seat directly across from me, which was good and bad. I couldn't accidentally touch him, but I got to stare at his too-perfect face for three hours.

I noted that Laous already had his head back, eyes closed. He was so damn relaxed. The Daelighter didn't strike me as the stupid kind—he'd already stated that this was probably a trap for him—so he knew we had no plans to just hand the stone over to him without a fight. So why all the confidence?

It made me uneasy.

My worries were cut off when the engines roared loudly around us and the wall behind my chair started to vibrate. Unlike a normal airplane, there was no long takeoff. We pretty much started to roll, and then *boom*, we were in the air. There were no windows for us to see the progress, but judging on how quickly my ears blocked up, we were rising quickly. Opening my mouth a few times, I shook my head to clear it.

"Are you doing okay?" Emma asked, shooting me a worried look.

I blinked at her for a moment, wondering what the hell she was talking about. Then I remembered. The last flying incident, which hadn't gone over so well.

"Uh, actually, I'm fine." I really was. I'd barely even thought about the fear that had rocked me on our flight from Hawaii. "Maybe ... my body is not as shocked because we flew just recently."

Emma nodded. "Yeah, I would guess that it would be a daunting experience the first time you fly ... when you're more used to swimming."

Yeah, I mean ... it had to be that. Right? What else had changed in the last few days? My eyes locked on Xander and I felt that pull inside of me, urging me forward. There was a bond between us. It had been there from the start, only cementing when we had sex. I wondered if that was helping me stay grounded, the same way his scent did because it was like my ocean.

If that was the case, what would happen to me when we had to part ways? I couldn't live without the water. I knew that without a doubt. But I was starting to fear I might not be able to live without Xander either.

19

The flight was fast. Still, by the time the captain announced that we were starting to descend and that they would be searching for a secure location to hide the aircraft, my butt was numb.

Jiggling on the spot, I bit my lip. Xander chuckled and my head shot up. "We'll be on the ground in about two minutes," he told me, his smile tearing at my insides. I managed to smile back, even though I was about as far from happy as it was possible to be.

Xander had barely taken his eyes off me the entire flight and I'd sucked up every moment of his attention, craving it, because he filled an empty part inside of me. I'd always thought it was because of my colder nature, being more fish-like. But I could see now it was a space in my soul for Xander.

A space he'd never get a chance to truly fill.

Before I could grow even more pathetic, we hit some turbulence and the entire plane shook and rattled. My insides squeezed together, like my stomach was going to burst out of my body, and I gripped my armrests tightly. I had to close my eyes. I felt the panic rising; this was no time to freak out. Why the hell did people fly when it was so damn dangerous? We were hurtling toward the ground at like forty billion miles an hour, and if for some reason the pilot didn't land it properly, we were all going to die.

It was a huge risk, seriously!

Warm hands gripped my face, and my eyes flew open instantly. "Xander!" I gasped, instinctively reaching for his forearms so I could hold on to him. "Get back to your seat, this is way too dangerous."

Xander looked relaxed, even though his eyes were blazing at me. "You underestimate me, Avalon. Nothing can take me down."

I had to snort out some laughter, even though I was still terrified he was about to be torn in half by the force of us landing. "Your arrogance knows no bounds. How did you even fit your head inside the door to this plane?"

He winked at me. "Arrogance is a human trait. I'm confident."

I hated to disagree with him; arrogance was definitely a trait Daelighters had in spades. Although, I supposed there was a fine line between arrogance and confidence.

"Hold on," the pilot announced, before the speaker cut off.

I tightened my grip on Xander, and he pressed in closer to me, like he was shielding me with his own body. "If you get hurt trying to protect me, I am going to kill you," I warned him, pulling him even closer to me.

He buried his face into my neck, and my head went light and fuzzy. "Thank you," I heard him whisper. "Thank you for showing me that there is more to Royale than what we are told to be."

Don't cry. For fuck's sake, this guy was destroying me. How could this feeling be so painful and yet also so addictive?

I'd never loved anyone before, I knew that for a fact. Attraction and love were not the same thing. Usually one night was enough to get the attraction part out of my system. But Xander … no time would be long enough. No amount of sex would be enough to lessen my want for him.

The plane's rattling cut off then, and for a second I wondered if we had landed and I'd missed it in all my Xander musing. No … it still felt like we were descending.

"They descended fast, but they'll land silently," Lexen said, from the other side of Emma. "Because we're now in stealth mode."

It was all so black ops. For a moment I wondered how the hell this was my life.

Xander leaned back a little; his gaze turned toward the front of the aircraft. "We're almost down," he whispered.

I understood why he was whispering; the lights were dimming and there was an air of secrecy washing over the cabin. Laous had his eyes open, and he looked focused. The bitch at his side was whispering something, but he just stared forward, determination in his gaze. Rao's head was down, and his eyes appeared to be closed. I wasn't sure if he was sleeping, or if he was just trying to escape reality.

When I couldn't bear to witness any more of his grief, I turned away, only to find Daniel wearing the same expression, his eyes locked on his brother. Callie was stroking his arm over and over in an attempt to keep him calm. I wondered if Daniel had been like that for the entire flight. I hadn't noticed, but I'd dozed on and off for parts and missed a lot.

The lights flickered out completely then, and Xander

quickly unbuckled the front clasp on my harness, pulling me to my feet. "Stay close," he whispered.

I did as I was told because there were only a few little lights up high, visibility was almost zero, and I wasn't keen on being stuck in a dark cabin with Laous. He was all mild and calm right now, but I'd heard the stories. That man was dead on the inside. He'd killed people. He'd kidnapped my friends. He wanted to steal a powerful stone that was keeping my world alive so he could use it for his own personal power and gain.

I fought against the urge to turn around and take my chances at getting in one good throat punch. Seriously. I'd feel so much better. Xander captured my hand before I could put that plan into action, drawing me closer as if he sensed my sudden violent intentions. When we reached the exit, the pilot slid the door open, his face appearing in the half light from the moonlit land outside. He held a finger to his lips, urging us to be quiet, before he leaned in close. "I've dropped you a few hundred yards from your coordinates. We have word that there are locals living close by, but if you stay under the radar, you should be fine."

He stepped back and let us leave. I glanced to the sky quickly, wondering if the other aircraft was closing in on us. Knowing backup was on the way, even if we had to do this next bit on our own, did help stem some of the icy nerves in my gut.

Lexen and Emma were first down the stairs. Laous brought up the rear ... well, Rao was the actual last, his head still lowered as he followed silently.

My friends and I formed a tight circle at the bottom of the stairs. "The pilot said he will wait for us unless their cover is blown," Chase said quietly. "If that's the case, they'll take off and disappear above until we need them."

"Where exactly is the stone?" Laous interrupted our whispers, not even attempting to keep his voice down. He clearly didn't care if we drew the attention of the locals.

There was an extended pause, and I wondered if maybe everyone was thinking about throat punching him now. "I'll have to use my phone to track the coordinates," Lexen said, swiping across the screen. He keyed something into it, and then stared for a moment.

"This way," he said shortly.

The guys made sure the four of us girls were in the center, keeping Laous as far away as possible. Laous, with his people, strolled along behind us like he didn't have a care in the world.

Despite the previous warning about the area we were in, there wasn't anything in the vicinity that was a cause for alarm. The only details clear in the moonlit night were bushes and trees, and what looked like a huge jungle off in the distance. No signs of human life.

The Draygo who had hidden the stone went to a lot of trouble to put it somewhere that was isolated and would hopefully remain isolated for many hundreds of years, considering he had no idea how long the stone would be hidden with us as secret keepers for it.

"How much further?" Laous asked gruffly, a darker emotion bleeding into his words for the first time. He finally sounded frustrated.

Lexen looked at his phone again, moving the screen with his thumb. I wondered if he was deliberately drawing out the moment. Annoying Laous was one of life's little pleasures.

"We're getting close," he eventually said.

Emma leaned toward me, and I lowered my head. "He's checking in with Astoria," she breathed into my ear. "We have to stall Laous until we know everyone is safe back there."

"How much longer?" I asked, trying to be quiet, but failing because I was getting spooked.

Emma shrugged, pulling me down again. "They took out that front group who were without hostages. Our people have taken their place in the hope they'll trick the other members of Gonzo scattered around. Roland managed to fry their comms, so it's working so far. Some of the other houses have gotten Daelighters situated around Astoria. So far, we're looking good."

My eyes flicked to the side. Laous was about twenty feet away and a little back from us. "Didn't he say he was keeping in touch?"

"Not sure how he could be," Emma said. "All of the over-lords are blocking the network, and 90 percent of the town is out of cell service. Roland left one small part so he could communicate with Lexen."

And we hadn't seen Laous, or any of his people, with a phone. So why was he so unconcerned? It was like he didn't even care what was happening back in Astoria.

A thought occurred to me. What if he wanted the Daelighters to take out Gonzo and whoever else was helping him? The little I knew of him, I'd never have guessed he was a guy who liked to share power. Getting rid of them would be in his best interest. Especially if he didn't need their help any longer. Which had to mean that he was supremely confident he could get the stone from us now, even though he was vastly outnumbered.

But how?

"He's up to something," I whispered, keeping my voice down.

Emma nodded rapidly. "I think so as well," she returned. "We just have to remain on guard, and make sure the stone does not come out of the ground until the town is secure. Then Laous will have nothing to use against us, and we are stronger than him."

My worry didn't abate even a fraction. It just didn't make sense that he would bring only three of his people with him, one being Rao, who was clearly too beaten down to do anything.

We walked on in silence, all of us on high alert. The land grew steadily darker as the night wore on and the moon shifted across the sky. There were still no signs of human inhabitants, but the rustling in the bushes when we had to push through them made it clear animal life was still active in this area.

Lexen's phone lit up and my attention went immediately to him. Emma gave my arm a squeeze and hurried to his side. I wondered if this was about Astoria and whatever was going on back there. "Stone is twenty yards away now," Lexen said, loud enough for Laous to hear.

"About damned time," Laous muttered. "I was afraid you were about to try and screw me out of this deal. And let me tell you, you definitely don't want to do that."

He tripped then, and it almost looked like a branch had slid across the ground where he'd been standing. Laous recovered quickly, his head darting around as he tried to figure out what he had fallen over. I saw Maya hide a smile, letting her head drop forward so her dark hair covered her face.

Chase.

I managed not to laugh, even though I really wanted to. It was the little things, seriously. We started to descend, the ground getting quite steep, and by the time Lexen stopped we were in a small gorge, a cliff face on one side and a creek on the other.

For the first time since we'd stepped into this land, there was evidence of humans: a fire pit, huge stones arranged in a circle with half-burned sticks inside. I could feel no heat from it though, and I hoped that meant this was just an occasional camping spot. There were also markings on the side of the wall. Emma went straight for them, her eyes alight.

"Amazing," she whispered. "It's like discovering hiero-glyphics from an ancient tribe."

She paused then, leaning closer. "Actually...."

I realized what she'd noticed, and I turned to Xander, lifting some of his blond hair so I could see the marks. He nodded. "Yes, they're definitely Daelighter symbols."

Laous regarded the wall, scowling. "Lucky you're all so diligent in helping me with my task. I never would have found this location otherwise. There are a lot of wards here blocking the network energy, among other things."

"Guess someone saw your evil ways coming a long time ago," Callie said, staring daggers at him.

He moved in a flash, reached out to smack her in the face ... or maybe grab her; it was hard to tell in the dark. Before he could touch her though, Daniel's hand shot out and wrapped around Laous's throat. He lifted the man with almost no effort, throwing him solidly back against the wall with the wardings.

Laous's people—except Rao—immediately went into attack mode, lashing out with something that flashed brightly in the darkness. Lexen's hand become a blur of white light; it looked like a path of ice followed the movement of his palm. He intercepted whatever had been thrown at us, sending it shooting off across the water that ran nearby.

"Stop," Laous shouted, stumbling to his feet. "Let's just get the damn stone."

He eyeballed both of his people, sending them a silent

message. The woman looked furious, but she backed up without another word, lowering her hands.

"So," Emma said wryly, breaking the last of the tension. "Anyone bring a shovel?"

Lexen, still looking all muscled up and pissed off, shook his head before sending a half smile toward his mate. "Always underestimating me," he grumbled, his voice very deep.

The white lights in his eyes were there again. They spread out across his body and down his arms. He grew larger but didn't do the full shift. His hands started to change first, scales almost completely covering them, which hadn't happened last time. His fingers curved into long, razor-sharp-looking talons.

"That's a little more dragon than usual," Emma said breathlessly, her eyes very wide.

He winked at her but didn't speak. I wondered if the more dragon he went, the fewer human abilities he had. His phone slipped out of the clawed hand and would have hit the ground if Chase's branch arm didn't shoot out and capture it.

It really said a lot about my life recently that my friends were dragons and trees and I barely even blinked when it happened.

"A little closer to the river," Chase told Lexen, examining the screen.

Lexen took two steps forward, his longer legs crossing the distance to the river in no time.

Chase nodded. "Start there."

The moonlight didn't show us a lot of details, but I could certainly hear Lexen tearing up the ground with ease. "What's the time?" I whispered to Xander. "Is it nearing dawn?"

"Maybe forty minutes until, judging by the feel in air," he replied, his voice a whisper across my neck.

That low tone immediately brought me back to our afternoon together. He'd whispered words across my skin the entire time we were together. Xander was very open and free with compliments, and at no time had any of them felt fake or cheesy. I had felt beautiful with him, sexy and desirable in a way I never had with any other man. Xander brought out a side in me I didn't even know was there. Wanton. Needy. Sex-addicted, apparently.

Lexen looked to be about three feet deep now, digging very fast. "I'm not sure this is the right spot," Callie said, leaning over the hole. "Shouldn't the stone like ... give off a lot of energy if it's as powerful as rumor says?"

We all leaned in closer, and just like Callie, I didn't notice a change in energy at all.

"Maybe the wardings block that?" Maya offered.

Lexen continued on for some time—at about ten feet down he gave up, jumping back onto the land in a single powerful leap.

"So, what do we do now?" Emma asked. "Should we just keep digging around here? Maybe the coordinates are a little off because the area has shifted in the years since the Draygo buried the stone?"

No one disagreed with her theory. Lexen moved to another section. For the next twenty minutes, Lexen dug one hole after another, but there was no sign of the stone.

Laous was also growing frustrated. "Do not make me go to war over this," he said finally, after huffing around for five minutes, staring at the symbols on the wall. "I'm very close to the completion of my plan. I will not let anyone stand in my way."

"Shut the fuck up," Maya snapped, and I wasn't the only one blinking at her. Maya was not really the swearing type. She seemed to be much calmer in general than the rest of us.

Her and Chase both. "We're all here because of you and your bullshit. You're a selfish asshole, and while I am sympathetic to your childhood, that gives you no excuse for your actions."

Flames licked up and down Laous's arms, but he didn't even seem to notice, his gaze locked on Maya. "I never should have told you that story," he admitted roughly. "I never expected you to escape and be able to relay that to anyone else."

Daniel opened his mouth but Laous cut him off before he could speak. "No, nephew, I do not have any interest in your thoughts on it. No one cared when I was locked in hell, and I will never be in that position again. There is only one way to assure that, only one power strong enough to mean I'll never be truly powerless again. And you have five minutes to find it or I'm going to start killing humans."

No one immediately piped up and said that he no longer controlled Astoria, which made me wonder if maybe we weren't 100 percent sure that he didn't still have hostages there. Or somewhere else we didn't know about.

Lexen moved to another section of land and started to dig again. His chest was heaving a little, and that was no surprise, considering he'd dug halfway to Australia by now. Needing to move, because I was starting to get sleepy again, I walked back toward the Daelighter symbols on the wall, making sure not to fall into any holes half-hidden in the darkness.

A shadow moved when I was close and I jumped. It was Rao, facing the wall, staring very intently at it, both hands pressed to the rock. I took a step closer, wondering what he was doing.

It looked like he was ... tracing the symbols—this guy, who apparently saw the future, was very focused on those symbols.

Should we have looked closer at what was written on the wall? Was there a clue there that we had missed?

I stopped about ten feet further along the cliff than Rao.

He didn't lift his head or acknowledge me in any way, and I made sure to do the same, because drawing Laous's attention felt like a bad move. I didn't want this poor guy to suffer any more than he already had.

Rao was still tracing his fingers across the symbols. I reached out to do that same with the ones in front of me. They were scattered across the wall as far as I could see along the cliff, but there were a lot the same. Repeated over and over.

The marks felt familiar to me—no doubt because I'd seen them recently on the overlords' skin and on the platform between all the houses. Xander's energy hit me a moment before he stopped at my side.

"What do they mean?" I whispered, continuing to trace one particular pattern that I was most drawn to. It was etched in a deep red clay, baked onto the stone.

"This is legreto," he said, his hand coming up to rest on top of mine, stopping my almost obsessing rubbing of the top part of the curved shape.

He lifted both of our hands, moving on to another symbol close by. "And this is caramina. The pair represents our people. Royales."

The caramina symbol looked like a continuation of the legreto symbol, flowing lines reaching for each other between the two. Like ... they should be joined, not separate.

"What symbols are for the other houses?" I asked. "Do they all have specific symbols like Royale?"

Xander nodded, lifting his hands up to a dark ocher pair. "This is Leights. They have the Galinta's symbols." He traced the first, then moved to another close by. "This one is to symbolize their bond to the tree gods."

They had two symbols as well, and just like Royale they were intersected with each other. Two parts forming one whole.

"That is Imperial," a deep voice said from close by. I turned to find Daniel pointing toward the wall. Two symbols were there, their color in shades of blue. One was a flame, the other like a swirling staircase. "The justices and our energy from below."

"Which leaves Darken," I murmured, my eyes resting on the final two symbols in this part of the wall. "Theirs looks like a mountain, and the other is slashes of lightning."

I noticed something, when I leaned back to see all eight marks together. "Your symbols ... there's symmetry here. Like what we have in our group," I whispered. "Eight marks, eight of us. Each symbol blends into the next, and doesn't it look to all of you like the eight of these could link together to form a single image?" I kept seeing the lines and swirls linking to each other, and it all looked similar to me.

Xander and Daniel wore confused expressions as they stepped closer, and then further back to see the entire wall.

"The eight are not supposed to be one," Daniel said, tilting his head. "Our houses are not that closely bound."

"But they were," I reminded them. "You said the original overlords were leaders of a single house. House of Daelighter."

"Could this be a part of our history lost?" Xander murmured. He pulled his focus from the wall, searching the ground, leaning down to forage through the stones and dirt. When he rose, he held a white piece of rock. He placed it on the wall, close to where the symbols were, and began to sketch.

He started with House of Royale, and this time he drew them all close together, joining the lines instead of leaving gaps.

"There," I said, pointing to where I thought Imperial should go.

He looked for a second, and then nodded. A few times it didn't fit, but once the first five were in place, the rest became very clear.

By the time he was finished, the others had drifted over to us—except Lexen, who was still digging, and Laous, who was not leaving the dragon dude's side.

"Well, I'll be damned," Daniel said, staring.

The symbols did all fit together, and no one had noticed before now because the houses normally had very little to do with each other. They did not draw their marks together.

"I think this is the reason we can't find the stone," I told them. "The Draygo clearly knew there was no safer security measure than forcing the four houses to work together. That only the eight of us, who are bonded for the first time in their history, would be able to do it."

Maya was bouncing on her toes. "Like the secret keepers led to the location, but all houses are needed to find the stone."

"How though?" Chase asked, his hand resting on the rock wall. "I can't feel any energy. What do we do with the symbol now?"

"What if we needed those crystals?" I asked. "The ones with energy from the ancients?" From the time the four houses were joined as one.

Xander shook his head. "No one has seen them in years, not since..."

"We were born?" I guessed.

He blinked a few times, nodding. "Actually ... yes. Shit. I'm not sure anyone put that information together, because of the year timespan between your births. I remember seeing the crystal as a child. Mother used to keep it in a special glass on the mantel."

Chase nodded. "Ours was embedded in an old Galinta, sitting in the center of our land. Stories say it's the first. I haven't visited there since I was very young ... the stone could definitely be gone."

"They're here," I decided, bursts of excitement filling me. "We need to find the crystals first, and then we'll find the starslight."

I don't know how I knew that, but everything inside of me was urging me to follow this path. We just had to figure out where the crystals were.

20

*D*awn was stealing away the last of the darkness, which at least made it easier to stare out across the pocket of land we were in. I stumbled away from the wall, stepping around my friends—and all Lexen's holes in the ground —and crossing to the small stream. When I reached the edge of the water, I just went on instinct.

"Legreto," I mumbled, before I kicked off my shoes.

The moment I stepped into the water, a shock of energy hit me—which I hadn't been expecting—and I fell to my knees. Water splashed up, soaking me thoroughly.

"Avalon," Xander called, reaching the edge of the water in about an eighth of a second. "Are you oka—"

His words cut off when he entered the stream. More energy rocked through us both. I cried out as I was slammed forward, my hands stopping me from faceplanting against the rocky bottom of the shallow water.

"It's in here," I groaned, pushing myself up. Or attempting to. "Or something powerful is."

Xander recovered much quicker, lifting me up to his side. My feet were off the ground but still dangling in the water, and the two of us together was enough, apparently, to start the ground shaking.

I was just freaking out that my theory was very wrong, when a fissure appeared just before us, extending about six feet long and two inches wide. A sparkle of blue glinted in the early morning light as a crystal slowly rose to the surface.

Xander didn't let me go. He held me against him as he reached out and lifted the stone, bringing it toward us. Emotion clogged my throat, and I tried to swallow down the newly formed lump in there. The crystal was so beautiful, colored like the ocean, the blues and greens swirling into each other in an almost mesmerizing pattern.

"It looks like Hawaiian waters," I choked out, my chest so tight that breathing was painful.

My hand reached for it before I could think the action through. The moment Xander and I were both touching it, a hot, almost sharp pain rocketed through my chest. My body suddenly felt so much larger ... filled with life and energy and warmth.

Emotions hit me hard, so many that I couldn't really filter through them to know what I was feeling.

"What just happened?" I asked, slowly, softly, attempting to swallow the lump in my throat.

I wasn't the only one asking questions either—our friends were on the edge of the water, shouting at us.

"We bonded," Xander said hoarsely. The voices died off— either everyone was in shock too or my ears had stopped working. "And not like the secret keepers and overlord bond we already share, but the bond that is a marriage in our world."

He shook his head. "I've never heard of a Royale bonding like this without an overlord blessing the sanction. I was there with my sister...."

"Was it the crystal?" Lexen asked. I blinked in his direction, still trying to figure out what had just happened. I knew what Xander had said, but my mind wasn't quite ready to accept it. "It contains the energy of ancient overlords, which is more than enough to cement a Royale bond."

"Your—" I choked. "Your mother is going to kill you," I managed to finish hoarsely.

Xander just lifted me higher, burying his face into my neck. "I don't give a fuck," he all but growled. "Even without the bond, there's no way I could have let you go. I planned on challenging her for you. I won't give this up without a fight ... I can't."

What? Had he just.... *What!*

What had changed since we were in Royale half a day ago and he all but told me that he could only offer me a few years at best?

Xander let out a low laugh against my neck. "I know what you're thinking, and I promise you ... I mean every word. I might have told you that politics would hold us apart, and at the time I was sure I'd have to choose duty over love. I was prepared to do it as well, because my people mean a lot to me. But then I realized something very important ... maybe the moment you swam into the sacred legreto, rainbow hues spreading around your beautiful face. I realized that without you I would not be the sort of leader my people need. You make me care. You make me a better Daelighter. I can't lead without you."

I felt too emotional to articulate my feelings, but I had to say something. "Xander, I ... I won't be the reason you fight with your family. The reason you might be forced to step away as overlord."

The others started murmuring behind us, talking about finding the other crystals. They wandered off, probably to give us some privacy.

"Do you want this bond?" Xander asked me, his blue eyes killing me with their intensity.

I nodded before I even had a chance to really think about it. It was the truth. "More than anything," I admitted. "It's been killing me thinking about not having a chance to explore the connection between us. But even with our bond you still have to deal with your mother. She hates me. She's never going to accept a human as your mate."

"We will figure it out," he said, kissing me hard. "But first, let's deal with the stone and Laous."

A ricochet of energy rocked him for a moment. We turned to find Callie and Daniel at the huge fire pit, flames dancing high above them, and a glint of crystal at the top of the flames.

"They found the Imperial crystal," I said.

Xander did not let me go, wading us back toward the land. When we stepped up, I pulled my hand back. We held the crystal together.

"The fact you want to fight for us means everything to me," I told him honestly. "If it doesn't work out, if this is all I get with you, I don't regret our short time together. Or this bond. I'm honored that fate decided to put you in my life."

My voice cracked. I bit my lip to keep the tears from falling. "I'm pretty sure I've half loved you from the first time you arrogantly ordered me out of the water. You make me ... feel." The damp heat in my eyes was too much. I felt the moisture slide down my cheeks.

Xander finally let me down so he could cup my face with both hands. "You are perfect," he told me. "I will fix this."

Someone shouted before I could reply. We turned to find everyone near the wall of symbols, three crystals visible in their hands.

"We found them all," Emma said.

"Now get my damn stone," Laous roared from behind the group. Flames burst up, visible over Lexen's head. "I have waited long enough. Find the starslight stone, and just know, I'm taking the crystals as well. Extra payment for keeping me waiting so long."

"He's losing it," Xander murmured. "We don't have a lot of mental illness in Overworld. The network keeps us all in balance, but for those who do travel down that path, it can be very dangerous. Especially for someone in the overlord blood-lines. The power inside of us becomes unpredictable. We can't control it."

That sounded scary. Didn't we already have enough scary going on right now?

Focused again on our task, no one argued with Laous. We didn't plan on letting him have any of the stones, but he didn't need to know that. The eight of us moved toward the wall, each of us holding our crystals.

Flames erupted to the side of us and we swung around to find Laous completely on fire, his people on either side of him standing as close as they could get without burning. "Find my stone," he said. There was no inflection in his voice at all, which made it scarier.

I exchanged a look with Xander. "Any idea what we do now?"

Callie, still watching Laous's out of control fire closely, said, "Maybe something to do with the symbols?"

We were already near the wall, so I reached out and put my hand against it. Xander placed his next to mine. The others followed our actions. "We should touch as well," Chase suggested, shuffling in closer from the side. Everyone moved so that our arms and bodies touched while our hands remained against the wall.

Energy, like we'd felt the first time the secret keepers had connected, flared to life between the eight of us. "Holy shite," Maya gasped. "It's strong."

The stone in Xander's hand started to vibrate. It sent out a low-pitched sound that appeared to be making the ground we stood on vibrate as well.

"The wall is changing," Emma said in a rush.

Focusing all of my attention on the symbols, I noticed five small indents in the wall now, between our symbols, deep enough for us to insert our crystals. Xander and I didn't wait. Laous's fire was even bigger than before; he had run out of patience.

Lifting our joined hands we shoved our crystal into the rock, and even though the hole hadn't looked that deep, the entire crystal disappeared completely. I tried not to freak out, hoping we'd just done the right thing.

The moment the Royale symbols started to swirl, the others hurried to do the same with their crystals.

"What's the fifth hole for?" Callie asked, peering into it like it was a peephole.

No one said anything, all of us wondering what we'd missed, until Emma moved forward. Her hand reaching for the neckline of her shirt. She lifted out a chain with a stone on the end.

"You think...?" Callie asked, trailing off as Emma undid her chain and slipped the stone off. A wistful expression crossed her face as she placed this last piece of stone in the center of the others, and it too disappeared into the rock.

"That's a piece of starslight," Xander told me. "A piece from the very stone we're looking for."

"My parents gave it to me," Emma added sadly.

The moment her stone disappeared, the ground rumbled strongly, and we all took a step back. Except for Laous, who was apparently beyond rational thought at this stage; even his minions were stepping back. I couldn't even see Rao. Hopefully he had taken this chance to escape.

"Yes!" Laous shouted, and I turned to find the wall opening before us. Literally.

The gap was about two people wide. It extended all the way to the very top of the cliff face. Laous rushed forward, but he was slammed back at the entrance, almost like there was an invisible net over it.

Springing to his feet, he swung around on us. "More layers of security. I would really like to kill that Draygo now."

"Looks like you need the secret keepers again," Callie drawled. "Bet you're glad you didn't manage to kill me." She shot him a sardonic grin. "You owe Daniel some flowers."

Laous regarded her with his dead, hooded eyes. "Get me my stone and I'll send you an entire garden."

Callie narrowed her eyes on him but didn't choose to engage again.

"Let's do this," I said in a rush, moving forward. I was ready for it all to be over.

Xander wouldn't let me go first, of course, and we had a silent argument. Finally, I conceded, because he was a stubborn bastard. "Don't get used to it, though," I hissed as he gently moved me back. "We do this shit together."

He just grinned at me, happy to have gotten his own way,

only to find that he bounced right out of the entrance as well. I snorted with laughter, and his grin turned into a furrowed brow. "Let me try," I suggested.

Stepping toward the entrance, I held my breath, waiting for my face to smash into whatever invisible barrier was there. Except I sailed right through, into the narrow and dark cave beyond.

"Secret keepers only," I said as I spun around. My brow furrowed as I looked at the worried expressions of the overlords. I wasn't sure why they were so stressed. It was far worse knowing we were leaving them out here with Laous, who I was still sure was up to something.

Emma, Callie, and Maya started forward and I held my hand up to them. "Wait! Why don't I just go and get the stone by myself. No need to risk all of us."

Xander growled loud enough that a bunch of birds lifted from nearby trees. "Get your ass out of there, Avalon. You have no power to defend yourself."

Before I could say anything, Callie shook Daniel off and took the leap across the entrance, standing with me. "I have power," she said. "I will keep both of us safe."

Emma and Maya rushed forward as well, and neither Lexen nor Chase stopped them. Lexen even stepped up to Xander's side, slapping his friend on the shoulder. "This is something the girls have to do alone," he said. "Our mates are strong and capable. They would not be fit to rule at our sides if they weren't. We have to trust them."

Xander relaxed minutely, even though his chest was still heaving. "In and out," he said to me. "Do not waste any time in there. For all we know the cave could collapse the moment the stone is taken."

I nodded, my eyes drinking him in like it might be the last

time I ever saw him. Then, with a deep breath, I turned and stepped into the cave.

My girls right by my side.

It was time to end this.

21

Callie's hand slipped into mine and I held on tightly. Only two of us could move through the cave at the same time, and I was glad that she'd taken the initiative.

"I'm grateful that you're all here with me," Emma said, from close behind. "This feels right. A fitting ending to this last four months of my life."

Maya coughed. "Please don't say ending. I'm not ready for it to be an ending yet. I still haven't done one tenth of the things I want to do. I still haven't had sex, for freak's sake."

I chuckled. "Well, you definitely have to do that before you die. Especially since Chase is sooo damn fine."

She laughed with me, and I was glad she didn't get jealous. It wasn't like it was a secret. All the overlords were superhot, but Xander was the only one I wanted. He was mine.

"He is gorgeous," she said with a sigh. "Sometimes he catches me just staring at him like a complete sap."

"It's weird that we're all eighteen and basically married, right?" Emma snorted that out. "Like, when Lexen first explained the mating thing to me, I kind of freaked out on the inside, but I never thought for one second I didn't want it."

I felt Callie shrug next to me. "When you know, you know. I don't think age is really that big a factor. And ... life is short, relatively speaking. I say embrace whatever good comes your way and worry about the future when it arrives."

Their confidence in their mates and the future of their relationships, was enviable. For the first time since meeting Xander, I had hope for the same thing. And sometimes hope was all that got me through.

The cave opened wider as we crept deeper, and thankfully the light remained consistent, despite the doorway no longer being visible behind us. "No sign of the stone yet," I said, my eyes locked on whatever was coming up ahead.

"So what happened with you and Xander in the water?" Callie asked out of nowhere. "Did he say you bonded?"

My throat tightened. "Yes, the stone bonded us ... like a Royale marriage." I pressed my free hand to my chest. "I can feel him in here. But ... I still don't know about the future. In Royale, overlords choose the mates of their children. His mother already has a caramina picked out for him. If he goes against them, he might have to step away from his entire family and responsibilities. I'm worried he will eventually come to resent me if that's what happens."

"He loves you," Maya declared. "Anyone can see that. I don't know Xander well, but the side of him we all know is sort of arrogant and self-centered. But he's not like that with you. He's softer ... kind. He shows that he cares, and not just about you. About all of us."

Xander had pretty much said the same thing. "Sometimes love isn't enough," I said sadly. "I mean, if we were no longer welcome in Royale, where would we live? What would Xander do? He's used to being a leader ... he would be unhappy if that was gone."

Before any more of this depressing conversation could happen, I caught sight of a gleaming reflection ahead. Slowing, I pulled Callie back.

"Did you see it?" I whispered, shifting my head to the side to find the glimmer again. "There's something back there."

With more caution, and staying quiet now, we shuffled forward. The cave widened considerably, and I reached out for Maya's hand so that the four of us were linked—she was already holding Emma's.

Warmth and energy filled me, and with that came a sense of calm. "Just in case we're about to die," Emma said, slight amusement in her tone. "I just want to say that I love you all. I'm grateful that we met."

"Love you all too," Maya added.

Callie sniffled. "Yes, same for me."

Overwhelmed, I choked out, "Meeting you guys and Xander is the best thing that has happened to me."

It hit me very poignantly then that a true friendship wasn't always about the length of time you'd known another person. Sometimes it was the people who came into your life in the right moment and stayed for the tough stuff. We were new friends in some ways, but our souls had known each other for our entire lives.

Our bond thrumming between us, we took a step forward, and another, the far wall closing in on us. It was the end of the line. The last part of this cave. A round space opened up from the tunnel we'd been in, and I noted how different the rock in this round section looked. It was smooth and refined, almost manmade.

As the four of us stepped over the threshold into the circle, we all stumbled. It was only the combined grip we had on each other that kept me on my feet.

"Holy fuck," Callie exclaimed. "The power...."

She sounded as breathless as I felt. My chest heaved up and down as I tried to suck air in. It felt like the energy in here was so thick the oxygen couldn't fit.

"We need to find the stone." I coughed, hunching forward.

All of us sucked in whatever air was left in the room, filling our lungs. With determination, we stepped forward.

"We can do it," Maya chanted over and over.

I joined her, and then so did Callie and Emma. Our voices got louder and louder as we pushed through the power. It was only at the last second, when one of us put on the brakes, that we managed to stop before hitting the back wall. I didn't think. I lifted both of my hands that were joined to my friends and slammed the bottom of our palms against the wall. The others followed; a ringing, like the ding of a bell, sounded around the cave.

Then the room fell silent.

The energy died away.

The rock before us slid across, like it was an automatic door, and light burst in from this new entrance. When my eyes finally adjusted, I was able to clearly see the stone rising from the floor.

"He literally buried it right at the equator," I said, shaking my head. The stone would have been almost impossible to find had Laous not pushed us into this situation.

The four of us stumbled forward, crossing closer to the stone. It was huge, about the size of a loaf of bread in width, and two loaves in length. The color was next to impossible to determine, sort of opaque and opal, with shifting galaxies of stars inside it.

"We should pick it up together," I suggested, hoping like hell the energy wasn't going to rip us apart.

Callie cleared her throat, and I jerked in surprise when she removed her hand from mine in one quick tug.

"Is everything okay?" I asked, stepping back as she let out a flare of strong heat.

She shook her head a few times, her short hair falling forward across her forehead. "I ... I don't kno—"

Before she could finish her sentence, her flames burst to life. Emma, Maya, and I slammed ourselves back against the closest wall, barely escaping an agonizing death by flames.

"Callie!" Emma shouted, the roar of the fire was noisy inside the cavern. "What are you doing?"

Callie slowly lifted her head then, and I gasped loudly. Her eyes were glowing ... and they were empty of all recognition as they brushed over us, looking right through us like we weren't even there. She stepped forward and picked up the stone.

It felt like I might be in a little shock, because I just stood there openmouthed and stared at her. "What is happening?" Maya cried, clutching my arm.

I shook my head, refusing to believe what I was seeing. "This is not her," I told them, completely sure. "This is not our Callie. Something is happening to her."

Laous. This had to be him.

Callie started to walk toward the new opening. "Callie!" Emma screamed, straightening to go after her.

We followed, but there was no way for us to get close. Her flames were hotter than I'd ever felt before, the rocks on the walls around her turning red as she passed.

"We need the guys," Maya said. "You two follow her, keep trying to get through to her. I'll go get them—they're going to be waiting for us to come back the same way we entered. They need to know about this new exit."

I hated separating, but she was right. We needed help with this. Only Lexen and Daniel could touch Callie when she was burning like this, so we had to get them here now.

"Be safe," I told her. "If you get to the front entrance and no one is there, do not step outside. We have no idea what Laous might have done."

I knew that bastard had been up to something. Whatever was happening to Callie, it had to do with him.

Maya nodded, hugging us both and sprinting back the way we'd just walked.

Emma and I wasted no time hurrying after Callie, who was just about to step out of the cave and into the morning light beyond.

"Come on," I said, gripping Emma's hand, picking up the pace so we could catch up.

Luckily we did, because the moment the stone left the round room, the entrance started to close. We had to dive through to avoid being crushed, and I felt the burn of stone right across my arm as I leapt.

"What is happening to her?" I asked, trying to piece it together in my head. "How is Laous controlling her like this?"

Emma's face went pinched. "It has to be the ... the Soul-stealer goo."

The what now?

"Callie was taken by him and placed in this tank of goo," Emma explained. "It's a weapon, designed to wipe away the enemy's mind and make them more compliant to suggestion. Laous wanted to use it to control her ... all the secret keepers. We thought Callie had fought it, that her bond with Daniel kept her mind safe. But what if...?"

"He's still managed to control a small part of her," I finished.

Emma nodded. "Yes, it must have been dormant, just lying in wait until he could use her."

She tripped over a stick and I caught her before she face-planted. We were pretty close to Callie now, who had also started running.

"Come on," I said, "we can't lose her now."

The fields were catching fire behind our fireball of a friend, which definitely made the chase more difficult as we dodged flames that were starting to spread across the dead grass and scrub. The sound of a helicopter grew louder in the distance, a few miles away across the open area. When it appeared, I let out a relieved sigh—it was the craft we had taken here. But then as it landed and the first figures appeared on the steps, I knew we were in big trouble. Laous, the bitch, and the dude who never said anything had somehow commandeered the aircraft and were now waiting for their prize to run to them.

They were here for Callie.

"Maya should have gotten back to the guys by now," I said, fear lacing my tone. If Laous was here ... where were our guys? There's no way they would have let him just walk away from them without a fight, especially when we were out of sight.

Emma didn't say anything, but her grip got tighter on my hand and I knew she felt the same worry.

"Callie!" I shouted, praying with everything I had that something would get through to her. "Fight him, Callie, you are stronger than Laous."

Her footsteps slowed, but she didn't turn back to us.

Emma joined my chorus. "You got this, Cal. There is no one tougher in this world. You can fight him."

Her footsteps slowed again, and she shook her head more than once.

"We're getting through to her," Emma cried, picking up the pace, her breathing heavy and gait uneven. But she didn't slow down or stop, she kept powering along.

"Come to me!"

That voice boomed unnaturally across the land, and I looked past Callie to see Laous standing on the top of the stairs, his hands raised to the sky. Whatever small part of Callie had been trying to fight was lost then. She started to full-on sprint, the stone held out in front of her.

More of the land lit up in her wake, and the heat and smoke from the fire was starting to get to me. My breathing turned into a series of coughs. Emma was in the same position. The next time she tripped, both of us went down in a heap, barely managing not to land in a bush blazing with flames.

The fire moved fast, so I rolled to the right, dragging Emma with me. My skin screamed as I scraped it across the ground, but hitting the fire would be much worse, so I just gritted my teeth and kept moving.

The air was a lot clearer down here, and both of us sucked in deep breaths when we got out of the main path of the flames. Cool wind brushed across my skin, and I looked up to find Lexen in the sky above. I could have cried as he zeroed straight in on Emma, diving down for her.

She was on her feet in an instant, screaming and pointing toward Callie—who was almost to Laous. Lexen's fury washed across the sky in a rush of dark clouds and lightning, and when I peeked around the corner of our bush I was relieved to see strikes slamming into the area where the bitch and quiet creep had been. We needed to take out Laous's backup. Then we would only have him to deal with.

"Avalon!"

I swung my head around to find Xander running so fast he was almost a blur. Daniel was close to his side, moving just as quickly. The moment Xander reached me, I was up and in his arms, his chest heaving as he held me close. "What the hell happened?"

Daniel didn't wait for an explanation, storming past in a rush of heat and growling.

"Laous is controlling Callie somehow," I said, already tugging him out into the open so we could follow.

"It's from the Soulstealer goo," Emma added. "It has to be."

Xander swore, then the three of us were sprinting. Xander had to slow down to keep pace with us—we had no chance of catching Callie at this stage. Even Daniel and Lexen looked like they weren't going to make it in time.

"Are Chase and Maya okay?" I asked, wondering why they weren't here.

Xander nodded. "Yes, we had a little trouble with some of the locals right after you left. The timing was conveniently good. I'm guessing Laous and his guys used the distraction to slip away and get the aircraft. Maya and Chase are just cleaning up the last of the trouble."

Xander didn't sound worried, so I tried not to stress about it either. They'd be here as soon as they could.

"We're not going to catch her in time," Emma cried.

She was very right. "Go ahead," I said to Xander. "Your friends need your help, and our human legs are too slow."

He hesitated for a beat, then kissed me hard and sprinted away in a flash.

"Come to me," Laous shouted again, his flames warding off the worst of Lexen's storm.

"No!" I screamed, seeing that Callie was only a few feet away now. We were too late!

Out of nowhere—or so it appeared from my angle—a figure raced in from behind Laous. A tall, bulky man. For once his head was held high, scarred face filled with determination. He ran at full speed toward Callie, tackling her down to the ground.

She immediately started screaming, kicking and fighting.

"Rao!" I gasped, wishing we were closer so I could see better.

Emma choked on her next words. "He's ... trying to stop her. He's giving our guys time to get there."

Callie's flames rose higher then and I couldn't see her anymore. She had completely covered herself and Rao in fire, and I hoped Rao was immune to Imperial flames. Otherwise he had just sacrificed his life to save the stone.

22

Callie

DARKNESS HELD MY MIND, the same way it had when I'd been trapped in the *concrestia* goo, the Soulstealer, running through an endless land of nothing, screaming, desperate to get back to my family. The only positive this time was I knew what was happening to me. I knew it, but I couldn't figure out how to fight it. My bond to Daniel flickered on and off, but I could never hold on to it long enough to actually free myself.

Words flashed across the darkness again, one of the few differences to last time. It reminded me of a computer doing an update, where the script would appear on the dark screen, scanning down the page.

Some of the words were in English too. I'd catch glimpses of familiar phrases, but they moved too fast for me to read them. My stupid fucking brain was useless.

Calm, Callie. Breathe and calm your mind. You'll never be able to read when you're trying this hard. Your brain is stressed.

Emma's words came back to me, something she'd said often in the hours we'd spent learning together. She was so patient, never getting upset or frustrated by my shortcomings.

Her voice wasn't the only one I had heard. There was Ava's too, calling me back to them.

"Help me," I screamed.

Why was I back here again? What had happened to the starslight stone?

"Come to me."

That insidious voice slithered inside of me and my legs picked up speed, moving even faster than before. Toward what, I had no idea, because there was only darkness around. When I tried to stop myself from moving, I found that I had lost all control of my body. It didn't run because I wanted it to, it ran because someone else did.

Laous? Could he have had done this to me again?

I couldn't rely on Daniel this time. I had to figure out how to save myself, because I sensed that this was bad. Time was running out for us all. I would be strong enough. My mom didn't know me as well as she thought when she called me stupid and weak. I would be more than she'd ever dreamed for me.

Words appeared across the sky again, and I found myself focusing on the first word. *One word at a time*, Emma always said. *Don't look ahead or you'll get confused.*

"Sto-ne," I said slowly. "The stone." Moving on to the next word, I sounded it out, one by one. Each time the words disappeared, I came back to where I'd been up to, just like Emma had been drilling into me.

"The stone will ... set ... you ... free." I sobbed. "I read it. I actually freaking read it."

The stone will set me free? What did that mean? The starslight stone? Or another completely random one? The words faded out again. I was trying to stop my legs again, because there was no way I could find a stone sprinting like this, when something hit me hard from the side.

I got my wish to stop, because the heavy weight knocked me right off my feet.

"Come to me!"

I began to scream, kicking and fighting and thrashing to be freed from whatever held me. Sweat dripped down my brow as the heat kicked up a notch.

"Callie, stop fighting me."

It was another voice, low and thrumming with pain. "Just let go," he said. "Don't fight any longer."

I wanted to stop so badly.

"Callie."

The low, stilted way he said my name ... I recognized it.

"Rao!" I shouted back to him, knowing he wasn't here in this world, but wondering if he might be in the physical plane. With my body.

A scent of burning flesh hit my senses hard. I thought of his burned face. The fresh burns. The old burns. And now ... there was so much heat around us.

No! Oh, my gods, no. Please ... no. Please don't let me be the one burning him this time. He's already been through so much. Too much.

I was praying and screaming and crying, trying to figure out how to wake from this nightmare. All the while the heat grew stronger around us.

"Let ... stone ... go," he choked out.

Stone. Until that moment I had not noticed the weight in my hands, I had not felt the burden I carried, but the second he mentioned it, I remembered the words and opened my hands.

And let the stone go free.

23

Avalon

LEXEN REACHED THEM FIRST, followed closely by Daniel and Xander. Callie and Rao were not moving, flames roaring up around them. Daniel waded right into the flames, the only one of us able to touch them.

"You can't go in?" Emma asked Lexen when she reached his side.

"No." He shook his head. "These are Flames of Ether, right from the justices themselves. Daniel is the only one who can touch them."

With a growl, Lexen pulled away from us and stormed toward Laous. Xander followed close behind him. Emma looked like she was about to follow as well, but I grabbed her arm.

"He's fine, Em," I said. "Look..."

Laous, who was covered in flames as well, was not fighting

them. He was crashed out on the ground, like he'd used all his energy and now he was slowly fading away.

Lexen reached down and hoisted Laous up. The smaller man found a second wind and started to fight him, his flames shooting out. Lexen and Xander didn't appear to be fazed by the fire, but Emma lurched forward, and I wondered what she had seen.

Then I saw it too. Laous's flame was zooming across the ground, like an accelerant lit its path. Right toward the huge aircraft.

"Xander!" I screamed already moving. Emma was screaming for Lexen as well.

Our guys turned their heads toward us a microsecond before the world lit up and we were thrown backwards with the force of the explosion. Everything went white and then dark for a moment, my ears ringing. I groaned and tried to pull myself up from where I'd been thrown, shaking my head as I crawled forward.

My eyes zeroed in on where the guys had been standing last, but there was nothing except a giant crater in the ground. I screamed until my throat burned, tears pouring down my cheeks as I continued dragging my injured body forward. I wasn't exactly sure what I'd hurt, but my legs weren't really cooperating with me. My arms still worked though, and slowly I got closer to where I'd seen Xander last.

He couldn't be gone. He was strong enough to survive an explosion like that. He had to be.

I collapsed as gut-wrenching sobs ripped through me. We might have saved the stone, we might have stopped the worlds ending, but what had we lost in the process?

I twisted at a noise beside me, only to find Emma half crawling, lurching toward me. She stopped by my side, hand scraping along the ground to clutch mine. "Can you see them?" she choked out.

"No," I sobbed, my throat closing so no more words could escape.

A breeze brushed over me then, lifting the loose strands of my braid so that my hair was flying around me. Emma and I managed to roll over, sprawling on our backs.

A helicopter was closing in on us ... more than one, actually.

There were dozens on the horizon, coming closer and closer. At first I thought this was more of Laous's people, and I was already saying my goodbyes, because we had nothing left to fight them with. Then I noticed two of the most beautiful things I'd ever seen in my life.

One was the American flag etched on the side of the closest metal beast in the sky. The other was Lexen, soaring in between two choppers, Xander holding on to one of his arms. They flew in like angels, maneuvering so that they could land right by us. The helicopters started landing as well, but my focus was on Xander, on every perfect strand of golden hair on his head. On the beautiful eyes that were locked on me. The gentle hands that stroked my cheeks, taking the tears with them.

"I thought you were gone," I said, my head pounding as I fought to hold on to consciousness.

Xander fitted one of his hands under my head; the other he gently slid under my butt, and he lifted me up to cradle me in his arms.

"Laous was determined to take us out with him," he said huskily. "But I managed to counter with water; it formed a barrier between us for long enough so that Lexen could fly us out of the main blast zone. Laous wasn't so lucky." His lips pressed to my cheek, chasing the tears as they fell. "I will never leave you, Avalon. You're stuck with me for life."

In that moment, I let myself believe his words.

A loud wailing drew our attention. Xander spun with me in his arm, heading straight for the spot Callie's huge fire had been. It was gone now, but three bodies remained sprawled there, the starslight stone on the ground beside them.

Callie was wailing, screaming, holding on to the body underneath her. "It's not fair," she sobbed hysterically. "He never had a chance. He never had a life."

At first I thought it was Daniel, then I remembered that their souls were tied together. If Daniel had been dead, Callie would be too.

It was Rao.

His body was burned beyond recognition. Ash covered Callie from head to toe so that she was almost unrecognizable.

"I killed him."

More screams ripped from her and I wanted to run away and hide, because her pain was hurting my heart so badly that I couldn't breathe. I wouldn't be a weak-ass bitch like that, though. She needed me.

"We have to go closer," I said to Xander.

His eyes were hard, jaw rigid as he nodded. We were all mourning, all of us sharing Callie's pain. Especially Daniel, who had just lost his second brother in a matter of a month.

"Put me down with her," I said, needing to be even closer.

Xander didn't argue, and Lexen followed suit, placing Emma down as well. Daniel shifted to the side from where he had been holding her, allowing us to crawl through the blood and soot and wrap our arms around her. I don't know when Maya joined us, but there was a new thrum of energy from our bond when she arrived.

It took a long time, but eventually Callie's sobs died off. Her body still shook, but I held her tightly, kept her together as best I could. There were voices all around us, but I never heard any of it. Later they'd tell us that the stone was back in the hands of the humans and the council. The bond between us and the stone was gone, but somehow we didn't lose the bond between the four of us. Colita said it was soul deep, that nothing could break it.

We took a helicopter to a private field, a plane to somewhere else, and then another helicopter to take us right to Daelight Crescent. I barely remembered any of it. The guys let the four of us stay close while a healer fixed up our physical injuries.

It wasn't until we landed back in Astoria that I was able to focus enough to listen to the conversations around me. "Gonzo is gone," one of the military men at my right was telling Lexen. "We managed to take out a large percentage of their numbers. The rest fled. We're ferreting them out as we speak."

"They placed too much of their trust and manpower in Laous," Chase said quietly. "It was their greatest mistake."

It was a silver lining from a really shitty day. Daniel still hadn't spoken a word, he was simply holding Callie's hand like it was a lifeline. She lay across his lap.

When the chopper finally touched down in Daelight Crescent, Callie, wearing a haunted look on her face, stepped out first. She seemed to need the space, running as soon as her feet hit the ground. She headed toward one of the mansions on the street and Daniel followed right after her.

"That's their home," Xander told me. He swept me close and I let myself rest against his strength, needing this one moment before reality returned. Some of my hair spilled across us; it was almost black. "I really need a shower," I whispered, a morose chuckle escaping me. I was covered in death, literally.

One side of his lips quirked up; he brushed my hair back. "I'm going to take you to my home here. I'll have to come back and debrief with the overlords and council for a short time though. Are you okay to be alone?"

I nodded, even though I really just wanted to hide away with Xander for a few hours. He had responsibilities, and I had to respect them. "I won't be gone long," he promised. "I need to be with you, and only you, right now."

"I need to be with you as well," I told him.

He swept me into his arms, and I protested. "I can walk now. I'm fine."

"I know. This is for me. I need to hold you while I can."

"While I can" was not a phrase I wanted to hear from him, but I was not worrying about the future in this moment. The present was already too raw and painful.

When Xander stopped at a massive metal and wood gate, I just stared up at the impressive and intimidating structure. "Trying to keep the riffraff out?" I joked.

He laughed, and it was a beautiful sound. "My mother likes to make sure everyone is suitably intimidated whenever she does something."

"I'm starting to see that," I returned, as we waited for the gates to open.

When he stepped inside, I gasped. The house was set quite far back on the massive property, all white and glass, stunningly pretty. But the part that was my favorite, by a million, was the pool. It basically filled the rest of the land, water as far as I could see, even drifting in and out of the lower levels of the house.

"Bedrooms are on the next level up," Xander said, pointing

toward a row of windows beside pearlescent pillars. "The pool is filled with legreto from home."

I struggled down and he let me go. Before I could dive into the pool, he captured my face in his hands. Holding me tightly, he pulled me closer. "I love you, Avalon," he said, his tone soft but sure. "You're my mate. I will have no other."

Then his lips were on mine and I couldn't think anymore. I just felt.

When he pulled back, I fought the urge to drag him into the water with me. "Come back to me," I said, stepping away, even though it was painful.

He nodded, unsaid emotions filling his face. Then he turned and walked away.

I stood there for a long time, then sucked in a deep breath and fell backwards into the water. My shoes were still in another country. I hadn't slept or eaten for days. And I might have just said goodbye to the love of my life while he went off to be betrothed to another woman. I was still scared that Lettie would win the battle. So, kicking my legs as hard as I could, I swam and swam until I couldn't breathe, until I felt like I would pass out and had no choice but to rise to the surface. Closing my eyes, I floated around, letting the water soothe me just as it had done my entire life.

Only it wasn't working. I felt restless; my energy was spent but I couldn't stay still. My skin felt two sizes too small, and my insides were trying to stretch their way out. I was so caught up in my own head, I never even heard Xander enter the water. It wasn't until his arms wrapped around me and I let out a shriek that I realized I wasn't alone.

"You look like you have heavy thoughts, baby," Xander said, cradling me closer.

I spun myself around, wrapping my legs around him and

hugging him close. My hair, silvery and tangle-free again, spun out around us like a translucent cloud. "You came back," I said, burying my face in his neck.

Xander's hands, which had been running up and down my back, slowed. "You didn't think I would? You let me go knowing that I might not return to you?"

I pulled my head back so I could see him. "I know you meant what you said, but Lettie is a determined woman. I was preparing myself."

He chuckled, jerking me closer so the center of my body was pressed intimately to the hardness of his. "Why do you think it took me so long? I told her I would walk away. That if she made me choose, I would choose you every single time without hesitation. I think for the first time in my life, she knew that this was not something she could order me to do. So she agreed."

"She agreed?" I gasped. "She's not going to fight you? Or ... like kick you out of Royale?"

Xander laughed, brushing his thumb across my cheek. "She tried, but father stepped in. He gave his blessing. He forced my mother to think about her actions, and ... she's still not happy, but she is going to break the mate alliance."

I kissed him like a starving person, openmouthed, tongue tangling against him, body straining to move even closer. Our clothes were gone in seconds. I wasn't even sure how that happened, but I didn't care. Xander was inside me so fast that my head spun, and I cried out as all the pleasure he could bring thrummed through my body.

Having him like this, in the legreto from our home world, was a dream.

My body, which had already been primed, started to unravel. I knew I was not going to be able to hold out any longer, even though I desperately wanted to feel this sort of pleasure forever. I must have said something to that tune, because Xander growled, his speed increasing. "You'll feel it forever. I can promise you that. This is just the beginning."

For the first time since meeting him, I let myself truly believe that I might have this forever.

Home.

24

*A*ll I saw was white. For a moment I wondered what had happened, then a warm arm slid across me and dragged me closer, and I remembered everything.

I was with Xander. In his bed—our bed, as he told me last night. We were still in the house in Daelight Crescent, on the second floor in the master suite. It was massive, taking up ten times the space of my last shared apartment.

"Good morning," I said, burying my face into his chest. We were both naked. We had not gotten much sleep through the night. The morning got here way too quickly in my opinion. When we weren't making love, we were discussing everything that had happened yesterday. The council still wasn't sure how Laous had managed to invoke the Fires of Ether through Callie, but they had assured us that he was definitely dead now. Daniel confirmed this, because his soul was in Imperial, awaiting judgment.

"What if Laous chooses to be born again?" I asked, needing to know he'd be punished for what he did. For Rao and Marsil.

"Reborn souls are pure," Xander told me, running his hand along my side. "If Laous chooses to be reborn, his soul will have another chance at a good life."

Still didn't seem fair, but I guess a new soul shouldn't be punished for its previous life's actions.

"How are you feeling?" Xander asked, changing the subject. His tone was serious enough that I lifted my head to see him clearly. Ocean blue eyes framed by thick dark lashes met my gaze.

"I feel...." I hesitated, trying to determine what I really felt. "I'm not really sure, to be honest. Overwhelmed. Shocked. Happy."

All of that was true. While a small part of me was waiting for the bad thing to crash into us again, I was happy.

"I've never been this happy," Xander said, still serious. Then he smiled, and my breath caught, just for a moment. "I can't actually believe you're here with me."

I swallowed roughly, reaching out to caress his face. He wore light stubble across his chin and cheeks now, and I was digging it. "I can't really believe it either," I confessed, my hands pausing to cup his cheeks.

I kissed him then, because I could. Because in this moment, he was mine.

"I can feel you in my chest," he said against my lips. "Our bond, it's growing stronger."

He'd told me that might happen, that after we were bonded sex and emotions would tie us closer to together. "I feel it too," I said, snuggling against him.

His hands were just starting to move across my skin, around to cup my ass, when his phone buzzed on the bedside table.

Xander let out a low curse, followed by a deep breath before he rolled over and grabbed it. I noticed that he wasn't one to let his phone go without checking it, just in case it was an emergency back home. Being on Earth made network contact harder, so their phones were always on.

The white sheets pooled around him, making his skin look an even darker bronze than usual. This was enough of a distraction that it took me a few moments to realize that he was still reading his phone quite seriously.

"Is everything okay back in Overworld?" I asked, drawing his attention to me.

He nodded as he lifted his head. "Everything is fine. Daniel is having his initiation ceremony today. He's already overlord, or acting as overlord, but the official ceremony will give him complete control of his house and the justices. He's asked if we can be there."

"Is that not normal?"

Xander shook his head. "No, we've always kept that sort of thing quite separate. But ... we're changing the way our world is run now. We're going to make sure that no one can divide us again."

"Laous brought about something good after all," I decided.

We were both silent, thinking about everything that had happened.

"He didn't beat us," I said out loud, needing to hear it. "We learned that the four houses are stronger together."

Xander dropped his phone and then his hands were around my waist as he lifted me onto him. As I settled down against his body, my insides hummed.

"Do we have time?" I asked.

His eyes darkened. "Always."

~

HOUSE OF IMPERIAL WAS UNDERGROUND, literally. We took a transporter to the top level of the justices, along with a lot of other Daelighters. All four houses would be here today, spread out across the incubation level.

Xander and I stood at the head of Royale. A select few of his people were there, and I was so happy to see Dawn among them. She had given me a hug and expressed her joy at my mateship with her brother.

Lettie wasn't quite so happy, but since she mostly ignored me, I took that as a win. I knew I would have to keep an eye on Xander's mother in the future—she was going to do everything she could to drive a wedge between Xander and me. Whatever her long term plan was though, I would not let her steal this life from me. She was in for a fight.

I was happy to see Emma and Lexen with House of Darken. Star was also there with a tall, good-looking guy. They were holding hands.

"That's Brad," Xander explained, noticing my stare. "He's Maya's best friend."

Ah, this was the human best friend. He actually looked a lot like a Daelighter as he stood there hand in hand with a Darken princess. I mentioned that to Xander, and he nodded.

"He's eating some of our food to extend his human life. He's hybrid now."

That's what the secret keepers were as well. Humans changed by Daelighter energy.

"It's nice to see Ambra is finally out again," Xander said sadly. "Lexen's mother has barely left her room since Marsil died."

Lexen's mother was ethereal and beautiful, but there was no hiding how pale and thin she looked. Jero, the other brother, stayed at her side, holding her hand. He looked strong and sure, standing tall. But a deep pain was etched across his face as well.

It was too great. The losses were too much.

Another group exited the incubation level and I had to stop myself from running to Maya. It felt like years since I'd seen them all, even though it had only been one night. I missed them.

"Who's that with Maya?" I asked, seeing a tiny Asian woman and a large, robust man on either side of her. "Her parents?"

Xander nodded, his lips brushing against my ear. "Yes, they're here as well now, staying with Maya in Daelight Crescent. They work for the human-Daelighter section of the government, so they're used to our ways. It worked out pretty well."

Maya appeared to have the best kind of family there was, the kind that loved and accepted unconditionally. House of Leights still fascinated me the most. I'd see a lot of them before, of course, but I was in love with their nature-based life-style. Living with their trees. And they were all gorgeous, in a supermodel, I-have-cheekbones-for-days kind of way.

Maya fit in perfectly, even if she was almost the shortest among them. Her mother was the only one I could see who was even smaller.

"It's starting," Xander told me, and I turned to face forward.

Daniel and Callie, along with a bunch of their people, were standing right on the edge of the justices' cliff. Council members stepped closer carrying stones and crystals. Not the ones from our trip to Columbia. Nope, they were all gone forever. These were just ancient energy stones that would bind Daniel to the network and his house.

I had no idea what was being said. The ceremony was not in English, but there was a magical feel in the air.

Daniel did not hesitate when it was his turn to repeat the words, his hands on the stones. But before he finished, he did something that must have been unexpected, judging by the hushed gasp that went through the crowd of Daelighters. He reached back and grabbed Callie's hands, bringing her forward, placing her hands on the stone with his.

"I'm going to guess this is not how it usually goes?" I murmured to Xander.

He shook his head. "No, the overlord couple rules together, but there is only one true overlord. Daniel is ... sharing his power with Callie, giving her full access to the overlord energy he will control."

Callie looked like she was going to resist at first, but Daniel whispered something to her and she just shook her head at him, relaxing. They both repeated the final words together, and the dress she was wearing, floor length and black with a scooped neckline, started to shimmer. White and blue energy rocked across her body, moving to Daniel.

"This is the part where one of them could be rejected," Xander said, sounding worried.

I felt nervous for them. They were our family. I wanted them to be able to take this new step together. Light shot up and I gasped, not sure if that was a bad sign. Another beam of light, from whatever was above, shot down to meet their beam.

"The network accepts them," a council member shouted.

The cheers that erupted were almost deafening, and my heart swelled at the thought that all the houses were joined together in this moment. In celebration. The rest of the ceremony was over pretty quickly after that, then all of the overlords met to congratulate each other, while the members of the houses started to make their journey home.

Daniel asked all of us to stay until the end, sending messages to his friends via the network. "You're going to have to show me how this network works soon," I joked to Xander.

He gave me a wink. "You got it, babe. You have forever to learn about my world. I can't wait to discover everything with you."

He was perfect. Most of the time, anyway. The arrogant asshole came out on occasion, but to be honest, I loved that side of him almost as much as his sweet side.

Emma just about barreled me over as she tackle-hugged me. "I missed you," she exclaimed.

I burst out laughing. "I missed you too. I was wondering if I might be a little crazy, since it was only one night apart."

Maya joined us then and we pulled her into the hug. "Nope, not crazy," she told us. "I was almost going to sneak out of Chase's place last night and come find you all."

"Tell me that Chase's place in Daelight Crescent is a tree house," Emma said with a laugh. "And we can have sleepovers there?"

Chase joined us then, after saying farewell to his parents. "It's a very large tree house. And you're all welcome anytime. There's enough room for us all to live together and still have our own wings, if you'd like."

Everyone laughed even though he'd said nothing particularly funny. It was just nice to think about the future. About being together. And I guess ... we were all happy.

"Callie!" Emma cried when our friend finally escaped from the council and others gathered around the new overlord couple. "You're an overlord major."

Callie hugged all of us, her face glowing even though her eyes were tired and somewhat haunted still. "I can't believe it, but ... I feel the energy now. Inside. The same way my fire is there. And while I'm really happy, Daniel is still getting his ass kicked for dropping that on me with no notice."

Her mate chuckled as he wrapped his arm around her. "You'd never have turned up today if I told you what I had planned. It all worked out for the best."

She shook her head at him but didn't argue. The last of the crowds were disappearing, and I realized how huge this top section of Imperial actually was.

"So, what did you want us to wait here for?" Lexen asked Daniel.

Daniel and Callie's faces went somber. I worried for a moment they had more bad news.

"I've been waiting for my full powers," Daniel said. "Because I wanted to offer you all one last chance to say goodbye."

Lexen froze, like he knew exactly what Daniel meant. "You should call your parents, Jero, and Star back as well," Daniel prompted his friend, who still looked frozen. "It's a one-time offer."

"Are you sure?" Lexen said hoarsely. "I've never heard of anyone doing that before. I don't want to get their hopes up."

Daniel clasped his friend on the shoulder. "I will break the rules for you all. Just this once."

Emma started to cry, and so did Callie. My eyes felt very damp as I stared at the ground, still not totally sure how Daniel was going to allow them to say goodbye to Marsil.

"He's in redemption?" Emma asked, sobs escaping her.

Daniel nodded. "Yes, he sacrificed himself to save two worlds. His soul went straight to redemption."

Emma nodded rapidly. "Of course it did."

Lexen's parents appeared from the huge building that was near the back of this level. Star and Jero were with them. Lexen met them halfway so he could explain everything. Ambra started to cry, burying her head in her hands, while Roland comforted her. Jero and Star, though, both looked happy, their faces almost bright as they hurried across to our group.

"They all accept your gracious gift," Lexen told Daniel.

Roland cleared his throat. "You're breaking a lot of rules today, Overlord Daniel."

Daniel shrugged. "First day on the job—everyone makes mistakes on their first day."

Roland chuckled. "I can see you're ready to bring about the sort of change Lexen has always pushed for. I can't wait until the day the four of you stand at the pillar of Overworld. That will be a fine day indeed." His wife lifted her head, her dark blue eyes rimmed in red. Roland's arm was still around her, solid, supportive. "Ambra and I are going to seriously discuss when to hand the mantle over to Lexen. Whenever he and Emma are ready for it."

Emma went very pale, but she also looked pleased that they had included her.

"Can I see my son now?" Ambra asked, her eyes brimming with fresh tears. "I need to see him one last time."

Cue waterworks again. This was going to be one emotional visit, and I wondered...

"If you'd like this to be a family thing," I offered quietly,

"I'm happy to stay behind. My heart is breaking for all of you, but I don't know Marsil personally, and maybe I'm—"

I didn't get a chance to finish before Ambra and Roland stepped forward, and then they ... hugged me. Tight. Like parents would. Which had my heart cracking right down the center.

"You are family," Roland said, his deep voice rumbling all around me. "Lexen told me everything that happened while you were gone, and there is no doubt in my mind that the eight of you ... you're family."

"We would like you there," Ambra added as they both released me.

I couldn't speak, my throat clogged with emotions, so I just nodded.

Daniel stepped over to the edge of the justices, leaning out very far over the tree-filled land below. Light spread out from his hands, starting small, before it shimmered all the way down the huge cascading steps.

The beam got wider and longer, and when Daniel dropped his hand, the light did not disappear.

"Redemption time," he said, before he sat down on the beam and pushed off.

"A giant rainbow slide ... well, okay then," I murmured as one by one everyone got on and pushed their way down the light.

When it was my turn—Xander right behind me—I dropped down, surprised to feel my body almost mold into the light. It was warm and soft, and as I started to slide, there was no out-of-control feeling, just a smooth glide all the way down. I was so fascinated with watching the lands below, trees and fire and monsters and water, that I almost missed the fact that I was closing in on the end. Luckily Daniel was there; he caught me before I could do an impressive tumble across the land. "Oh, thanks," I said, when he set me on my feet.

"No problem. I figured most of you would be distracted."

Not Xander. He sailed down like a boss, landing smoothly. The mood in the group was a strange mix of somber and excited as Daniel strode further into the pretty land. It was very fairy-tale-esque, with streams and green rolling hills, and that perfect warm temperature where you felt comfortable and not hot.

"There are souls here?" I asked, looking around. It seemed deserted.

"Yes," Lexen said quietly. "But they're not visible to us, not normally. They exist in their own version of paradise."

Daniel, who had disappeared briefly behind some trees, reappeared then, and he wasn't alone.

Ambra let out a choked cry, her hand going to her mouth as she ran toward them, Roland, Lexen, Star, and Jero right behind her. The rest of us let them go across first, strolling very slowly toward the group.

Marsil looked just like his brothers: dark hair, stocky build. A little shorter. A little less beautiful than Lexen but definitely still a Darken. He had his arms wrapped around Ambra; she trembled against him. "I love you, Mom," I heard him whisper as he held her tight.

"How long do they have?" Callie asked Daniel.

"I'll give them as much time as I can," he replied, voice hoarse. "But there's only so long I can draw Marsil into this realm without depleting my energy to the point of endangering my house."

Eventually Marsil was hugged by all of his family, and the tears were flowing all around again. But there was a ... happy feel to the emotion this time.

"You chose redemption," Star said. "I'm surprised."

Marsil grinned at her. "Do you remember Jenna—we grew up together? She was my best friend, and when she was killed in that cave-in ... I haven't felt whole since."

"It was a freak accident, right?" Roland said, remembering.

Marsil nodded. "Yes, it was. She has always held my heart, and I hoped she was here. I chose to remain as I was in this life so that I could see her again. And all of you, if it was possible."

Ambra sobbed, reaching forward to push her son's hair back.

"Did you?" Star asked, her eyes bright.

"I found her," he said, happy. "Please know that I'm content. I will wait for you to join me one day. Redemption is the perfect kind of—"

His words were cut off.

Daniel lunged forward and grabbed Marsil's arm, stopping him from flickering away.

"I can't hold you much longer," Daniel warned. "Don't talk about the afterlife. It's not for anyone to know until it's their time."

Marsil nodded, before he stepped forward again and hugged his family, one by one, each of them whispering last words of goodbye. I had to step away, because I wasn't sure I could watch this for one more moment and not sob my heart out.

"I love you," I heard Emma say, and I turned enough to see her hugging him. "Thank you for everything. I will never forget you."

"I love you too," Marsil whispered. "Look after my brother. He needs someone to keep him in line."

Lexen didn't smile. He looked like his was gritting his teeth actually, jaw rigid, brow furrowed. He was hurting.

"It's time," Daniel said a few moments later. "I'm sorry."

All of the Darkens held their hands out towards Marsil, and he did the same back. Slowly, he started to fade. Just before he disappeared completely, he said: "Oh, and there's one last thing..."

He was gone then, but in his place two figures slowly appeared, neither of them familiar to me.

The Darkens held each other in their grief, but Daniel stepped forward, astonishment on his face. "Rao ... Fraizer," he said. "You're both here?"

Rao? I had not recognized him at all. He looked tall and handsome, the scars completely gone from his face. He stood beside Fraizer, who was a younger, happier, hawk-haired version of Daniel.

Fraizer spoke first. "I'm so sorry I betrayed you. I just wanted to save Rao." He turned his head toward Maya then. "I'm sorry, I hope Laous didn't hurt you."

Maya waved a hand at him, tears streaking down her cheeks. "I'm perfectly fine. Sorry we couldn't save either of you."

Fraizer shook his head, smiling broadly for the first time. "I was saved. Rao is my family, something I've searched for my entire life. We're together now."

Daniel was crying. Not in an obvious way, but I could see the glints of moisture on his cheeks. "You both made it to redemption. How could I not know this?"

Rao chuckled, which made all of us smile. "You not had much time," he said, in broken English.

Daniel chuckled too, wiping at his face. "Yes, that's true. I was afraid to search for your names as well. Afraid I'd try to save you from the justices."

"Told you I was a good guy," Fraizer said with a wink. "You just had to have faith."

Daniel stepped forward, sucking in a deep breath. "Stick together," he told his brothers. He reached out and pulled them closer. "I'll see you both on the other side."

The three hugged, a bittersweet moment, which hurt as much as it was beautiful. Then Daniel stepped back, and Fraizer faded away. Rao stayed a moment longer ... just long enough to hug Callie.

"I'm so sorry," she sobbed against him. "You tried to help me so much, and I ended up killing you."

"Shhh," he said gently. "Not your fault. Saved me. Thank you."

Her tears increased, her body actually shaking as she sobbed and cried. "I'm happy," Rao said simply, before he leaned down and kissed her cheek. Then he was gone.

Daniel caught his mate as she collapsed.

"How ... how did they appear?" Lexen asked Daniel, who was lifting Callie up into his arms.

Daniel shook his head. "I have no idea. I guess there is a lot I don't know about my world. About the justices. Maybe if I figure it out, we'll be able to see them again. I hope so, anyway."

Everyone was emotionally spent, that much was clear, as Daniel called for a transporter to take us back to the surface.

"Where do we go from here?" Emma asked.

"Wherever you want, baby girl," Lexen told her. "But my first suggestion is a long vacation for us all. I mean, what's the point of a private airplane if we don't use it?"

"You all have to go back to school," Roland told them, his voice hoarse with emotion. "Some of you still have to graduate high school."

Everyone groaned except Emma, who clapped excitedly. His words had lightened the mood, and by the time Xander grabbed on to the light beam to take us home, I felt better. My chest still hurt, but it wasn't as deep.

This was the start of the rest of our lives.

And I for one couldn't wait.

25

One month later

THE FIRST MORNING light was just cresting across the familiar sky as I kicked my legs out, staring at my ocean. My favorite time and place. I was just missing my favorite mate.

Xander would probably be pissed that I'd snuck out of bed this morning—we'd only flown in late last night—but it had been so long since I'd seen Hawaii. I couldn't miss the first sunrise. Our vacation had taken longer than expected to get to. There was just so much that needed to be dealt with first.

But we were finally here.

I was in his pool, the ocean spread out before me. Xander owned one of the superfancy resort-style estates right along the ocean. He said we could stay here as long as we wanted. I was hoping for forever.

Royale was great, and the fact that I'd finally got to sleep under the water in our pod was all kinds of awesome, but this was my home. It didn't help that his mother still hadn't really warmed to me. But the Dawn situation was looking up. I finally convinced Xander to tell his parents and they went ballistic. They had her back in their pod straight away, under the excuse that she was needed for official overlord business.

Then they sent their warriors to search for the creature. So far no one had found anything, and everyone was half convinced that Donovan had already done away with it. Whether it was alive or not, there was no way any of her family was letting her go back to him, especially not now they knew she was pregnant. Something Donovan did not know. House of Royale was a world of water and drama; living amongst them was like being in a soap opera.

Which only made the peace and quiet here that much sweeter.

I was so enthralled with my ocean that I didn't even hear Xander enter the water. It wasn't until his arms wrapped around me, pulling us close together, that I realized he was there. "I've missed this place," he said.

I nodded. "Me too. So much. I'm not sure we can ever leave."

He laughed. "I'm good with that, especially since I have a surprise for you."

Spinning in his arms, I smiled up at him. "Another surprise? Seriously, you don't have to keep giving me things."

"There are not enough things in the world for me to give you that would equal what you've given me," he said seriously.

I kissed him, wrapping my legs around his waist, and realized he was wearing board shorts and held my bikini in his hands. Normally we'd swim naked, so that was a little odd.

"What's going on?" I asked him.

"Ava!" That familiar shout from Emma sent bubbles of

excitement through me.

"They're here?" I asked breathlessly, already reaching for the bikini.

He nodded, a broad smile crossing his face. "They left a few hours after us because Daniel had some duties, but we're all together for this vacation. One month of sun, surf, and food."

By the time I got my swimsuit on, the pool was filled with my family, most of them dressed in their travel clothes, but they didn't care.

Emma, Callie, Maya, and I hugged for the longest time. "I'm so happy to see you all," I cried, pulling them in again.

"Careful," Chase said with a laugh, reaching down to haul his mate up out of the water. "She's a shorty and can't touch bottom here."

We all laughed, and Maya flipped him off. "I was perfectly fine."

Chase kissed her cheek, and then let her go back to us. He returned to the guys, who were lounged back on the wide step.

"So, tell me everything," I said as I leaned against the edge of the pool and lifted my face. The sun was almost fully up now. I loved the warmth across my skin.

"My safe house is up and running," Maya started. "Chase helped me set everything up. My old nanny is managing it for me. She's already whipped them all into line, creating a safe and warm environment for the women and children. The initial launch went so well that we're talking about branching out to a few other cities."

"I'm so proud of you," Emma said, kicking her legs slowly. "You're going to change the lives of so many women impacted by domestic violence."

Maya's smile was filled with genuine happiness. "It helps

that my mate is a billionaire, and that he is so supportive. I never could have done this without him."

"Those assholes really are the best things that ever happened to us," Emma said, staring at Lexen.

"I wonder if they'd say the same thing about us?" Callie mused, shooting a half grin at Daniel. "Hey, Dan!" He turned. "What's the best thing that ever happened to you?"

He didn't hesitate for a moment. "You are."

She blew him a kiss.

Xander dived under the water then and was at my side in about a second, his arms around me as he shot up, taking both of us out of the water. He caught me as we came down again, water splashing across everyone. I couldn't stop laughing, while everyone else wiped at their faces.

That was the start of water wars. We splashed and played for hours, Xander's staff bringing us food and drinks throughout the day.

"This was a perfect day," I said later that afternoon, all of us sprawled on loungers, soaking up the last rays of the sun.

"Except for the fact that I'm going to be redder than a lobster," Emma said, "I couldn't agree more."

Rolling over, I reached out to Xander, capturing his hand. "I vote we stay here forever," I whispered sleepily.

"Seconded," Callie chimed in immediately.

"All in favor?" Maya asked.

There was not even a second's pause before a chorus of ayes rang out.

We all knew there were too many responsibilities on Over-world for us to stay here forever, but in that moment we were all happy and content.

And most importantly, we were together.

We were home.

BONUS SCENE

Avalon

I sucked in a deep breath, smoothing the skirt down, wishing I was back in my denim cutoff shorts. "Are you sure this is really necessary?" I complained to Emma, who stood on my right, wearing an exact replica of my outfit.

She flashed me a grin, her ponytail bobbing as she nodded. "Oh yeah, you need this high school experience. All of us do. It's only a few weeks until graduation."

"I'm only agreeing to this because Emma needs to graduate," Callie cut in from the other side of her. The four of us were standing in a line beside a water fountain in front of Starslight Prep.

Maya cleared her throat. "I need to graduate as well, even if I'm not sure about college or my future ... outside of Chase of course."

With another breath, I reached out and linked my arm through Emma's. "Okay, let's do it, then. I'm sure I can handle a few more weeks of school if it means I get to hang with you all."

We started to move together, all of us dressed in the uniform that set this fancy school far apart from the public schools I'd gone to. I didn't really have plans for the future either. College kind of seemed like a waste of time when I was going to be spending most of my life under the water with Xander. But Emma, and possibly Maya, were still planning on attending college, so they had to suck it up and finish the year.

"I have no idea how you both managed to catch up on the schoolwork in such a short time," Callie said, her face paler than usual. "It would have taken me five years to read through all of those assignments."

Emma shook her head. "No way! You can do anything, Cal. You saved us all. You read those words in your head that helped you release the stone. Laous was trying to play on what he perceived as a weakness, and you went boss-lady on his ass."

Callie shook her head, but she did smile, and some of the color returned to her face. "Thanks to you," she murmured, hugging one arm around Emma. "If you hadn't helped me so much, I'm not sure I would have had a shot at reading in my panicked state."

Emma moved to return the hug and I released her arm so she wasn't being pulled in two directions. "Not a doubt in my mind that you'd have killed it without any help from me," she said softly to Callie.

The rest of our conversation was cut off when we entered the main building. I paused just over the threshold, staring around and trying to figure out how this was a school.

"Let me guess," I said with a snort of laughter. "This was ... designed by our *other* friends."

The girls just nodded and laughed with me. "Yeah, they really need to work on their *blending* abilities." Maya snort-laughed.

Students were pushing through the doors as it got closer to being time for the first bell. I was surprised to see so many of them staring at our group, especially Emma and Callie. They didn't know Maya and me, but we still got a fair share of stares.

"I was invisible in my high school," I said, fighting the urge to duck my head. This was when my height was a pain in the ass. "Guessing that's not going to be the case here."

Emma actually laughed so hard she had to rest her hands on her knees while she tried to suck in deep breaths. "Oh, God. You just wait, Ava. Our guys are part of an elite world here in Astoria, and they are worshipped."

Which explained why there were so many dirty looks tied in with all the curious ones coming our way. Clearly no one liked Emma and Callie stealing their gods. "Speaking of," I said, "weren't they supposed to meet us here this morning?"

All four had been called into a last-minute overlord meeting, and had reluctantly agreed that we could go on ahead to the school early. With Callie among us, there wasn't much humans could do to hurt us.

A shout rang out before anyone could answer. "Hey!" Star was waving as she rushed toward us, an amused Brad following close behind.

Maya greeted her best friend with a hug. Emma greeted her sister-in-law the same way. I watched it all with a warm happy feeling in my chest. I hadn't had a chance to get to know Brad or Star that well yet, but they were both extremely nice. And extremely in love.

Lucky Roland and Ambra were all about their children's happiness first and duty second, because I imagined it might have been difficult for Star to tell them that she loved a human dude. Emma was at least special in their world. Brad was only a bystander caught up in it all.

"What's your first class?" Star asked, pulling a folder from her backpack.

Emma didn't even have to look at hers; she already had it memorized. "We're all in AP Calculus. Lexen made sure that we're all in the same classes, except for Maya, who had some special requests."

The rest of us were just here for the social aspect. We were exempt from tests and assignments. Somehow the overlords worked that out. Probably helped that we were the mates of the founding fathers of this entire school and half the town.

A bell rang and more students rushed past. We were drawing attention, but no one seemed game to stop until a blond girl skidded to a halt and let out a scream. Emma immediately shrieked as well, and the pair rushed together, hugging like they hadn't seen each other in years.

"I can't believe you're back," the girl said, pulling away, her bright green eyes filled with tears. "When they said you had a huge family emergency, I thought for sure I'd never see you again." She swallowed roughly, her eyes holding a fresh look of horror. "Then when those men came ... well, I was glad you didn't have to go through that."

Emma's face crumpled, and she hugged her friend tightly again. "I wish I'd been here with you all. The worry that they'd hurt you was far worse than not being here."

They remained in a tight hug for an extended moment, and when they pulled back both wiped at their eyes. Emma reached out and grabbed the other girl's hand. "Come on, let me introduce you to the other members of my family."

The girl looked both apprehensive and excited as she was

dragged our way. "Guys, this is Cara," Emma said happily. "She was my first friend in Astoria."

She then went around and introduced each of us to Cara. "And that's Ava," she finished. "Xander's girlfriend."

By this time Cara had her mouth wide open, staring between all of us. "Are you telling me," she finally said, "that you four are all dating the guys from the elite families? OMG! I should have known, though. You're all so stunning. Like a group of freaking supermodels." She dropped her eyes to Maya. "Petite supermodel for you."

Everyone laughed, but she just kept gaping at us. "I have to tell everyone," she said suddenly. "All of these thirsty bitches in this school need to know to get their hands and eyes off your men." She nodded decisively. "I've got your backs, don't you all worry about a thing."

With one last hug for Emma, she was gone in a flash. I laughed. "I like her. She's much nicer than most of the chicks in my old school."

Emma pressed her lips together, eyes still watery. "I can't believe Laous almost murdered an entire town. Those Gonzo were bad news, and he just left everyone with them, knowing he never planned on coming back with the stone."

Five people had died in the hostage situation. Emma hadn't known any of them personally, but that didn't make it any better. Not to mention there had been more than one rape reported as well. "Cara never got...." I trailed off, but she knew what I meant.

"No, thankfully. Her father got them into their underground bunker. He's a bit paranoid, monitoring police radio and stuff like that."

Paranoid or not, it had paid off if it kept his family safe. I was probably going to be one of those crazy mothers ... if I was ever blessed with children. Just the thought of little Xanders running around had my heart pretty much a puddle of mush in my chest. Kids were not in my short-term plans, but I really did want to start a family. I was the only one among the girls who did, though. Emma, Callie, and Maya were all about being irresponsible humans for as long as they could.

A hush washed over the hall. I thought maybe it was because the second and last bell was about to ring and everyone was in class. I turned to double-check and realized that nope, it was nothing to do with the bell at all.

"It's almost too much." Emma sighed, stepping forward. "Seeing the four of them together."

It was too much. The overlords stepped in through the main entrance, the four of them wearing the uniform in an attempt to fit in with the humans. No ties for them though; they had open collars, their dress shirts fitted across broad shoulders and muscled chests. They also had about half a foot or more height on most of the school. So yeah, they really didn't fit in at all.

I wiped at my mouth to make sure I wasn't drooling.

"We owe fate some flowers," Maya said seriously. "Like bunches of flowers."

"And chocolate," Emma added.

"Wine!" Callie and I said together.

Despite the crowd starting to gather around them, the guys found us immediately. As they started to move toward us, the students parted, hushed whispers following them.

"They're back...."

"Holy shit, they're all together."

"... died and gone to orgasm heaven."

I chuckled at the last one. That girl had not even bothered to whisper as she gushed to her friends. As Xander stepped closer, I forgot about the noise and students. I didn't hear any of the words or murmurs. All I saw was him. His blond hair was a little longer than usual, falling in a mess of waves across his forehead. His eyes were intense, devouring me as he prowled toward me. He was lethal and sexy, and his appeal only increased every moment I was with him.

When he reached my side, he swept his arms around me. "I missed you," I said, and the air fled my lungs as his lips pressed to mine.

By the time he let me go, teachers had arrived to usher everyone to class and I was completely disoriented. "I missed you too," Xander said, still holding me close. "And I just realized something."

"What's that?" I said breathlessly.

His smile was tender. "I've never loved you more than I do right in this moment. My love for you ... it grows every single day."

Perfect. He's perfect.

"Do you think it will ever stop growing?" I whispered, pressing closer. "How many years before you reach maximum love?"

Xander shook his head, wearing the smallest of smiles. "There is no end point, Avalon. Love has no limit. I for one can't wait to see what a thousand years of love feels like."

I felt exactly the same as Xander did. I loved him more with every second he was in my life. I loved him more in this moment than I had yesterday. And the day before.

"Love has no limits," I repeated, burying my face in his chest. "And I can't wait either."

Love. Family. *Home.*

Forever.

BONUS SCENE

Callie

School was still the same: stressful. But I no longer felt like I might have heart palpitations if the teacher called on me to answer a question. I was actually finding that despite my difficulties in reading, I was pretty well-educated. Plus, it was almost the end of the year and the teachers were past giving a shit.

So that made school stressful and ... fun. Who would have thought it?

"Hey."

His low voice had every muscle in my stomach clenching. As I turned to find those soulful eyes on me, I had to touch him. "Hey, Overlord," I said with a wink. "Fancy meeting you here."

I was at the bottom of the stairs that led up to our eating area. It would be empty up there. Most Daelighter students were gone now, back to Overworld or off to their next adventure. But Emma and Maya wanted to finish out their high school journeys, and we all stuck together. It was kind of nice to have the entire space to ourselves.

I still wasn't used to the intense scrutiny we were under. The humans in this place were fascinated with the overlord kings of the school. If only they knew they were an alien race with powers that could decimate them in seconds. Who was I kidding, they wouldn't care. That would only make the guys hotter.

Daniel wrapped me up in his arms and everything inside me sighed with happiness. Between our soul bond and my intense love for him, being held like this was singularly the best feeling I'd ever had in my life.

Well, that and sex. Which drove me absolutely crazy. I was thinking I had a problem. Might even need a support group.

"You need to stop thinking that, Callie," Daniel murmured, pulling me even closer. "We're in the middle of school."

I threw my head back and laughed. "You can't read my mind, so how do you always know when I'm thinking about sex?"

His grin was lethal; those damn dimples. "Because your eyes darken and you chew on the corner of your lips." He rubbed his thumb across my lip. "And because I feel the emotions swell inside of you, and I know that's exactly how I feel when I think about touching you."

My breathing was ragged. I tried to control it, because he was correct: this was definitely not the right place for this sort of intensity. But, my God, he was going to kill me.

I got a breather when the rest of our friends arrived. The eight of us wandered up to the next level with its amazing array of food that we basically had to ourselves.

"Should we ... maybe share this?" I asked. Despite my love of the privacy, it still felt wrong.

Lexen chuckled and Emma shot him a look. "I told you it was shitty of us to have all the best food up here," she told him, "and not share it."

Lexen leaned toward her, doing the same thing Daniel did so well, loving her with just one look. "I know, Em. Which is why...." He trailed off with a sweep of his hand.

It took them a second to show their heads, creeping up the stairs. A dozen or more students made it to our level, and they were the last humans I ever expected to see up here. The scholarship kids.

Emma legitimately had tears in her eyes when she turned back to her mate. "I love you!" she all but squealed. "Thank you."

Lexen shook his head; he brushed a kiss across her lips. "You should know by now," he told her in a low voice, "there's nothing I won't do for you."

I'd have swooned and been jealous as hell, except I had my own. He showed me multiple times a day how much he would do for me.

Right after the incident with Rao, I was broken. I never knew my heart could hurt so much and me not die because of that pain. And the guilt. Oh, God, the guilt had eaten me alive. It helped when I saw him in the justices, but it didn't completely erase what I had done. Whether Rao was happy or not, he was still dead because of me. He never got a chance at happiness, and that wasn't fair.

Daniel had been so patient with me, just holding me, letting me cry and scream and rage. When some of that calmed, we went to New Orleans and stayed there for weeks. It was the best time of my life. I even said goodbye to my mother, despite not knowing the exact location of her cremation. But I knew she was somewhere in that area.

I loved him so much.

"I love you, too," he said, pressing a kiss to the spot just below my ear. Somehow he always knew what I was thinking. He cared enough to learn my tells, my facial expressions. It made me feel loved and cherished.

I was blessed in more ways than I thought I deserved.

BONUS SCENE

Maya

This school was the best! Seriously. Not only were the teachers cool, letting us call them by their first names, and basically giving us zero assignments outside of the necessities, but there was an entire level in the cafeteria with three-star Michelin-rated food.

"Why did we not go to school here our entire lives?" I asked Brad, who had been late coming to lunch but was still managing to eat more than all of us combined. Okay, not more than the overlords, but he was holding his own with them. Which was impressive.

"I know," he said as he swallowed. "Their football team looks amazing. They were complaining about losing Lexen and his brothers halfway through the season, but they still managed to win most of their games."

I blinked at him, shaking my head. He grinned. "Right, I

know. You don't care about football. How's it looking for graduation?"

A happy feeling fluttered into my chest. "Great, actually. With a little help from Chase, and being able to add my charity to my résumé, it looks like I have early acceptance into my top three schools. I'm still not sure about college next year, but it's nice to know I got in."

For someone who had been actively hoping to avoid the college decision, this was quite the change for me. But Chase had been the empty part of my soul, the part always searching. Now that he'd filled my life, I felt freer to plan a future.

"What about you?" I asked him, having to wait while he shoveled more pasta in his mouth.

"Pribsfljsf agot got—"

"Whoa…" I held up a hand to interrupt him. "No. Just because Star is not here doesn't mean you can act like a heathen. Swallow before you talk, dude. How many times have we had this convo?"

Brad winked at me. "You love my heathen side," he said with an empty mouth this time. "And what I was saying … I'm not sure I want to go to college next year. Roland has a role for me in Darken, if I want to take it. And … since that's where Star is going to be … I want it."

I would never have imagined my player of a best friend would fall so hard and fast, but Star had him completely consumed. "I'm really happy for you," I said, reaching out to grab his hand. He returned my squeeze, his face softening.

"I'm happy for you too, Maiz."

He went back to his food and I let him be; the bell was going to ring soon. I found Chase leaned back in his chair, silently watching the table.

And me.

Our bond tingled within me; I could feel him in my chest.

"You know," he said, reaching out to drag my chair closer to him. "If you want to go to college, I will support you all the way. I will be at college with you, and we will have all of the human experiences."

I tilted my head up to him, desperate to kiss him. He said the sweetest, most considerate things. "I'm not sure it's the right path," I admitted. "Part of me wants the experience, but a larger part of me will miss our home. The Galinta. The other Leights. I think that returning to..." I lowered my voice considerably because some students were up here with us now. "Overworld ... is the right thing for our future. Besides, I don't age. I can go to college in fifty years if I feel like it."

Chase captured my lips, giving me exactly what I wanted. "I love you so much, *sayana*. Thank you for my life."

I could never find the right words to tell him how much I loved him. But I was determined to spend the rest of my life showing him. The same way he showed me every single day.

BONUS SCENE

Emma

Why in the hell had I suggested we finish up the final weeks of school?

"Come on, you need to run faster than that. This is just the warm-up."

I glared at the coach as I huffed past. If looks could kill, he'd be so close to death right now. "Exercise is not right," I spluttered, shaking my head as my wobbly knees almost gave out. "It's not natural."

I finally lost the fight with my balance, but before I could hit the deck, strong familiar arms swept around my waist and held me up. "I got you, baby girl," Lexen drawled, laughter in his voice.

I glared at him too, but only strong enough for a slight injury. "You still haven't developed the ability to maim with your eyes," he said, lips tilting up at the corners. "But I love your persistency."

Dammit. Another unfair thing. Callie got a cool power. Why not me?

With a sigh, I admitted, "I'd probably only abuse it anyway. It's for the best."

Lexen actually laughed out loud. It was still my favorite sound in the world. I felt like I had achieved something great when I made him laugh. He must have noticed the way I was looking at him, because the amusement on his face faded away, to be replaced with an expression I knew very well. Fire started low in my body, and I was wondering if maybe I did have some sort of energy in there. How else could Lexen make me burn like this?

We had stopped running now. The rest of the class had gone on ahead with their torture, and the coach knew better than to question Lexen. So no one bothered us.

"Are you happy?" he asked me, hitting me from the left with that random question.

I swallowed hard, unsure if I should be upset. "Um ... why are you asking me that?" I finally said. "Do I seem unhappy?"

Lexen shook his head. "No, not at all. But I was reading this book, and they said that you should always check in with those you love. That sometimes ... sometimes humans put on a brave face."

My lips twitched and I tried really hard not to smile. Lexen was a tough guy, scary, but there was this spot deep down that was so caring. I almost couldn't believe some of the things he had done for me. He showed me that he loved me in a million ways. Reading psychology books on humans to try to understand me better was just one of the latest.

I stepped into him, the tips of our shoes bumping. Tilting my head back, I let all the love I had for him pour out of me. "I am happier than I ever thought I could be. Despite the losses, which still hurt, I am not broken, and that is because of you. You keep me together. You make me."

It was a very un-modern thing to say, and I didn't mean that I needed Lexen to be a better woman. Or that I needed Lexen to make me feel okay. I meant that we were two halves of the same whole. I would not be the Emma I was today without him.

"You make me as well," he said. And that was the part that made it okay.

Together we were whole.

ACKNOWLEDGMENTS

Thank you! Thank you to every single one of you that took a chance on my secret keepers. These characters have completely captured my heart, and I can't imagine not living in their worlds now. You might have noticed that I left a few side storylines vague and unfinished ... this is because I want the option to come back one day and write about them again.

Because something tells me that they're going to call to me if I don't.

Thank you to Heather, my amazing PA, for making my life such smooth sailing. Your help, encouragement, and love for my worlds means everything to me.

Thank you to Tamara for the incredible covers. I adore you. Thank you to Lee and Liv from Hot Tree Editing. You make my words shine.

Thank you to my review team and my Nerd Herd. You know I

heart you all. Your enthusiasm for my books is one of the best parts of my day.

CPSIA information can be obtained
at www.ICGtesting.com
Printed in the USA
LVHW011537170520
655738LV00005B/186

9 781925 876017